#1 BESTSELLING NOVEL, #1 BESTSELLING AUTHOR!

"THE MAN IS A MASTER OF THE THRILLER. HE KNOWS HOW TO SELL, WRITE SUSPENSE, AND PLOT HIS TALES WITH PRECISION...*ALEX CROSS, RUN* IS PATTERSON AT THE TOP OF HIS GAME...One of the central pleasures of the Alex Cross series that is furthered quite a bit in this newest adventure is that Cross is a whole person. We don't just see him at work. We get to know his family. We see him interacting with his wife, mother, children, and friends. These moments make Patterson's story stand out and offer more voices than a typical thriller...A HELL OF A READ BY A MASTER STORYTELLER."

—Breitbart.com

"A SHOCKER...PATTERSON SHOWS NO SIGN OF SLOWING DOWN AND GIVES EVERY INDICATION THAT HE HAS NOWHERE NEAR EXHAUSTED HIS SUPPLY OF IDEAS OR, MORE IMPORTANTLY, UNFORGETTABLE CHARACTERS."

—BookReporter.com

"ENTERTAINING AND EASY TO READ."

—ReadersRefuge.blogspot.com

"FANTASTIC...ONE OF THE BEST OF THE ALEX CROSS SERIES."

—ThePhantomParagrapher.blogspot.com

DOUBLE CROSS

"THE SUSPENSE, CHILLS, AND THRILLS ARE THERE, AND AN ENDING WHICH I NEVER SAW COMING. ANOTHER GREAT OUTING FROM PATTERSON, AND ONE THAT I SIMPLY LOVED. HIGHLY RECOMMENDED."

—NewMysteryReader.com

"EXHILARATING AND INTENSE…FANS WILL BE THRILLED."   —NightsandWeekends.com

"VINTAGE PATTERSON…IT IS FAST MOVING AND SUSPENSEFUL AND TAKES THE OCCASIONAL SURPRISE TWIST…Life for a Patterson fan doesn't get much better than this."

—1340MagBooks.com

CROSS

"THE STORY WHIPS BY WITH INCREDIBLE SPEED."   —*Booklist*

"ANOTHER GREAT ONE FROM JAMES PATTERSON. HOLD ON TO YOUR SEAT!"

—ArmchairInterviews.com

"SMART AND STRAIGHTFORWARD, IT BUILDS INTEREST AND MOMENTUM IN SHORT, TIGHT CHAPTERS THAT CAPTIVATE, CREATING AN ADDICTIVE READ."   —TheMysterySite.com

MARY, MARY

"THE THRILLS IN PATTERSON'S LATEST LEAD TO A TRULY UNEXPECTED, ELECTRIFYING CLIMAX."
                                        —*Booklist*

"*MARY, MARY* FLOWS EFFORTLESSLY AND WITH MOUNTING SUSPENSE TO ITS FINAL, SHOCKING TWIST; A FASCINATING PSYCHO WILL CAPTIVATE THE AUTHOR'S MANY FANS."
                                        —*Library Journal*

"PATTERSON'S HYPNOTIC THREE-OR-FOUR-PAGES-TO-A-CHAPTER PACE WILL KEEP YOU UP READING FAR INTO THE NIGHT...A GREAT PLOT TWIST."   —*Fort Worth Star-Telegram*

LONDON BRIDGES

"EXCITING...A FULL PACKAGE OF SUSPENSE, EMOTION, AND CHARACTERIZATION...THIS THRILLER WORKS SO WELL...ANY THRILLER WRITER, WANNABE OR ACTUAL, WOULD DO WELL TO STUDY [*LONDON BRIDGES*]."
                                        —*Publishers Weekly*

"AS WITH THE BEST OF PATTERSON'S WORK, IT IS IMPOSSIBLE TO STOP READING THIS BOOK ONCE STARTED."   —BookReporter.com

THE BIG BAD WOLF

"THE BIGGEST, BADDEST ALEX CROSS NOVEL IN YEARS." —*Library Journal*

"VASTLY ENTERTAINING...THE FINEST CROSS IN YEARS." —*Publishers Weekly* (starred review)

"POWERFUL...YOUR HEART WILL RACE." —*Orlando Sentinel*

FOUR BLIND MICE

"THE PACE IS RAPID...ACTION-PACKED." —*People*

"CHILLING." —*New York Times*

"BRISK...SATISFYING." —*San Francisco Chronicle*

VIOLETS ARE BLUE

"PARTICULARLY JUICY...ENJOYABLY SPOOKY... BOTTOM LINE: BLOODY GOOD CREEPFEST." —*People*

"AS ADDICTIVE AS ALL OF PATTERSON'S BOOKS...YOU HAVE NO CHOICE: YOU MUST READ IT." —*Denver Rocky Mountain News*

ROSES ARE RED

"THRILLING...SWIFT...A PAGE-TURNER."
                                        —*People*

"THERE ARE NO FASTER READS THAN PATTERSON'S ALEX CROSS BOOKS. I CAN'T WAIT FOR THE NEXT ONE."
                    —*Denver Rocky Mountain News*

POP GOES THE WEASEL

"Fast and furious...In the Patterson pantheon of villains, Shafer is quite possibly the worst."
                                    —*Chicago Tribune*

"PATTERSON DOES IT AGAIN. THE MAN IS THE MASTER OF THIS GENRE. We fans all have one wish for him: Write even faster."   —Larry King, *USA Today*

CAT & MOUSE

"THE PROTOTYPE THRILLER FOR TODAY."
                            —*San Diego Union-Tribune*

"A RIDE ON A ROLLER COASTER WHOSE BRAKES HAVE GONE OUT."   —*Chicago Tribune*

JACK & JILL

"FORTUNATELY, PATTERSON HAS BROUGHT BACK HOMICIDE DETECTIVE ALEX CROSS... He's the kind of multilayered character that makes any plot twist seem believable." —*People*

"CROSS IS ONE OF THE BEST AND MOST LIKABLE CHARACTERS IN THE MODERN THRILLER GENRE." —*San Francisco Examiner*

KISS THE GIRLS

"TOUGH TO PUT DOWN...TICKS LIKE A TIME BOMB, ALWAYS FULL OF THREAT AND TENSION." —*Los Angeles Times*

"As good as a thriller can get." —*San Francisco Examiner*

ALONG CAME A SPIDER

"James Patterson does everything but stick our finger in a light socket to give us a buzz." —*New York Times*

"When it comes to constructing a harrowing plot, author James Patterson can turn a screw all right...James Patterson is to suspense what Danielle Steel is to romance." —*New York Daily News*

ALEX CROSS, RUN

Books by James Patterson
Featuring Alex Cross

ALEX CROSS, RUN

JAMES PATTERSON

VISION

NEW YORK   BOSTON

Copyright © 2013 by James Patterson
Excerpt from *NYPD Red 2* copyright © 2013 by James Patterson

Vision
Hachette Book Group
237 Park Avenue
New York, NY 10017
www.HachetteBookGroup.com

Vision is an imprint of Grand Central Publishing.
The Vision name and logo is a trademark of Hachette Book Group,
Inc.

The Hachette Speakers Bureau provides a wide range of authors for
speaking events. To find out more, go to
www.hachettespeakersbureau.com or call (866) 376-6591.

The publisher is not responsible for websites (or their content) that
are not owned by the publisher.

Printed in the United States of America

Originally published in hardcover by Hachette Book Group
First oversize mass market edition: February 2014

10 9 8 7 6 5 4 3 2 1
OPM

Prologue

DIE YOUNG AND LEAVE A
BEAUTIFUL CORPSE

ONE

IT'S NOT EVERY DAY THAT I GET A NAKED GIRL ANSWERING THE DOOR I knock on.

Don't get me wrong—with twenty years of law enforcement under my belt, it's happened. Just not that often.

"Are you the waiters?" this girl asked. There was a bright but empty look in her eyes that said ecstasy to me, and I could smell weed from inside. The music was thumping, too, the kind of relentless techno that would make me want to slit my wrists if I had to listen to it for long.

"No, we're not the waiters," I told her, showing my badge. "Metro police. And you need to put something on, right now."

She wasn't even fazed. "There were supposed to be waiters," she said to no one in particular. It made me sad and disgusted at the same time. This girl didn't look like she was even out of high school yet, and the men we were here to arrest were old enough to be her father.

"Check her clothes before she puts them on," I told one of the female officers on the entry team. Besides myself there were five uniformed cops, a rep from Youth and Family Services, three detectives from the Prostitution Unit, and three more from Second District, including my friend John Sampson.

Second District is Georgetown—not the usual stomping grounds for the Prostitution Unit. The white brick N Street town house where we'd arrived was typical for the neighborhood, probably worth somewhere north of five million. It was a rental property, paid six months in advance by proxy, but the paper trail had led back to Dr. Elijah Creem, one of DC's most in-demand plastic surgeons. As far as we could make out, Creem was funneling funds to pay for these "industry parties," and his partner in scum, Josh Bergman, was providing the eye candy.

Bergman was the owner of Cap City Dolls, a legit modeling agency based out of an M Street office, with a heavily rumored arm in the underground flesh trade. Detectives at the department were pretty sure that while Bergman was running his aboveboard agency with one hand, he was also dispatching exotic dancers, overnight escorts, masseuses, and porn "talent" with the other. As far as I could tell, the house was filled with "talent" right now, and they all seemed to be about eighteen, more or less. Emphasis on the less.

I couldn't wait to bust these two scumbags.

Surveillance had put Creem and Bergman downtown at Minibar around seven o'clock that night, and then here at the party house as of nine thirty. Now it was just a game of smoking them out.

Beyond the enclosed foyer the party was in full swing. The front hall and formal living room were packed. It was all Queen Anne furniture and parquet floors on the one hand and half-dressed, tweaked-out kids stomping to the music and drinking out of plastic cups on the other.

"I want everyone contained in this front room," Sampson shouted at one of the uniforms. "We've got an anytime warrant for this house, so start looking. We're checking for drugs, cash, ledgers, appointment books, cell phones, everything. And get this goddamn music off!"

We left half the team to secure the front of the house and took the rest toward the back, where there was more party going on.

In the open kitchen there seemed to be a big game of strip poker in progress at the large marble-topped island. Half a dozen well-muscled guys and twice as many girls in their underwear were standing around holding cards, drinking, and passing a few joints.

Several of them scrambled as we came in. A few of the girls screamed and tried to run out, but we'd already blocked the way.

Finally, somebody cut the music.

"Where are Elijah Creem and Joshua Bergman?" Sampson asked the room. "First one to give me a straight answer gets a free ticket out of here."

A skinny girl in a black lace bra and cutoffs pointed toward the stairs. From the size of her chest in relation to the rest of her, my guess was she'd already gone under the knife with Dr. Creem at least once.

"Up there," she said.

"Bitch," someone muttered under his breath.

Sampson hooked a finger at me to follow him, and we headed up.

"Can I go now?" cutoffs girl called after us.

"Let's see how good your word is first," Sampson said.

When we got to the second-floor hall, it was empty. The only light was a single electric hurricane lamp on a glossy antique table near the stairs. There were equestrian portraits on the walls and a long Oriental runner that ended in front of a closed double door at the back of the house. Even from here I could make out more music thumping on the other side. Old-school this time. Talking Heads, "Burning Down the House."

Watch out, you might get what you're after.
Cool babies, strange but not a stranger.

I could hear laughing, too, and two different men's voices.

"That's it, sweetheart. A little closer. Now pull down her panties."

"Yeah, that's what you call money in the bank right there."

Sampson gave me a look like he wanted to either puke or kill someone.

"Let's do this," he said, and we started up the hall.

TWO

Sampson's voice boomed over everything else. He gave one hard pound on the paneled mahogany door—his own version of knock and announce—and then threw it open.

Elijah Creem was standing just inside, looking every bit as pulled together as the pictures I'd seen of him—slicked-back blond hair, square cleft chin, perfect veneers.

He and Bergman were fully dressed. The other three—not so much. Bergman had an iPhone held up in front of him, taking a video of the freaky little ménage à trois they had staged there on the king-size sleigh bed.

One girl was laid out flat. Her bra was open at the front, and her bright pink thong was down around her ankles. She was also wearing a clear breathing mask of some kind, tethered to a tall gray metal tank at the side of the bed. The boy on top of her was buck naked except for the black blindfold around his eyes, while the other girl stood over him with a small digital camera, shooting more video from another angle.

"What the hell is this?" Creem said.

"My question exactly," I said. "Nobody move."

All of them were wide-eyed and staring at us now, except for the girl with the mask. She seemed pretty out of it.

"What's in the tank?" I said as Sampson went over to her.

"It's nitrous oxide," Creem said. "Just calm down. She's fine."

"Screw you," John told him and eased the mask off the girl.

The buzz from nitrous is pretty short lasting, but I didn't assume for a second that it was the only thing these kids were on. There were several blue tabs of what I assumed was more XTC on the nightstand. Also a couple of small brown glass bottles, presumably amyl nitrate, and a half-empty fifth of Cuervo Reserva.

"Listen to me," Creem said evenly, looking me in the eye. As far as I could tell, he was the ringleader here. "Do you see that briefcase in the corner?"

"Elijah? What are you doing?" Bergman asked, but Creem didn't respond. He was still watching me like we were the only two in the room.

"There's an envelope with thirty thousand dollars in that case," he said. Then he looked pointedly from a brown leather satchel on the antique setback cabinet, over to one of the three windows at the back of the bedroom. The fringed shades were all drawn, but it was pretty clear to me what he was going for.

"How much time do you think thirty thousand dollars is worth?" he said. He was unbelievably cool about the whole thing. And arrogant. I think he fully expected me to go for it.

"You don't seem like the climb-out-the-window type, Creem," I said.

"Ordinarily, no," he said. "But if you know who I am, then you know I've got quite a bit at stake here—a family, a medical practice—"

"Six and a half million in revenue last year alone," I said. "According to our records."

"And then there's my reputation, of course, which in this town is priceless. So what do you say, detective? Do we have a deal?"

I could tell he was already halfway out that window in his mind. This was a man who was used to getting what he wanted.

But then again, I wasn't a seventeen-year-old girl with a self-image problem.

"I think my partner put it best," I told him. "What was it you said, John?"

"Something like screw you," Sampson said. "How old are these kids, Creem?"

For the first time, Dr. Creem's superior affect seemed to crack right down the middle. His silly grin dropped away, and the eyes started moving faster.

"Please," he said. "There's more cash where that came from. A lot more. I'm sure we can work something out."

But I was already done with this guy. "You have the right to remain silent—"

"I don't want to beg."

"Then don't," I said. "Anything you say can and will be used against you—"

"For Christ's sake, you're going to ruin me! Do you understand that?"

The narcissism alone was kind of staggering. Even more so was the cluelessness about what he'd done here.

"No, Dr. Creem," I said as I turned him around and put the cuffs on. "You've already done that to yourself."

THREE

TWO MONTHS TO THE DAY AFTER ELIJAH CREEM'S UNFORTUNATE SCANDAL broke in the headlines, he was ready to make a change. A big one. It was amazing what a little time, a good lawyer, and a whole lot of cash could do.

Of course, he wasn't out of the woods yet. And the cash wasn't going to last forever. Not if Miranda had anything to say about it. She was only speaking to him these days through her own attorney, and he hadn't been allowed to see Chloe or Justine since the future ex–Mrs. Creem had packed them off to her parents' house in Newport. Word from the lawyer was that they'd be finishing out the school year there.

The silence from the girls had been deafening as well. All three of his blond beauties—Miranda, Justine, Chloe—had swiftly turned their backs on him, just as easily as closing a door.

As for the medical practice, there hadn't been a consult, much less a booking, since it had come out in the press that Dr. Creem (or Dr. Creep, as a few of the less savory rags were calling him) had traded surgical procedures for sex with more than one of Joshua Bergman's unfortunately underage protégées. Between that, and the little video collection Creem had accumulated on his home computer, there was still the very real possibility of a jail sentence if they went to trial.

Which was why Elijah Creem had no intention of letting that happen. What was the old cliché? *Today is the first day of the rest of your life?*

Yes, indeed. And he was going to make it count.

"I can't go to prison, Elijah," Joshua told him on the phone. "And I'm not saying I don't *want* to. I mean, I *can't*. I really don't think I'd make it in there."

Creem put a hand over the Bluetooth at his ear to hear better, and to avoid being overheard by the passersby on M Street.

"Better you than me, Joshua. At least you like dick."

"I'm serious, Elijah."

"I'm joking, Josh. And believe me, I'm no more inclined than you are. That's why we're not going to let it come to that."

"Where are you, anyway?" Bergman asked. "You sound funny."

"It's the mask," Creem told him.

"The mask?"

"Yes. That's what I've been trying to tell you. There's been a change of plans."

The mask was an ingenious bit of latex composite, molded from human forms. The very newest thing. Creem had been experimenting with it since the scandal broke, and his own famous face had become something of a social liability. Now, as he passed the plate-glass window in front of Design Within Reach, he barely recognized his own reflection. All he saw was an ugly old man— sallow skin, sunken cheeks, and a pathetic remnant of dry, silver hair over a liver-spotted scalp. It was spectacular, actually. Poetic, even. The old man in the reflection looked just as ruined as Dr. Creem was feeling these days.

Dark-rimmed glasses masked the openings around his eyes. And while the lips were tight and uncomfortable, they were also formfitting enough that he could talk, drink, eat—anything at all— with the mask on.

"I didn't want to let you know until I was sure this would work," Creem told Bergman, "but I've got a surprise for you."

"What do you mean? What kind of surprise?" Bergman asked.

"Joshua, do you remember Fort Lauderdale?"

There was a long pause on the line before he responded.

"Of course," he said quietly.

"Spring break, 1988."

"I said I remembered," Bergman snapped, but then softened again. "We were just a couple of fetuses then."

"I know it's been a while," Creem said. "But I've given this a lot of thought, and I'm not ready to just go quietly into the night. Are you?"

"God no," Bergman said. "But you were the one who—"

"I know what I said. That was a long time ago. This is now."

Creem heard his friend take a long, slow breath.

"Jesus, Elijah," he said. *"Really?"*

He sounded scared, but more than that he sounded excited. Despite the mousy tendencies, Bergman also had a wonderfully twisted streak.

He'd always been more excited by the murders than Creem.

For Creem, they'd been cathartic as much as anything else. A means to an end. And this time around, he had a whole new agenda.

"So...this is really happening?" Bergman said.

"It is for me," Creem told him.

"When?"

"Right now. I'm waiting for her to come outside as we speak."

"And, can I listen?"

"Of course," Creem said. "Why do you think I called? But no more talking. Here she comes now."

FOUR

CREEM POSITIONED HIMSELF ACROSS THE STREET FROM DOWN DOG YOGA AS the seven forty-five evening class let out. Among the first to emerge onto Potomac Street was Darcy Vickers, a tall, well-proportioned blonde.

He couldn't take credit for the tall or blond part, but as for the well-proportioned elements, those were all thanks to him. Darcy's ample bust, the perfectly symmetrical arch of her brows and lips, and the nicely tapered thighs represented some of Dr. Creem's best work.

Not that Darcy Vickers had ever expressed the first drop of gratitude. As far as she was concerned, the world was populated with her lackeys. She was a typical specimen, really—a K Street lobbyist with a steroidal sense of entitlement and a desperate need to stay beautiful for as long as possible.

All of it so very familiar. So close to home, really.

He waited outside Dean & Deluca while she ran in for whatever it was women like her deigned to eat these days. He watched while she held up the line at the register, talking obliviously away on her cell phone. Then he crossed the street again, to follow her down the quaintly cobblestoned alley toward the garage where Darcy's Bimmer was parked.

There was no need to keep too much distance. He was just some geezer in a windbreaker and orthopedic shoes—all but invisible to the Darcy Vickerses of the world. By the time they reached the deserted third level of the garage, he'd closed the gap between them to less than twenty feet.

Darcy pressed a clicker in her hand, and the Bimmer's trunk popped open with a soft click. That's when he made his move.

"Excuse me—Miranda?" he said, half timidly.

"Sorry, no," Darcy said, dropping her grocery bag and purple yoga mat into the trunk without even a glance.

"Funny," he said. "You look so much like her." When the woman didn't respond, he stepped in closer, crossing that invisible line of personal space between them. "Almost exactly like her, in fact."

Now, as she turned around, the annoyance on her face was clear, even through the Botox.

"Listen," she said, "I don't mean to be rude—"

"You never do, Miranda."

As he came right up on top of her, she put a hand out to deflect him. But Dr. Creem was stronger than the old man he appeared to be. Stronger than Darcy Vickers, too. His left hand clamped over her mouth as she tried to call out.

"It's me, sweetheart," he whispered. "It's your husband. And don't worry. All is forgiven."

He paused, just long enough to see the surprise come up in her eyes, before he drove the steak knife deep into her abdomen. A scalpel would have been nice, but it seemed best to stay away from the tools of his own trade for the time being.

All the air seemed to leave Darcy Vickers's lungs in a rush, and she collapsed forward, bending at the middle. It was a bit of work to get the knife out, but then it came free all at once.

With a quick sweep of his leg, Creem kicked her ankles off the ground and lifted her into the trunk. She never even struggled. There were just a few gurgling sounds, followed by the glottal stoppage of several half-realized breaths.

He leaned in close, to make sure it would all reach Bergman's ears over the phone. Then he stabbed again, into the chest this time. And once more down below, opening the femoral artery with a swift, L-shaped motion, so there could be no chance of recovery.

Working quickly, he took a hank of her long blond hair in his hand and sawed it off with the serrated edge of the knife. Then he cut another, and another, and another, until it was nearly gone, sheared down to where the scalp showed through in ragged patches. He kept just one handful of it for himself, tucked into a Ziploc bag, and left the rest lying in tufts around her body.

She died just as ugly as she had lived. And Dr. Creem was starting to feel better already.

When it was done, Creem closed the trunk and walked away, taking the nearest stairs down toward M Street. He didn't speak until he was clear of the garage and outside on the sidewalk.

"Joshua?" he said. "Are you still there?"

Bergman took a few seconds to answer. "I'm...here," he said. His breath was ragged, his voice barely above a whisper.

"Are you..." Creem grinned, though he was also a little disgusted. "Joshua, were you masturbating?"

"No," his friend said, too quickly. Bergman had an ironic sense of modesty, all things considered. "Is it done?" he asked then.

"Signed, sealed, delivered," Creem said. "And you know what that means."

"Yes," Bergman said.

"Your move, old pal. I can't wait to see what you cook up."

Part One

WIN, LOSE, OR DRAW

CHAPTER
1

IN THE PREDAWN DARKNESS OF APRIL 6, RON GUIDICE SAT BEHIND THE WHEEL of his car, keeping an eye on the house across the way.

Alex Cross's place was nothing special, really. Just a white three-story clapboard on Fifth Street in Southeast DC. The shutters were ready for a coat of paint. There was a tidy little herb garden on the front stoop.

Cross lived here with his grandmother, his wife, and two of his three children, Janelle and Alex Jr., aka Ali. The oldest Cross child, Damon, was home for spring break, but he spent most of his time at boarding school these days. And there was a foster kid, too. Ava Williams. It wasn't clear whether she was on track for adoption, or what. Guidice still had some digging to do. He liked to know as much as possible about his subjects.

There were a dozen Metro police officers on his list, and he'd been keeping tabs on all of them, mostly as a point of comparison. But Cross was special. Alex was the one that Guidice wanted to kill.

Just not yet.

Killing a man was easy. Any half-wit with a gun could put a bullet in someone's head. But really *knowing* a man—learning his weak spots first, getting to know his vulnerabilities, and taking his life apart, piece by piece? That took some doing.

Meanwhile, whether Cross knew it or not, he had a big day ahead of him.

Guidice watched the front windows, waiting for a light to come on. It wasn't strictly necessary to spend this much time on a subject, but he enjoyed it. He liked the quiet of the early morning hours, even if it meant just sitting and absorbing the seemingly inconsequential details—the missing chunk of concrete on the stairs, the eco-friendly bulb in the porch light. It was all part of the larger picture, and you never knew which tiny piece might take on some kind of significance in the end. He passed the time scribbling observations into a spiral notebook on his lap.

Then, just after five, a soft stirring came up from the backseat.

"Papa? Is it time to get up?"

"No, sweetheart," he said. He kept his chin down and his eye on the house. "You can go back to sleep."

Emma Lee was cuddled up in an army sleeping bag with her favorite Barbie, Cee-Cee. Her pillowcase had Disney's Cinderella on it. She'd chosen it for the picture of the little helper mice, whom she adored, for whatever reason.

"Will you sing me something?" she asked. " 'Hush, Little Baby'?"

Guidice smiled. She always called songs by their first words.

" 'Hush little baby, don't say a word,' " he sang quietly. " 'Papa's going to buy you a mockingbird....' "

The front hall light came on in Alex's house. Through the frosted glass of the door, Guidice could see the tall, dark shape of the man, descending the stairs.

Guidice continued to take it all down while he sang. " 'If that mockingbird don't sing, Papa's gonna buy you a diamond ring....' "

"A real one?" Emma Lee interrupted. It was the same question, every time. "A real diamond ring?"

"You bet," he said. "Someday, when you're older."

He looked back over his shoulder into the soft, sleepy eyes of his daughter and wondered if it was even possible to love someone more than he did her. Probably not.

"Now go back to sleep, Baby Bear. When you wake up again, we'll be home."

CHAPTER
2

I GOT THE FIRST CALL AT HEADQUARTERS AROUND TWO O'CLOCK THAT afternoon.

A woman had been found dead in the trunk of her car, in a Georgetown parking garage. Pretty unusual for Georgetown, so my hackles were up more than usual. I took the elevator straight down to the Daly Building garage and headed out with an extra-large coffee in hand. It was going to be a long-ass day.

That said, I really do like my job. I like giving a voice to the people who can't speak for themselves anymore—the ones whose voices have been stolen from them. And in my line of work, that usually means through some kind of violence.

The responding officer's report was that a garage attendant at American Allied Parking on M Street had found what looked like a pool of dried blood underneath a BMW belonging to one Darcy Vickers. When the cops arrived, they'd forced open the trunk and confirmed what they already suspected. Ms. Vickers had no pulse, and had been dead for some time. Now they were waiting for someone from Homicide to arrive and take it from there.

That's where I came in. Or at least, so I thought.

It was a beautiful spring day. The best time of year in DC. The National Cherry Blossom Festival was on, and we hadn't yet gotten hit with the first wave of summer humidity—or summer tourists. I had my windows down and Quincy Jones's *Soul Bossa Nostra* up loud enough that I almost didn't hear my phone when the second call came in.

Caller ID told me it was Marti Huizenga, my sergeant at the Major Case Squad. I juggled the volume down on the stereo and caught the call just before it went to voice mail.

"Dr. C.," she said. "Where are you?"

"Pennsylvania and Twenty-First," I told her. "Why?"

"Good. Take a right on New Hampshire. Another body just popped up, and it sounds god-awful, to tell you the truth."

"So you thought of me."

"Natch. I need someone over there right away. It's a bad scene, Alex—a dead girl, hanging out of a sixth-floor window. Possible suicide, but I don't know."

"You want me on this instead of Georgetown?"

"I want you on both," Huizenga said. "At least for now. I need one set of eyes on both scenes, as fresh as possible. And *then* I want you to tell me this is all just a coincidence, okay? I'm asking politely here."

Huizenga's sense of humor was as dark as mine could be sometimes. I liked working with her. And we both knew that the difference between two *unrelated* dead bodies and two *related* ones was the difference between not getting much sleep for the next forty-eight hours, and getting none at all.

"I'll do my best," I said.

"Vernon Street, between Eighteenth and Nineteenth," she said. "I'll tell Second District to get started without you at the garage in Georgetown, but try to be there as soon as you can."

That's kind of like telling the clouds when to rain. I had no idea how long I'd be at this new scene. You never do until you're there.

And this one turned out to be a nightmare.

CHAPTER
3

VERNON STREET IS JUST A SINGLE TREE-LINED BLOCK OFF THE WEST END of U Street. It's a quiet residential area, but I could see a crowd of people pooled on the sidewalk as soon as I turned the corner from Eighteenth. Most of them were looking up and pointing at a mansard-roofed brick building on the south side of the street.

As soon as I got out of my car, I saw the girl. It was like a check in the ribs. She hung suspended by her neck on a length of rope, about three feet below one of the dormered sixth-floor windows. Her face was visibly discolored, and her hands seemed to be tied behind her back.

Jesus. Oh Jesus.

There were two cruisers and an ambulance parked out front, but the only personnel I saw was a single cop on the door of the apartment building. The rest of the sidewalk was filled up with looky-loos, snapping away on their phones and cameras. It pissed me off as much as it amazed me.

"Get this street roped off, right now!" I told the cop on my way into the building. "I don't want to see anyone on that sidewalk by the time I'm up there looking down, you got it?"

I knew he had his hands full, but I couldn't help

feeling revved up by the whole thing. This girl was someone's daughter. She had a family. They didn't need her picture on some goddamn Facebook page for the world to see.

I left the cop to it and took the stairwell instead of the elevator. It seemed like a more likely exit, if this was in fact a murder we were talking about. And you only get one chance to see a crime scene for the first time.

When I came out into the sixth-floor hall, another cop and two EMTs were waiting outside an open apartment door. The building had three units on this level, all facing the street. Our dead girl was apparently in the center one.

"Door was locked when we got here," the police officer told me. "That splintering on the frame is us. We were inside just long enough to get a flatline on the girl, but it wasn't easy. I can't guarantee we didn't move anything in there."

The apartment was a small alcove studio. There was a closet kitchen to one side, an open bathroom door on the other, and a futon couch that looked like it doubled for a bed. As far as I could tell, there were no signs of a struggle. In fact, the only thing that looked out of place was the old-fashioned coat tree, braced sideways against the open window, with a loop of rope hanging down from the center.

I forced myself to enter the room slowly, checking for drag marks, or anything that might have been left behind. When I got to the window and looked down, I could see the top of the girl's head, just out of reach. Her heel had broken through the window of the apartment below, and the cord around her wrists seemed to be more of the same rope that had been used in the hanging.

That didn't rule out suicide, either. A lot of people will bind themselves just before they do the deed, to keep from trying to struggle free in the heat of the moment.

Down below, another cruiser had arrived and the street was clear. But now I had another problem. When I looked straight across, I could see at least a dozen people in the windows of the facing apartment building, looking my way—more phones, more cameras. I wanted to give them all the finger, but I held back.

Still, I wasn't going to let this go on for one second longer than I had to.

"Give me a hand over here!" I shouted toward the hall.

Technically, the body at any crime scene belongs to the medical examiner, not the cops. But I wasn't thinking about technicalities right now. I was thinking about this girl and her family.

I already had my own phone out, and I fired off a bunch of shots. I got the coat tree, the window frame, the rope, and the girl, from above. I needed to preserve as much detail as I could before I did what I was about to do.

"Sir?" a cop said behind me.

"Help me pull her in," I said.

"Um...don't you want to wait for the ME?"

"No," I said, pointing at the audience we had across the street. "Not anymore. Now give me a hand, or get me someone who will!"

CHAPTER
4

WE LAID THE GIRL OUT AS CAREFULLY AS WE COULD ON THE FLOOR OF THE apartment, and left the rope around her neck. As long as she was out of the public eye, that's all I needed. The rest I could leave to the investigation.

Her name was Elizabeth Reilly. According to the driver's license I found in a purse by the front door, she was just two weeks shy of turning twenty-one. The apartment had all the signs of someone who lived alone, from the Lean Cuisines in the freezer to the single towel and washrag hanging neatly in the bathroom.

Obviously there was more to the story here, but I wasn't seeing it yet.

When the ME did arrive I was glad to see it was Joan Bradbury. Joan's an easygoing, sixty-something Texan. As far as I knew, she never came to work in anything but top-stitched cowboy boots, even after twenty years in DC. She's opinionated, but also easy to work with, and didn't give me any big lectures when she saw what I'd done with the body. Joan has four daughters of her own; I think she instinctively got it.

While she started her initial exam, I got our team of investigators out knocking on doors, especially across the street. This hanging had gone down in broad daylight. Someone had to have seen something.

I also got some more info from Sergeant Huizenga on our victim. Elizabeth Reilly had been a nursing student at Radians College on Vermont Avenue until the previous December, when she'd dropped out. There was no word yet on recent employment, but other than one unpaid parking ticket her record was squeaky clean.

By the time I got back to Joan, they were ready to wrap and bag the body for transport to the morgue.

"I'm going to need a full autopsy," she told me, "but I'm thinking this girl was dead before she went out the window. Maybe strangled with the same rope."

She reached down and pointed at some dark, purplish marks on Elizabeth Reilly's lower neck.

"You see these contusions? These are all consistent with manual strangulation. But up here, higher, where the rope caught her? Just faint bruising. If there was any blood flow when she was actually hanged, those marks would be darker."

I rocked back on my heels and ran a hand over the bottom of my face.

"This is what I was afraid of," I said.

"There's more, Alex."

Normally Joan was pretty matter-of-fact, even at the roughest scenes, but there was a tightness in her voice I'd never heard before. This one was getting to her.

"The abdomen's still flaccid, and she's got obvious striations around her midsection and breasts," she told me. "As far as I can make out, our girl here had a baby recently. And, Lord help me, I mean *recently*."

CHAPTER
5

IT WAS LATE EVENING BY THE TIME I FINALLY GOT OVER TO THE AMERICAN Allied Parking garage in Georgetown. The site was well preserved, but Darcy Vickers's body had already been removed. I'd have to fill in some blanks with the crime-scene photography later and glean what I could for now.

Ms. Vickers's silver BMW 550i was parked on the third level. That's where she'd been found. One of the Second District detectives, Will Freemont, walked me through it. He seemed like he wondered what I was doing so late to the party, but that was the least of my worries right now. My thoughts were still consumed by the Elizabeth Reilly case.

"So, they found her in here," Freemont said, pointing into the open trunk. "Stab wounds were here, here, and here." He pointed with two fingers to his own chest, abdomen, and upper leg. "This lady didn't die too well, but you can bet she died quick, for whatever that's worth. And just for shits and giggles, I guess, he cut off her hair, too."

Left behind were a yoga mat, a briefcase, a few shopping bags, and a garment bag, all covered in a combination of dried blood and a mess of loose blond hair, some of it matted with the blood.

There was also a good-size dark stain—more blood—pooled on the cement under the car.

"He would have needed it to be quick," I said. "It's a pretty risky site for a murder."

"He?" Freemont said.

"I'm guessing," I said. It was all about first impressions at this point. "What do we know about Darcy Vickers?"

The detective flipped open a small notebook, the same kind I carried, and looked down at it.

"Forty-two years old. Divorced, no kids. Works for Kimball-Ellis on K Street, mostly retainer work for a couple of the big tobacco companies. Supposedly she had a real cutthroat reputation, from what I've got so far."

In other words, Darcy Vickers had plenty of enemies. Most lobbyists do. But not every lobbyist ends up stabbed to death in the trunk of a car. Who, exactly, would want to do this? And why?

And for that matter, could this possibly have anything to do with Elizabeth Reilly's hanging?

Nothing obvious had been taken. Darcy Vickers's wallet, cash, phone, and jewelry were all still there, as far as anyone knew. That led me to believe that the killing itself was the motive, either to satisfy some impulse for violence or to get rid of this woman in particular—or maybe both.

In those respects, the two cases seemed the same. But the m.o. was completely different.

Assuming Elizabeth Reilly hadn't committed suicide, her killer wanted the body put on display for everyone to see. He would have had to go to some trouble for that. Whereas with Darcy Vickers, it was all about the act itself—the stabbing, and then for whatever reasons, the cutting of the hair.

My gut was telling me these were two different cases, but we still had a lot of background work to do. Maybe these two women shared some connection, somewhere.

"Any witnesses?" I asked Freemont.

"Not exactly," he said. "But security cameras picked up something interesting."

He unfolded several sheets from his pocket, and showed me a series of black-and-white screen captures.

"This is nine oh four last night. We've got Ms. Vickers, coming in the east entrance from the alley over there. Then, right behind her, we've got this guy."

The image showed a middle-aged, or maybe elderly, white male. The picture quality wasn't great, but it was clear enough for a few details. He was bald, with dark-rimmed glasses, and what looked like a Members Only jacket, with the snaps on the shoulders.

"At nine oh nine, we've got the same guy leaving a different way, out toward M Street, and still on foot," the detective went on. "What he was doing in here for five minutes is anyone's guess."

"What about cameras on this level?" I said.

"Right there." He pointed toward a badly battered unit in a corner of the ceiling. "Someone took it out just after eight o'clock last night. Threw a rock at it, or something."

"So, then..." I stopped to think about this. "If the old guy has anything to do with it, why just take out one camera? Why let himself be seen on two others?"

"I know," he said. "Good question. We've got a BOLO out on him right now. If we can get him in, we might start to put together some answers."

Maybe, I thought. But something told me it wasn't going to be that easy.

CHAPTER
6

I GOT HOME AROUND FIVE THAT MORNING, HOPING TO CATCH A COUPLE HOURS of sleep.

And I guess that's what happened. I barely remember crawling into bed next to my wife, Bree. The next thing I knew, light was streaming in through the windows, and we were under attack by a small band of munchkins.

"Wake up, wake up, wake up! Doo-do-doo! It's a big day!"

Ali, my youngest, had already crawled right up the middle of the bed, and was kneeling there between us. My daughter Jannie stood at the end, all dressed and ready to go.

"It's seven thirty, Daddy," she said. "We're supposed to be there by nine!"

"Oh...right," I said.

"You didn't forget, did you?"

"No," I said. "Of course not. We'll be right down."

Of course—I had forgotten. I'd been planning on being at the ME's office first thing for the morning briefing, and then sitting in on Elizabeth Reilly's autopsy.

But the kids were right. Today was a *big* day.

This was lottery day at Marian Anderson Public Charter School, the best high school in Southeast, and one of the best in the city. Jannie, as well as Ava, who was living with us now, had both put in applications, along with four hundred and twenty other eighth graders, looking for one of the hundred and five spots available in that fall's freshman class. By law, charter schools have to hold a lottery when supply exceeds demand—which it always does—and we were hoping against hope to get both girls in.

"You know, you don't absolutely have to be there," Bree said, rubbing my back on the side of the bed. "I saw the news last night. I know you're buried at work. Nana and I can cover this."

"No," I said. "I'm coming. I just need to get this cement out of my head."

Over the past several months, I'd missed Christmas Eve, Ali's play, Damon's quarterfinals, and most Sunday mornings at church, to name a few. This felt like my last line in the sand, and I wasn't going to cross it. I'd call someone to cover for me at the ME's office until I could get there.

Downstairs at breakfast, Nana Mama had the griddle fired up, and all the kids had stacks of pancakes in front of them when Bree and I came in. It was a full house these days, with Damon home for spring break, and now Ava bringing our total up to seven.

"Good morning, children," Nana said, of course meaning me and Bree. She's the undisputed matriarch of our family, and the kitchen is her throne room. "Blueberries or no blueberries?"

I went straight for the coffee.

"What're you doing up? Didn't you just get

home?" Nana muttered at me from the stove. I mumbled back something about *big day.* I wasn't thinking about a whole lot more than caffeine at that moment.

"So who's feeling lucky today?" Bree asked from the head of the table.

Everyone's hand went up but Ava's. She just kept shoveling her food in, eating fast like she always did.

"What about you, Ava?" I said. "Are you excited?"

She shrugged, and answered with a mouthful of pancakes. "S'not like I'm gonna get in."

"Don't be so gloomy, Gus," Nana said from the griddle. "Attitude is everything."

If I'm being honest, though, it wasn't hard for me to understand Ava's pessimism at all. She was far brighter than she let on—maybe even brighter than she knew. It wasn't about that, though.

She'd landed in our laps some months back after her mother, a junkie, had OD'd and left her to live alone on the streets of Southeast. There were still plenty of issues for Ava to work through, and I'd set her up with my own therapist, Adele Finaly. In the meantime, we had our good days and bad days.

Basically, Ava had been hardwired not to expect too much from life—and consequently, not to want too much. Every now and then I caught a smile, or an unguarded moment, and in a way it showed me the potential she had waiting for her, if we could just help her see it, too. The one thing she didn't have was hope. It's what I'd call an inner-city epidemic—and nothing holds a person back more than that.

If there was anything we could do to change the shitty hand life had dealt Ava so far, we were going to do it.

One good day at a time.

CHAPTER
7

FILING INTO THE GYM AT MARIAN ANDERSON, YOU MIGHT HAVE THOUGHT THERE was a carnival going on. There were balloons flying everywhere, and faculty and staff in bright yellow and green T-shirts, greeting everyone with big smiles.

Inside, the bleachers were all pulled out and chairs were set up on the gym floor. Between the kids who had applied, their parents, siblings, and school staff, there were nearly a thousand people in that gym, and the place was buzzing with nervous tension.

Nana's lips were pursed from the second we got there. She tried to stay upbeat, for the girls' sake, but she'd also been a teacher for forty-one years. She had some definite opinions about this particular ritual.

"*Mm-mm-mm,*" she said, looking around. "You know why we're here today? Because we adults can't get off our duffs to offer more than a random chance at a good education in this city, that's why."

I think the gridlock on education reform in Washington pisses Nana off more than anything else in life. There was no escaping the fact that three quarters of the people in that gym were go-

ing to leave disappointed today. Some of them—
especially the poorer families—were going to be
devastated. The only other free option for high
school in our area was one of DC's so-called
dropout factories, where less than sixty percent of
entering freshmen graduate.

We found a block of seats on the floor and settled in. Jannie stayed on her feet, looking around
for some of her friends, but Ava just sat quietly in
her chair.

Finally, just after nine, the school's principal got
up on stage to welcome everyone. And then they
got right to it, pulling cards out of a rolling hop-
per and calling out the names, one by one.

"Monique Baxter...Leroy Esselman...Thomas
Brown..."

With every new draw, there was a shout, or a
scream, or some flurry of movement from somewhere in the gym. It really was like winning the
lottery. Each kid whose name was called got to
walk up on stage, cheered along by the faculty,
where they got a welcome packet, and then they
were ushered back out again in a flurry of applause.

As the names went by, lots of people were
making hatch marks on pieces of paper in front
of them, or counting down on their fingers. I
had Jannie on one side of me and Nana on the
other. The tension coming off both of them was
palpable.

Within about ten minutes, the lottery was already starting to wind down. We got up to name
number eighty-two, eighty-three, eighty-four...
and then—

"Janelle Cross!"

Just like that, we were the ones jumping up and hugging each other, swept along in the excitement of the whole thing. I'm not going to pretend I wasn't thrilled, because I was. This was a great opportunity for Jannie. But even as I headed up to the stage with her, I couldn't help looking back to see what Ava was doing.

She was just sitting there and staring at the floor like nothing had happened. Like she was made of stone—at least on the outside. Bree had an arm around her, and waved me on toward the stage. It was a tough bit of mixed feelings for me to juggle.

But maybe, just maybe, we could get lightning to strike twice before this whole thing was over.

NO SUCH LUCK.

By the time Jannie and I had circled all the way around and back to our seats, the lottery was over. Most of the people were on their feet now, milling around and getting ready to leave.

Ava was still in her chair, scuffing her feet back and forth. She looked numb, as much as anything else.

Nana looked angry. Bree looked heartbroken.

"I'm sorry, Ava," I said, sitting down next to her. "I wish it had come out differently."

"Wha'ever," she said. "I knew I wasn't gettin' in."

It was frustrating to me, when the world behaved exactly as Ava expected it to. If I had to guess, I'd say she wanted in just as badly as Jannie, if for no other reason than to feel like she'd won something for once.

Jannie came over and sat on the other side of her. Several families around us were holding each other, and a lot of their kids were crying. Some of the parents, too. It had all gone by so fast.

"This sucks," Jannie said. "Sorry, Ava."

"No, you ain't." Ava turned on her with a sudden glare. When Jannie tried to take her hand, she snatched it away and stood up fast. "Come on," she said. "It's time to go. The lottery's over." Then she started walking out ahead of the rest of us without looking back. There was nothing to do in the moment but soldier on and follow her out.

Nana took my arm as we went. I could feel her shaking with anger.

"It's insanity, is what it is," she said. "Why in God's name should children have to win a damn lottery to get a good education? And right here in the nation's capital! What does that say about our country to the rest of the world, Alex? What?"

Even the "damn" was unusual for her, but I knew how she felt. The problem was so big, and so intractable, it was hard to even know who to be mad at anymore. The school chancellor? The teachers' union? The mayor? God?

"I wish I had some answers for you, Nana. I really do," I said.

"Well, I'll tell you what," she went on. "Miss Ava Williams will not be falling through any cracks, thank you very much. That girl is going to get the education she deserves if I have to give it to her myself."

In other words, Nana Mama was going to get done whatever the chancellor, teachers' union, mayor, and God hadn't seen fit to accomplish.

And I had every faith that she would. One hundred percent.

CHAPTER
9

RON GUIDICE SAT IN THE BLEACHERS AT MARIAN ANDERSON HIGH SCHOOL, taking notes as the school lottery played out. The place was jam-packed. Not too many white folks, but enough that he didn't stand out, anyway. Nobody would even notice that he didn't have a fourteen-year-old of his own in tow.

Emma Lee played quietly the whole time at his feet, undressing and redressing Cee-Cee without a peep. She had the patience of a little saint, that was for sure.

Maybe she got that part from me, he thought.

Meanwhile, he sat and watched the Cross family as the lottery wound down. Interestingly enough, he found himself glad to hear Jannie's name called out over the public address system. And then he was sorry when it became clear that Ava hadn't made it in.

Poor Ava. That girl couldn't catch a break, could she? Unless you counted getting in with the Cross family to begin with. They were "good people," on paper. Guidice was even starting to like them a little more than he would have preferred. The grandmother and the kids, anyway. It happened all the time. He couldn't help getting involved with his subjects.

Would they be devastated when Alex was dead and gone? Of course they would. That was the part that couldn't be helped. The world was full of innocent victims.

He'd been one himself, once. Thanks to Alex.

But none of that mattered—not as long as he kept an eye on the bigger picture. Always the bigger picture.

That's where Alex Cross was a dead man walking.

CHAPTER
10

I SKIPPED LUNCH WITH THE FAMILY AND GOT MYSELF STRAIGHT OVER TO THE new Consolidated Forensic Lab at Fourth and School Streets. It's an amazing building—two hundred and eighty thousand square feet of facilities under one enormous roof. MPD finally had firearms, toxicology, DNA, fingerprint analysis, and the medical examiner's office all in one place.

As soon as I got there, I threw on a surgical gown and mask and pushed in through the swinging door of the examination suite where Joan Bradbury was already halfway through Elizabeth Reilly's autopsy.

"What have we got so far, Joan?" I asked.

"A lot," she said. "Come on in."

The body was open on the table, with a long Y cut down the middle of the torso, which had been flayed open by now. I've sat through more autopsies than I can remember, and my stomach's way past any kind of trouble with this stuff. At the same time, I never let myself forget the reason I'm there. I owed Elizabeth that much, at least.

"I did a tox screen on her blood last night, just to get a jump on things," she told me. "We got a positive read for antidepressants, and, get this— Pitocin."

"Pitocin? You test for that?"

"Not usually, but under the circumstances, I thought I might check. Glad I did, too. Pitocin doesn't stay in the system too long, only around forty-eight hours. Which means Elizabeth Reilly induced her labor less than two days before she died."

My mind started spinning around this new piece of information. So far there were no hospital records for Elizabeth Reilly in the area, and no record of any live births under that name, much less an induced labor.

Was it possible she'd done this on her own for some reason? She'd been a nursing student. She could have easily known how to get her hands on some Pitocin, and maybe even known how to administer it.

But why?

And meanwhile, was there a three-day-old baby out there somewhere? I needed to find out, ASAP.

"By the way," Joan went on. "We didn't find any rope fibers on her fingers or palms at all. Someone else put that noose around her neck. And if all that weren't enough, the break in the second and third vertebrae was definitely post-mortem. I've got a few hours to go here, but I can tell you right now, my report's going to rule out suicide."

Ultimately, cause of death is the ME's to call. I hardly ever disagreed with Joan's conclusions, and I didn't have any reason to do it today, either. This was now officially a homicide investigation.

Maybe also a missing persons case.

I had my work cut out, that was for sure.

CHAPTER
11

THE FIRST THING I DID WHEN I LEFT THE MORGUE WAS FIND SAMPSON. HE WAS catching up on his reports at the Second District station house, and I pulled him outside for a talk.

I've known John all my life, and I trust him as much as anyone at MPD. He's also been around long enough that he knows people all over the city. More specifically, he knew which people at which agencies were going to be willing to talk to him about a missing baby without eighteen and a half signatures on two dozen forms first. I understand why we've got a lot of the paperwork we do, but there's a time and a place. This wasn't it. If speed was my number one priority right now, discretion was a close second.

We stood out by my car in the station house parking lot, downing some sandwiches and going over the details.

"All indications are that this was a vaginal birth. No signs of episiotomy, or any hospital intervention at all," I told him. "Given the Pitocin in Elizabeth's system, and the fact that nobody we've talked to said anything about any pregnancy, it seems pretty clear she was trying to keep this a secret."

"It's not so hard to hide a pregnancy," John

said, flipping through the file I'd given him. "Especially if nobody's looking."

"Exactly. Her neighbors barely knew her, and she dropped out of school five months ago."

"What about family?" he asked. "Next of kin?"

"Not much. She's got two grandparents down in Georgia who raised her, and that's about it. According to them, she fell off the radar a while ago. They haven't heard from her since Christmas."

"In other words, this baby could be—"

"Anywhere. Yeah."

John chugged the last of his Diet Coke and obliterated the can in his huge hand. There's a reason we call him Man Mountain. "I'm going to need something stronger here," he said.

"Talk to Youth Division, see if any of this rings a bell," I told him. "Harry Keith over there will keep his mouth shut, if you need some help. Go district by district if you have to. Check the NCMEC database as often as you can, and talk to their people over in Alexandria. Just don't say anything about me or this case."

This was the thing. Elizabeth Reilly's pregnancy was the only card we were holding close anymore. If our killer had any connection to her baby, I didn't want him to see us coming, and I was already publicly attached to this very public story. That's where Sampson came in.

The other possibility was that there might not be a baby to find anymore. We didn't know if Elizabeth's pregnancy had been full term; if the baby was delivered stillborn; or God forbid, if it had been killed for some reason I didn't understand yet.

Right now, all of that was a question mark. But for the baby's sake, as well as the mother's, we had to assume that there was still someone out there to save.

CHAPTER
12

FOR THREE DAYS WE GOT NOWHERE. THERE WAS NO SIGNIFICANT MOVEMENT on the Darcy Vickers or Elizabeth Reilly murders, and the phone call I kept hoping to get from Sampson never came. You could just feel these cases going cold.

Then on that Saturday morning, we had a new development. The worst kind. Another body popped up in Georgetown.

I was home when I got the call from Sergeant Huizenga. She wanted me to keep going in the direction I'd been going, and monitor this homicide alongside the other two. The trick would be to see this scene on its own merit first, without comparing it to anything. Sometimes if you go looking for connections, you start to see what you want to see instead of what's really there.

I took Pennsylvania, and then M Street, all the way to the Key Bridge and parked just below it. Several cruisers were already on-site, and they'd strung an outer perimeter of yellow tape across Water Street, on the south side of the Potomac Boat Club.

A maintenance worker had found the boy's body that morning, lodged under one of their docks. By now someone had pulled him onto the shore and left him there, on a little spit of dirt and grass just beyond the white-clapboard-and-green-shingled building.

The first sight of him was a shock, even for me. The apparent cause of death was a gunshot to the face, with an ugly, wide-open entry wound that told me he'd been hit at close range. It was hard to know what kind of powder burns or stippling had washed away in the water, but there were still a few dark marks around the remains of his cheek-bone. A couple of smashed teeth were exposed where the flesh had been blown away, and it gave him a kind of sideways grimace, almost as if he were still in pain.

That wasn't all. His jeans were stained dark all around the hips and crotch, presumably from stabbing. There were at least half a dozen ragged perforations in the denim of his pants, clearly cen-tered around the genital area. It was a horrible proposition to think about what had happened to this poor kid. I could only hope for his sake that he'd been shot dead first, and mutilated after. Not much consolation there.

The most depressing part was how young he was. He didn't look any older than eighteen, and his waterlogged letterman's jacket was from St. Catherine's, a private high school in Northwest DC. How he had gotten here, like this, was any-one's guess.

My one clear hit was that this had been done in anger—possibly at the victim himself, but also maybe out of the killer's own sense of self-loathing. Mutilation can be a signifier of that, as often as not. Either way, our perpetrator obvi-ously had some kind of demons to exorcise. You don't need a gun *and* a blade if your motivation is strictly murder.

In fact, it felt a little to me like this killer was getting out all of his ideas at once—stabbing, shooting, drowning. But why? What need did that satisfy?

After I'd taken in all the details I could, I slipped on some gloves and checked the boy's pockets. They were all empty, but I did find a name, Smithe, stenciled on the back of his jacket. I called it in right away.

It didn't take long to get word back, either. A few minutes later, a call from our Command Information Center told me that an eighteen-year-old senior at St. Catherine's, Cory Smithe, had been reported missing by his parents two days earlier. Six one, blond hair, and a small birthmark on his right wrist. Check, check, and check.

"Have you got an address?" I asked the dispatcher.

"Already sent it to your phone," she told me.

Because we both knew what I had to do next.

CHAPTER
13

WHEN I HEADED BACK TO MY CAR ON THE FAR SIDE OF THE BOATHOUSE, I saw that the locust storm had descended—the kind with cameras, microphones, and broadcast towers.

Instead of the usual half-dozen reporters we might have seen by now, there were dozens of them, just waiting for the story. Trucks were lined up on Water Street, and without a designated press space everyone was right there on the tape line.

This was three bodies in less than a week, centered around one of DC's least violent neighborhoods. By comparison, the previous three murders anywhere west of Rock Creek had been spread out over a fourteen-month period. People were definitely sitting up and taking notice.

"Detective Cross, over here!"

"Who's the victim, Alex?"

"Are you considering this a serial investigation at this point?"

It's a little like being a rock star, without any of the fringe benefits. I gave them the bare minimum, which was all I could afford to do right now.

"Sergeant Huizenga will be out to brief you after the family has been notified," I told whoever was closest. "We won't be releasing any details in the meantime."

"Detective Cross, will you be overseeing all three of these cases?" Shawna Stewart from Channel Five asked me.

"I don't know yet," I told her.

"How are the Darcy Vickers and Elizabeth Reilly investigations coming along?"

"They're coming," I said, just as I reached my car.

"Hey, Alex, is it true you pulled Elizabeth Reilly's dead body out of that window before a proper examination?" someone else yelled out. "Doesn't that compromise the investigation?"

That one stopped me cold. Maybe I should have kept moving, but instead I turned around to see who had asked the question.

This guy struck me as a one-man operation from the first glance. I'd seen his type before—camera around his neck, a handheld recorder pointed my way, and a notebook sticking out of the pocket of his cargo shorts. He also had a full beard, and no press credentials that I could see. Everyone else around him had laminated badges from the city, clipped to their lapels or hanging on lanyards around their necks.

"I don't recognize you," I said. "Who are you with?"

"I'm just trying to get the facts, detective."

"That's not what I asked," I said. "I asked who you're with."

He raised his voice then, enough to make sure the microphones all around us were picking him up. "Am I a suspect, detective? Are you saying you want to detain me?"

He was baiting me. I've seen it a million times. If they can't get the story they want, they'll try to create one—especially the hacks and the wannabes.

"No, I'm not detaining you," I said. "It was just a simple question."

"Why? Am I required by law to identify myself?" he said.

Now he was just being a dick. The civilian in me wanted to shove that recorder right down his throat.

"No," I said again. "You're not required to identify yourself."

"In that case—no comment," he said, fighting back a smile. It got a laugh from a few in the crowd, but not from me. The best thing I could do right now was get in my car and leave.

I had somewhere more important to be, anyway. And it couldn't wait.

CHAPTER
14

BY THE TIME I PULLED UP IN FRONT OF CORY SMITHE'S HOME, I FELT LIKE I HAD a fifty-pound bag of gravel sitting on my chest. Family notifications are the hardest part of my job, hands down.

The Smithes lived in one of the thousands of early twentieth-century row houses that line the streets of Northwest DC. This one was on Shepherd Street in Petworth, with a tiny, terraced stamp of green lawn halfway up the stairs to the front door. In the middle of the grass was a statue of the Virgin Mary, surrounded by a bed of spring tulips. Maybe the Lady would give these people some comfort when they needed it most.

I'd already notified the Fourth District missing persons unit. They had Victims Services on the way over, but this part was all on me. I climbed the stairs and rang the bell.

Cory's father answered the door almost right away. He looked a lot older than I would have expected, and had a cane hooked over his wrist.

"Can I help you?" he asked, a little warily.

"Mr. Smithe? I'm Alex Cross from the police department," I told him. "I'm here to speak with you about Cory. May I come in?"

There are a few things you want to avoid in

this kind of situation. One of them is mentioning up front that you're from Homicide. Notifications need to unfold at the right pace—not too fast, but not too slowly, either.

"Come in," he told me, and opened the screen door. "My wife's in the back."

He hobbled on ahead of me, and I followed him through to a screen porch off the kitchen. Mrs. Smithe was there, in slippers and a flowered housecoat. She clutched the neck of it closed and stood up as I came in. The cordless phone on her lap fell onto the floor, but neither of them seemed to notice.

"What is it?" she said. I could tell by her face that she'd already been contemplating the worst. I quickly reintroduced myself, and then got right to it.

"I wish there was an easy way to say this," I told them.

"Oh Lord. No..."

"I'm so sorry, but Cory's been killed. He was found this morning."

It was like her voice cracked the air. There weren't any words now, just a gut-wrenching expression of grief. Loss. Devastation. She sank down onto her knees and leaned against her husband, who was still holding the cane, trying not to go down himself, I think. He bent his head toward his wife's with his eyes squeezed shut, the cane shaking between the two of them.

"Where?" Mr. Smithe choked out. "Where was he?"

"In the Potomac," I said. "At the Georgetown waterfront." There's no sense holding back information at this point. It was better for them to get it from me than some other version on the news later.

"Killed?" he said. "As in—"

"Somebody did this to him, yes," I said. "Again, I can't tell you how sorry I am."

I think a lot of people assume that's lip service when cops say it, but the truth was, I could have cried right there with them. The loss of a child is a tragedy, whoever's it is. You learn to keep it inside.

I waited until I felt like they could hear more from me, and then moved on.

"I know how hard this is," I said, "but if you could give me a little information about Cory, it could be a big help."

Mr. Smithe nodded, still on his feet. His wife was back in her chair, quietly weeping.

"What do you need to know?" he asked.

"The kinds of things Cory liked to do, where he hung out, the friends he spent the most time with. That sort of thing," I said.

His mother looked up then. "Was he in some sort of trouble?" she asked.

"I don't know," I told them honestly.

"He was a good boy," Mr. Smithe said. "I know every parent must say that . . . or maybe they don't. But Cory walked hand in hand with God. He prayed with us every night. In fact, he's supposed to start at Catholic University in the fall. A theology major."

Later I'd learn that Mr. Smithe was a deacon at the family's church, and his wife had been a nun for twenty years. This had to feel to them like the cruelest possible blow from God.

I pressed them for as much as I could, and took

down the names of Cory's closest circle. There was a girlfriend, Jess Pasternak, they said. She lived only a few blocks away. That was as good a next stop as any.

Then I gave the Smithes my card with my cell number written on the back, and left them to grieve in private. The best thing I could do for them now was keep moving.

As usual, time was not on my side.

CHAPTER
15

"IS THAT WHAT THEY TOLD YOU? CATHOLIC U? ALTAR BOY, AND ALL THAT?"

Half an hour later, I was sitting in my car with Jess Pasternak. She had her legs pulled up on the seat, hugging her knees to her chest and crying bitterly while we talked.

When I'd shown up at her house, she'd asked to speak with me outside. Since she was eighteen, like Cory, that was her prerogative. After a tense exchange with her parents at the door, she'd followed me down to the curb.

Now, whatever it was she had to say, it wasn't coming easily.

"Why?" I asked her. "Is there something Cory's parents didn't know about?"

She pounded the seat with her fist, literally fighting back the tears. It was like she was two parts devastated, and one part pissed off about something.

"I warned him," she said. "I really did."

"Jess? What are we talking about?" I said. "I know this is hard, but you've got to tell me everything."

She sat up straighter and wiped her eyes. It left a dark streak of makeup on the back of her hand,

and she absently wiped it onto the knee of her torn jeans.

She was a pretty girl, but not in the traditional, St. Catherine's kind of way. Her blond hair was cut short above her ears, and she wore a wifebeater with thin leather suspenders over it, along with calf-high black boots. She looked more rocker chick than cheerleader to me.

"Cory wasn't even going to college," she said. "We were going to travel in the fall. You know— France, Italy, la-la-la." She corkscrewed her hand in the air like it was all so much folly, now.

"How does that relate to what's happened?" I asked. I hadn't given her any of the specifics of Cory's murder, but she seemed to assume that something awful had been done to him. Which it had.

"I swore I'd never say anything," she told me, twisting the withered tissue in her hand. I could tell she was getting close, so I just sat quietly and waited.

Suddenly, she hitched up on the seat and pulled a silver phone out of her back pocket. I thought she was about to make a call, but instead she went onto the web and navigated to a page of some kind.

"There." She dropped the phone on the seat between us. "I didn't say a word, okay?"

When I picked up the phone, I saw she'd opened up a site called Randyboys.com. More specifically, it was a profile for Cory Smithe— or Jeremy, as he called himself there. When I thumbed down the page, I saw there were pictures, too—Cory, with his shirt off; in his underwear; nude from behind, with his face obscured.

The profile said he was available for outcalls only, no overnights, no travel. No Sundays either, I noticed.

"They told me you were his girlfriend," I said.

"Yeah, well…" Jess let out a scoff between her tears. "I mean, don't get me wrong. Mr. and Mrs. Smithe are super nice and everything. They're just kind of clueless about the whole gay thing. Much less"—she gestured at the phone without looking at it—"all that."

"Do you know anything about the men Cory was hooking up with?" I asked. "Were there regular customers?"

She held up her hands in a shrug. "He just said they were all letches and chicken hawks. Guys with money, I guess."

"Do you know where he'd meet with them?"

"Wherever they wanted," she said. "At a hotel, in the park, down by the waterfront…"

She rolled her eyes, and it seemed to hit her all over again that her friend was gone. Then the tears started back up.

"I told him to be careful. I really did, but he wouldn't listen. That asshole!"

I gave Jess my last tissue and let her cry. I didn't read too much into the anger, other than a defensive kind of reaction to feeling overwhelmed. As far as I could make out, she was telling me everything she could about Cory.

And, if I was lucky, she'd just given me a little bit about his killer, too.

CHAPTER
16

TALK ABOUT HAVING TO PULL IT TOGETHER. AFTER SPENDING THE DAY ON WHAT would be any parent's worst nightmare, I had to turn around and show up at home with something like a smile on my face. Especially tonight. This was Damon's last night before he had to go back to school for fourth quarter, and I was taking everyone out to dinner at Kinkead's.

For once I was glad to be running behind when I got home, if only as an excuse to grab a few minutes by myself. One shower, shirt, and blazer later, I was at least looking fit for public consumption.

By the time I was sitting down at my favorite restaurant, with my family chattering and laughing all around me, I was even starting to feel halfway human again. David Yarboro was on piano that night; I had a nice glass of pinot noir in front of me; and for just a little while, I could pretend that my biggest problem was deciding between the salmon and the New York strip with Kinkead's Scotch whiskey sauce.

Life was good. It really was.

After everyone ordered dinner, I pushed back my chair and stood up with my glass. It got some glances from around the room, and I noticed Jannie looking a little mortified—but if embarrassing your kids isn't one of the privileges of being a dad, I don't know what is.

"I'd like to make a toast," I said.

"White, wheat, or rye?" Nana joked, and got a laugh all around the table. My grandmother reads me as well as anyone. I'm pretty sure she could tell I needed a boost that night.

"To our guest of honor," I said. "Damon, you make me proud, every single day. We're going to miss you like crazy while you're gone, but in the meantime—here's to you. Here's to a great quarter at Chapin. And most of all, here's to summer vacation, when we get to see you again."

"Here's to summer vacation!" the kids chorused back.

"Close enough," Bree said, and we all clinked glasses around the table.

After that, Damon stood up to make a toast of his own. I could see all too well that my oldest boy, standing there at the head of the table in a jacket and tie, wasn't really a boy anymore. It didn't help that he was fifteen but looked twenty.

"Here's to Ava," he said, looking right at her. "I know you and I haven't really spent that much time together, but I just want to say, welcome to the family."

"Welcome to the family!" everyone echoed back.

I looked over at Ava and was a little shocked to see her grinning from ear to ear. Ever since the school lottery, she'd been scowling her way through the day, and spending long stretches of time alone in her room. Now it was like someone had turned on the lights for the first time in a long time.

And that's why my boy Damon is a star. With just a few words, he managed to get something out of Ava that I'd barely been able to do in four months. He may be the quietest of my kids, but that's the thing about the quiet ones. When they do speak up, it's usually for a good reason.

Or even a great one.

Suddenly, my eyes were stinging and the room went a little fuzzy. I never even saw it coming. It was like the whole day just washed over me in one big wave—all that stress on the way in, and everything I was so grateful for on the way out.

"Daddy?" Ali leaned over and looked up into my face. "Why are you crying?"

"I'm not," I said, wiping my eyes. "Well, maybe just a little." I pulled him up onto my lap and put my arms around his little string-bean body. "But they're happy tears," I said.

"Don't mind him, children," Nana told everyone. "Despite appearances, Mr. Dragonslayer over here is just an old softie at heart."

"True that," I answered.

Then Nana gave me a wink and raised her glass to make one more toast. "Here's to old softie, who can cry all he likes, but he's still paying for dinner!"

CHAPTER
17

RON GUIDICE GOT HOME AROUND TEN THIRTY THAT NIGHT. AFTER GETTING up at five, and crisscrossing the city all day, he was exhausted. Still, there was plenty of work to do. It was probably going to be another all-nighter.

Just inside the door of his simple Cape house in Reston, he stepped out of his shoes. It was an old habit from growing up in New Hampshire, with its long winters and subsequent mud seasons. He set his Timberlands in the rubber tray by the door, alongside Emma Lee's little sneakers and his mother's old slip-ons.

"Hey, Mom, I'm home," he called out.

Lydia Guidice jerked awake on the couch, with a chubby hand to her chest. She'd been sacked out in front of *NCIS,* or *CSI,* or *SVU*—whatever it was. Guidice could never tell one of those shows from the other.

"Good Lord, you scared the bejesus out of me," Lydia said. "I still can't get used to that beard of yours. Makes you look like some kind of terrorist."

"Uh-huh." Guidice leaned into the fridge and pulled out a Bud. "Emma Lee eat okay?"

"All her chicken nuggets and seconds on applesauce. She went down about eight thirty."

"Good, good. You want anything?"

"I wouldn't mind a little ice cream," his mother said.

In fact, ice cream was the last thing Lydia Guidice needed. She hadn't weighed herself since she slipped past the three-hundred-pound mark. But the ugly truth was, his mother was a lot easier to take when she was stuffing her face.

"Where were you tonight?" she asked, pushing herself up to sitting.

"Work," he said.

"You might have called."

"We've been over this, Mom. If I don't call, it means I'm working late. I don't understand what's so complicated about that."

"I just worry, that's all. Would it really kill you to pick up the phone?" she asked.

Guidice took a long hit of his beer. It was the same dance, every goddamn time.

"You know," he said, "if you want, I can just as easily take Emma Lee and find a smaller place—"

"No, no," his mother said.

"Take my benefit checks with me, too. I think they're hiring over at the Safeway right now. You want me to pick you up an application tomorrow?"

"Don't start," she said, and put out a hand for her dessert. Guidice stopped short, holding the quart of Breyers mint chip just out of her reach.

"Who's in charge, Mom?" he said.

"Oh, for pity's sake."

"Say it."

Lydia grunted testily and shifted her eyes up to meet his gaze. "You're in charge, Ronald. Always have been," she said. "Satisfied?"

Guidice handed her the ice cream and leaned down to kiss the top of her head.

"Then let's stop having this conversation, Mom, what do you say?"

The fact of the matter was, Lydia Guidice had never finished the tenth grade, never married Ron's father, and never held down a real job in her life. Now, at age sixty-two, three hundred and some pounds, and no Social Security coming in, she was about as marketable as a used condom, and they both knew it.

Guidice didn't enjoy making his mother squirm like this. That's why he only did it as often as necessary.

"I'm going to give Emma Lee a kiss, and then I'll be working in my room," he told her.

"Okeydoke."

"Love you, Mom."

"Love you, too, son," Lydia answered as she tucked into her ice cream. "Don't stay up too late."

GUIDICE TIPTOED INTO EMMA LEE'S ROOM AND STOOD OVER HER BED. SHE WAS all curled up like a little hedgehog in one corner under the covers, sleeping peacefully.

There was nothing more precious than this. Nothing.

He leaned down and stroked his daughter's sweet little cheek. Brushed her sand-colored hair away from her eyes. Kissed her forehead.

Halfway out of the room, he changed his mind. He could just as easily work in here. He parked himself in the white-painted rocker by the door instead and listened to the metronome of Emma Lee's even breathing.

Once his laptop was powered up, Guidice plugged his earbuds into the computer's audio jack and started opening Windows. There were notes to transcribe from the day, sites to check, listservs to monitor—but first, he wanted to make sure everything was up and running at Alex's house.

With the family out to dinner that night, there had been plenty of time to install an Infinity transmitter on each level of the Cross home. Each one was hardwired behind an existing outlet so there would be no issues with battery life or losing power. There were also three corresponding match-head-size microphones tucked into the kitchen, the master bedroom, and Alex's office on the third floor. If anything, Guidice was going to net more information than he would ever have time to weed through, but too much was definitely preferable to not enough.

He opened all three channels now, and let them stream simultaneously in his ears while he worked. Mostly it was quiet over there. Someone was watching TV, and it seemed that maybe Alex was in his office, just from the sound of shuffling pages and the occasional clearing of a throat.

It was a bizarre mash-up, really—sitting here gathering source material from the privacy of his daughter's bedroom. A peaceful moment in the middle of the storm.

There was still Lydia to worry about, but so far she was more use to him than she was trouble. In a way, it was like his mother knew which questions she could get away with, and which ones to leave alone. Like how they were affording to live, for starters.

Guidice's reporting hadn't brought in any appreciable income for quite a while now. Not since everything had changed—and not since the cash settlement, after the cops had stolen his life away from him.

As if a wad of money could make up for what they'd done!

It was nothing more than routine incompetence, the way Theresa had been allowed to die that night, right there on the sidewalk like a common criminal.

And not just Theresa, either. No one else had

known it at the time, but their unborn child had died that night, too, along with the only woman he'd ever loved. Both of them, murdered in cold blood.

And all on Alex Cross's watch.

CHAPTER
19

ELIJAH CREEM PREFERRED TO SECTION HIS OWN GRAPEFRUIT IN THE MORNING. He liked the way the membranous flesh gave so easily, but how it also demanded a certain element of precision from the blade of his knife.

He took his time with it that morning, lingering over his fruit, steak, and egg breakfast while he read the *Post*. One story in particular had caught his attention there, and he perused it twice through as he ate.

"Kate?" he called out to the housekeeper.

"Sir?" she said, poking her head through the swinging kitchen door into the dining room.

"Would you bring me my phone, please? I think it's in the hall."

"Certainly," she said, and disappeared again.

According to the paper, a boy from Northwest DC had been shot, stabbed, and dropped into the Potomac, where his body had been found floating just the day before. The *Post*'s coverage, at least, indicated that the police had no leads whatsoever on who might have done this.

"Oh, I heard about that," Kate said, suddenly back with his phone and looking over Dr. Creem's shoulder. "It was on every channel last night."

"Was it?" Creem said. "Apparently, the boy died quite horribly."

He liked that she didn't turn away. Instead, she leaned closer to get a look at the black and white picture of the victim. Also, close enough for Creem to rest a hand gently on the curve of her ass.

"So young," she said, though she was barely older.

She hadn't flinched at his touch, either. Kate, with her green card problems and sick father, certainly knew which side her bread was buttered on.

"That's all, for now," Creem said, and winked at her as she freshened his coffee. She smiled pleasantly.

He watched her go and waited until she was back in the kitchen, out of earshot. Then he picked up his phone and called Josh Bergman.

"Elijah?" Bergman answered. "Is something wrong?"

"No," Creem told him. "I know we agreed to keep a little distance for the time being. But I'm looking at the paper here, and I just had to ask if you've been as busy lately as I think you have."

"Oh, that," Bergman said, feigning nonchalance.

"I thought so," Creem said. Joshie had really upped his game since the last time around. It was impressive.

"And how are you, Elijah? I've been thinking about you."

"Never better," Creem told his friend—and it was true, to an extent. Maybe the old life had been burned down around him, but this new one was rising, phoenixlike, to take its place. "It turns

out I hated my wife for the last sixteen years. I just
didn't realize it until she was gone," he said.

"What about the girls?"

"I miss them terribly," Creem deadpanned.
"But in the meantime, I wear what I like to the
table, I don't have any of those soul-sucking dinner parties on my schedule anymore, and I'm seriously considering that little dark-eyed housekeeper of mine."

"You mean Kate? Nice choice," Bergman said.
He'd always liked hearing about Creem's sex life,
and only sort of tried to hide the fact. "What's
stopping you?"

"Nothing, I suppose," Creem answered. "But
Josh, listen. One more thing. I want you to know
how much I appreciate you. How much I *have* appreciated you, through all of this."

"Elijah, have you been drinking?"

"I'm serious," he said. "I think you're the only
real friend I've ever had."

"Okay, fine," Bergman said. "Then let me listen
while you doink your maid."

Creem laughed it off. They kept each other en-
tertained, that was for sure. "I'm hanging up now,
Josh. Thanks for ruining the moment."

"Just remember—the ball's in your court,"
Bergman said.

"Yes, of course," Creem told him. "I can hardly
wait."

Then he hung up the phone, picked up the
small, serrated knife from the table, and headed
off to the kitchen.

CHAPTER
20

KATE WAS DOING DISHES WHEN HE CAME IN.

"Can I get you something, Dr. Creem?" she asked.

"No, no, I'm fine," he said, coming to stand over by the sink. "I just meant to tell you before that you should help yourself to anything left in Miranda's closet upstairs. I think she was about your size."

"That's very nice. Thank you," she said.

"Also, there's really no need for the uniform anymore," he said, indicating the gray-and-white aproned dress she wore. "That was really Miranda's thing, not mine."

Kate kept washing the glass in her hand, but she smiled beautifully. For a girl who had obviously never had any work done, she was quite the specimen.

"How do you get anything done in this, anyway?" Creem asked. He reached over and fingered the hem of her uniform, letting his thumb brush against her thigh. "Looks awfully uncomfortable to me."

"I don't know," she said, looking down.

"I think you'd be much more comfortable"—

Creem raised the knife in his hand, up to the white collar at the back of her neck—"like this."

He pulled the collar back and drew the blade straight down, cutting a ragged line all the way through to the skirt.

She squealed when he did it, and stiffened right up. So did Creem.

"It's all right," he said. "I'm a surgeon. You're in good hands."

Now she laughed nervously, but also pressed her body against his, grinding into him with her ass. She wanted him, didn't she? Of course she did. He was Dr. Elijah Creem. There were all kinds of things he could do for her.

And to her.

Creem reached around front and cut away the skin-thin fabric of her panties next. It wasn't the same as cutting actual flesh, but it had its appeal. Besides, his life was complicated enough right now. He couldn't afford to take out his own maid. What was the expression—don't shit where you eat?

Instead, he bent her over the sink, with the warm water still running, and entered her right there.

"Relax," he told her. "This should feel good."

With the very tip of his blade, he reached up again, and drew it softly down the exposed skin of her back. Using only the slightest pressure, just enough to raise a few skin cells, it left behind a fine white line, like a tiny chalk mark. She shivered as he did it—either loving this, or displaying some killer acting skills. Creem didn't care which.

He didn't last long after that, either. The ruined uniform, and the sight of the girl bent over the sink, catching warm water in her hair, was enough to get him off. But then, with one fleeting mental image of the knife taking his place inside of her, Creem was quickly past the point of no return.

Up and over.

Fourth of July fireworks, and all that.

When he was done, he sent little Kate upstairs to pick out something else to wear. He even gave her a wad of cash to go shopping with afterward, and the rest of the day off.

"Thank you, Dr. Creem," she said in her quaint accent. "Thank you so much."

"No, thank *you*," Creem said. "What a lovely way to start the day."

He smiled as she scooted out, letting her enjoy herself for now.

By the end of the week, she'd be looking for another job.

CREEM'S APPOINTMENT WITH HIS CRIMINAL ATTORNEY WAS SCHEDULED FOR nine thirty that morning. He showed up at the L Street offices of Schuman and Pace just after ten.

"Elijah," Bill Schuman said, coming around the desk to shake his hand. "Good to see you." He paused to let Creem apologize for his tardiness, but Creem only nodded. He'd probably be charged for the time, anyway.

"Have a seat. Please," the lawyer told him.

"Don't mind if I do."

He took the button-tufted tweed couch near the door instead of the leather swivel by Schuman's desk. Schuman seemed a little puzzled, but didn't say anything as he sat back down and started flipping through the file in front of him.

"Give it to me straight, doc. How long do I have to live?" Creem asked.

"You're in a good mood," Schuman said.

"Just got laid, if you want to know."

His lawyer looked at him with an expression somewhere between offended and envious. It was the look of a guy who hardly ever got laid himself.

"Anyway," Schuman went on, "things are moving along. We've got Lew Carroll coming down from New York for second chair, and I've already pinned down the two best jury consultants in the city for this trial."

"Fine, fine," Creem said. "Do we have a lot to go over?" Now that Joshie had thrown down the gauntlet with such determination, he had much more interesting things to think about.

"Well...yes," Schuman said. "Of course we do. Elijah, you've got to focus here. If you want to get your money's worth on this defense—"

"At eight hundred and twenty-five an hour, I don't know if that's possible," Creem said.

Schuman raised his voice. "—then you're going to have to show up. And I don't just mean physically. Now, this pandering charge is a non-starter, but I want to talk about the pornography charge. That's where things start to get a lot stickier."

Creem wanted to say "No pun intended," but he kept his mouth shut.

"A worst-case scenario could be actual jail time," Schuman told him. "Five years for possession, or as much as fifteen if the DA starts talking distribution. Are you hearing me on that?"

"When do you expect to go to trial?" Creem asked, his first serious question.

"June fourth," Schuman said, "unless I can talk the DA into something more palatable."

"Such as?"

"Well, a plea bargain, for one."

"No," Creem said.

"Elijah, at least listen to the range of options—"

"No." Creem got up and paced over to the window. "I'm not taking a plea on this. I'll wait for the trial. You just do your goddamn job."

"I *am* doing my goddamn job!" Schuman said,

showing his first bit of real spine. "I don't understand. Why aren't you—?"

He stopped short then, and dropped his head. "Oh...cripes. Please don't tell me...."

Now Schuman stood up and walked over to where Creem was watching the traffic down on L Street. When he spoke again, it was in a needless hush.

"Elijah, please tell me you're not planning on doing something stupid, like fleeing the country. Just tell me that much, at least."

Creem smiled again, looking down at Schuman. Maybe this tightly wound little man was smarter than he looked.

"Now why would I need to do that, Bill?" he said. "I've got the best lawyer in the city working for me."

CHAPTER
22

AT THAT AFTERNOON'S MAJOR CASE SQUAD BRIEFING, SERGEANT HUIZENGA GOT the ball rolling by letting us know that word had come down from on high, approving all overtime requests until further notice.

That got a round of applause—it's not unusual for cops to work off the clock when things get as tight as they were these days. But of course, on the clock was better.

"One guess," I heard someone mutter behind me. "Al Ayla."

Just a few months earlier, Washington had taken several hard hits by the Saudi-based terrorist organization, also known as The Family. Both the mayor and the chief of police had caught hell over that one, with accusations of mishandled resources and slow response time to the crisis as it played out.

The one good thing that had come out of it, apparently, was that we now had the kind of resources we could really do something with. Patrol units in and around Georgetown had been doubled during daylight hours, and in some cases tripled at night. A dedicated tip line had been established, and our neighborhood outreach people were on the street every day.

Some of that was about increasing the scope of the investigation, to be sure, but some of it was also about heading off the inevitable public flogging you get, no matter how hard you work.

Each of our three homicides now had a lead detective assigned, along with a full squad of investigators. I'd be running between all three, along with whichever personnel I could pull in from the districts, as needed. Huizenga was happy to have me working with Sampson on the search for Baby Reilly, since the Major Case Squad was out flat right now. As long as these three cases were all grouped under one umbrella, I was the guy holding the umbrella.

When Huizenga handed the floor over to me, I started by putting the three victims' morgue photos on the screen at the front of the room for everyone to see. It wasn't easy to look at, but my whole focus right now was about trying to draw some lines between these cases.

"These are now officially in chronological order, left to right," I told everyone. "The autopsy puts Cory Smithe's time of death at twenty-four hours after Elizabeth Reilly's, and forty hours after Darcy Vickers's."

People started taking notes. A few just watched and listened, absorbing the details, which is more my own style.

"Beyond the issue of timing," I said, "we've got a fair amount of common ground here, but mostly in pairs. Almost nothing I've found so far cuts across all three cases. Two of the victims were stabbed, for instance—although even there, Ms. Vickers's wounds were fatal, whereas Mr. Smithe was mutilated postmortem. In both cases it was done with a narrow, but not identical blade.

"Two of these victims, obviously, were women," I went on. "Two were found in Georgetown proper, although we don't know for sure where Smithe was put into the river, so the primary crime scene there is still an unknown."

The captain of our Homicide Branch, Frank Salazar, interrupted with a question—probably *the* question on everyone's mind.

"Alex, I know we're at the supposition phase, but what's your bottom line right now? How many perpetrators do you suppose we're looking at?"

I took a beat to think about it. The short answer was—*I wish to hell I knew.*

"Here's the problem," I said. "There's no scenario right now that doesn't defy logic, or at least, likelihood. We've never seen anything like this before, given the geography and the time frame. But I will say that it seems to me, a single killer is highly unlikely. The greater question in my mind is whether our perps are operating independently of each other, or not."

That went over like a lead balloon. People were getting anxious for answers, both inside and outside the department. But without more information than we currently had, we were still flying blind on all three of these murders.

Meanwhile, the whole time I'd been talking, I could feel my phone vibrating—once, twice, a third time, in quick succession. As soon as Huizenga started fielding a few of the questions, I took out the phone and checked messages. They were all from Sampson—two voice mails and a text. That seemed like a good sign to me.

Since I was still in the briefing room, I checked the text first, and sure enough, it was exactly what I'd been hoping for.

Alex—Package found. Give me a call, ASAP.

CHAPTER

23

FIRST THING THE NEXT MORNING, SAMPSON AND I CAUGHT THE EARLIEST possible flight from DC down to Savannah, Georgia.

Elizabeth Reilly's baby had been found three days earlier, newborn and alone, in a rental cabin on the northern edge of the Okefenokee Wildlife Refuge. If it weren't for CODIS, the national DNA database, that little girl would have been absorbed into the system, put up for adoption, and probably never identified. Instead, as soon as her sample went online, it was only a matter of time before Sampson got a crossmatch to Elizabeth Reilly. With DNA, that meant a hundred percent certainty that this was her child.

A Charlton County sheriff's deputy, Joe Cutler, met John and me when we arrived late that morning, at the entrance to Oke-Doke Cabins and Campground. The place had a dozen rental units spread out over a thirty-acre parcel, and Cutler briefed us while we drove back toward the cabin in question. I wasn't even sure what I was hoping for here, just something to start clueing us in about what had happened to this poor girl.

"I was the one who responded to the call," Cutler told us. "Found that little butterbean all wrapped up in a towel and crying her head off. She probably wasn't more'n a few hours old, but we got her right over to the NICU at Charlton Memorial, and she checked out just fine. No thanks to whoever left her here, of course."

"And you don't know who called it in?" I asked.

"Just an anonymous ten twenty-one," he said. "But I'd put my money on the mother. Probably some teenage girl who didn't have the guts to admit getting knocked up, you know?"

Maybe, I thought. Cutler obviously had his own feelings about what had happened here, but I was trying to keep an open mind as we drove back through the woods.

Eventually we came into a clearing, where a single log cabin sat up against a stand of enormous kudzu-choked oak trees. The woods were fairly dense all around here, and if there were any other buildings nearby, I couldn't see them.

This cabin was one of the so-called deluxe units, which only meant that linens were provided and there was an indoor bathroom. Still, Elizabeth could have theoretically had everything she needed to deliver her own baby here, including plenty of privacy.

At the front door, Cutler stopped to point out some gouge marks around the hammered iron knob. "Didn't actually rent the place," he said. "Just kind of helped herself. You can check availability online, so it wouldn't have been too hard to know which one'd be empty."

Inside the cabin was sunny, clean, and basic. There was a knotty pine floor with a farm table made out of the same wood, a small kitchenette, a queen-size bed under the dormered window. A bookshelf in the corner had a couple of games and some discarded paperbacks—Dean Koontz, Patricia Cornwell, Stieg Larsson. Nothing to indicate what might have actually happened here.

I tried to imagine the scene. Did Elizabeth set up her own IV by the bed? Would she have administered the Pitocin right away? How long did the delivery take?

She had to have been terrified, but that only meant that something even more terrifying had motivated her to come all the way down here.

Something—or someone. Was it the father? The killer?

Were those one and the same? I had no proof either way, but that was the version of the story that made the most sense to me, as John and I poked around, trying to put together the pieces of this invisible puzzle.

"I'll tell you something else," Cutler said, watching us from the door. "I kind of hope that baby's daddy never turns up. Considering the mother, I can't imagine he's any prize either, you know? I mean, seriously—what the hell was that girl thinking? That's what I'd like to know."

I didn't say anything, but I was starting to think that Elizabeth Reilly just might have been trying to save her daughter's life by coming here.

Also, that she just might have succeeded.

CHAPTER
24

SHELLMAN BLUFF, ABOUT TWO HOURS NORTH OF OKEFENOKEE, IS A LOW country fishing town in Georgia, with tidal marshes all along the coast, once you get that far. On the map the whole area looks like a maze of tributaries feeding into Sapelo Sound, which itself feeds right into the Atlantic.

Sampson and I didn't have any trouble finding Tommy and Jeannette Reilly's place, a small stilt house overlooking the causeway at the dead end of a quiet road in the village. This was where Elizabeth Reilly had grown up—and now maybe where her daughter would, too.

It was eighty-five degrees when we got out of the car. Not unusual for Georgia, but a little ahead of DC's temperatures. I was sweating in my jacket and tie.

Down by the water I saw an older woman standing on the dock. She wore a loose white dress, and had a long gray braid down her back. When she turned around, I saw she had a small bundle in her arms, too. John and I walked down from the dirt driveway to meet her halfway, on the dry brown patch of a back lawn behind the house.

"Grow 'em tall up in Washington, don't they?" she said, craning her neck, especially at

Sampson, who's six nine. We'd already spoken on the phone; there was no real need for introductions. "I'm going to guess you boys are hungry from your trip."

"We're fine, ma'am, thank you," Sampson said. "Looks like you've got your hands full there, anyway."

Mrs. Reilly beamed and turned to show us the tiny little girl. Baby Reilly, as I'd come to think of her.

"This is Rebecca," she said. "Our miracle child."

The baby was sleeping peacefully, wrapped up in a thin pink blanket. Her face was pink, too, from the heat, and her hair was the same sandy blond that her mother's had been. For me, there was a definite sense of relief, just laying eyes on her after all the searching and worrying about what might have happened. I think Sampson probably felt the same way.

Inside, we met Tommy Reilly, who looked to be in his early sixties, like his wife. I couldn't imagine taking on a newborn at that age, but he lit up just as brightly when he took Rebecca into his arms. It seemed clear to me that these people had already fallen deeply in love with their great-granddaughter. Maybe that's why they seemed so at peace here, all things considered.

Once we were settled around their kitchen table, I started in with some necessary business.

"Mr. and Mrs. Reilly, I don't mean to alarm you," I said, "but I have to ask. Have you considered relocating for the time being, or even putting Rebecca into county custody until this can all be sorted out?"

"You mean, until they find out who killed our Lizzie," Mr. Reilly said.

"That's right," I said. "Just as a precaution."

"You know, this isn't Washington, detective," he said, bouncing the baby gently on his shoulder. "I don't mean to come off naive, but it's pretty quiet around here. And for that matter...well, let's just say I'm a firm believer in the Second Amendment. I think we'll be okay."

"But we do appreciate the concern," Mrs. Reilly added.

I nodded, and took my time answering. I could imagine that giving up Rebecca, even just for a little while, could be traumatic under the circumstances.

"What if we talked to your sheriff's office about setting up a unit outside?" I asked. "Just for overnights, until we know a little more. I'd feel a lot better if we erred on the side of caution here."

"For Rebecca's sake," Sampson added.

The Reillys looked at each other across the table again. Without saying anything, they seemed to come to some kind of silent agreement, the way couples can sometimes.

"You do what you have to do," Mr. Reilly said. "I still think you're going to be wasting Earl's time, but I won't chase him off. How's that sound?"

Once that was settled, we were able to move on to the subject of Elizabeth herself.

"I know you've probably been asked before," Sampson said, "but is there anyone we should be talking to in Washington? Any friends, or boyfriends Elizabeth ever mentioned? Or for that matter, anyone who might have had some kind of grudge against her?"

Mr. Reilly shook his head and went to put Rebecca down in the raised bassinet by the window.

"I'm not sure Lizzie had a whole lot of friends up there," he said. "We kind of thought Washington was going to be a chance for her to spread her wings, and whatnot, but she never really did cotton to it. Or to the people, for that matter."

"There was one boy," Mrs. Reilly said. "I suspect he's the daddy, and maybe even—" She stopped, at a loss. "Maybe the one you're looking for. But honestly, I have no idea."

Sampson took out his pad and a pen. "Do you have a name?" he asked.

"Russell," she said, while John scribbled it down.

"Russell? Is that a first or last?"

"First," Mrs. Reilly said. "At least, I assume so. Lizzie only mentioned him in a few of her letters. Then he just kind of fell off the radar—last fall, I guess it was."

"I don't suppose you still have any of those letters?" I asked.

The smile I'd seen before came back onto Mrs. Reilly's face. "Oh, honey, I have all of them," she said. "Nobody writes real letters anymore, but Lizzie did. I figured those were worth saving. You just sit tight. I'll go get my Lizzie box."

CHAPTER
25

FOR THE NEXT HOUR, SAMPSON AND I SAT ON THE REILLYS' BACK DECK GOING through an old rosewood box, full of cards and letters Elizabeth had sent her grandparents during her two years in Washington. We put them all in order by postmark, and then started reading.

Most of the letters were on the same pink-and-gray stationery with Elizabeth's monogram at the top. They were usually decorated with funny little doodles and cartoons in the margins, and she always signed off with a heart dotting the *i* in her name.

At the same time, several of the letters were poignantly honest, about how lonely Elizabeth felt and how hard it was to meet people in the city. What I started to piece together here was a picture of a girl who had been a little naive about the world, a little young for her age, and probably all too vulnerable to a predator.

As for this Russell person, the first mention of him that we found was buried in the middle of a long letter from April of the previous year.

Want to hear something funny? I met a nice man the other day—at the Laundromat, of all places!! You never know, right? He talked to me the whole time I was there, and even offered to pay for my dryer. I thought that was cute, but I told him no thank you, maybe the next time.

And I'll tell you two a secret—I hope there IS a next time. Gentlemen aren't exactly easy to find in our nation's capital!!! Something tells me I'm going to have some extra-extra clean clothes over the next few weeks, ha-ha-ha.

The next mention came a month later, when she wrote to her grandparents that she'd run into "Laundromat guy (whose name is Russell, btw)" and that she'd accepted a dinner invitation this time. A subsequent letter described how Russell had driven her around to see the monuments at night. It was all very chatty, and never offered any other details about where this guy was from, what he did for a living, or who he actually was. Whether Russell had been keeping that information from Elizabeth, or if she was keeping it from her grandparents, I couldn't tell.

What I did know was that by early December, she was lying to them outright.

Dear Granny and Dodo,
I'm writing to tell you something that I'm too chicken to call and say. It looks like I won't be home for Christmas, after all. We've got exams coming up after the break, and I promised my study group I'd meet three times a week in the meantime.

PLEASE DON'T HATE ME!! And don't even think about coming up here. Xmas wouldn't be the same in DC, and hotels are crazy expensive anyway. Just know that I love you, and I'll be down to visit when I can.

Sending buckets of love,
Lizzie

That letter was dated December 11, which was a full eight days after Elizabeth had already dropped out of nursing school. She also would have been five months pregnant by then—too far along to hide.

And she never did make it home again, either. The last letter she ever sent was a birthday card for Tommy, in late March, where she wrote about classes I knew she wasn't taking, and mentioned several times how much she was looking forward to seeing both of them that summer—presumably after the baby was born.

By the time John and I had read through Elizabeth's correspondence, it was time to go. We didn't have all the answers I might have liked, but what we did have was a new person of interest in this case. As soon as we were in the car and headed back to Savannah, I put out a call to Bree.

I didn't want to wait on this. I didn't want to wait on anything right now. Also, we'd already had one leak in the press about Elizabeth's pregnancy. There weren't a whole lot of people I trusted with these questions anymore.

"I've got a name I want to run through NCIC," I told Bree, while Sampson drove. NCIC is the National Crime Information Center, a database operated by the FBI. Anyone who's ever been arrested, convicted, or detained in the US is in there.

It wasn't exhaustive for our purposes, but it was a good place to start. I'd also be going back through Elizabeth's phone records, looking at her mail, and reinterviewing her nursing school faculty—anything I could think of to get a line on this supposed boyfriend of hers.

"What's the name?" Bree said.

"Russell."

"Russell? Is that a first or a last name?"

I smiled in spite of myself. "First, I think, but we should try it both ways."

"You're joking, right?" Bree said. "Do you know how many records that's going to turn up?"

"I wish I was joking," I said. "For whatever it's worth, there's probably going to be a Washington area address sometime in the last two years. This guy may be the father of Elizabeth Reilly's baby. Maybe the guy who killed her, too."

"That's a lot of maybe," she said.

"I know, I know," I said.

But at this point, maybe was better than nothing.

ELIJAH CREEM PICKED UP A SMALL HORSEHAIR BRUSH FROM HIS DESK AND added several dots of liver-colored pigment to his newest mask. The masks themselves came fully finished from the fabricator in Arkansas, but there was something to be said for putting on his own touches. Not a bad way to spend a Friday night, really, considering the pleasure it would get him in the long run. The older and uglier he could make these faces—which was to say, the more invisible on the street—the better.

When the phone rang in his pocket, Creem ignored it. There were very few people he was interested in speaking with these days, much less the variety of scum who bothered to call anymore—lawyers, creditors, and the occasional reporter looking for a new angle on his now fast-fading scandal.

Instead, he applied a thin layer of spirit gum to the mask's upper lip, and spread a mesh-backed mustache carefully into place. Later, when it was fully dry, he'd thread it with silvery gray to go with the wig he'd picked out.

It was only when the phone stopped ringing, then started right back up again that Creem even thought about checking the caller ID, which he did.

It was Josh Bergman. Of course. So much for keeping their distance from each other.

"Josh," he answered. "To what do I owe the dubious pleasure?"

"Hello, Dr. Creem, it's Joshua Bergman. How are you today?"

Bergman's voice was stiff, and ridiculously bright at the other end of the line.

"Ah," Creem said. "I take it you're not alone?"

"Good, good. Glad to hear it. Listen, I have a young lady here in my office. I'm considering signing her at the agency, but I'd like her to have a quick consult with you first," Bergman said. "If you're up for it, of course. I know it's a bit late."

Creem grinned broadly, even as he felt his own pulse start to rise.

Referrals were nothing new between his office and Josh's. Bergman had sent over a good million and a half in business in the past few years, including a handful of "prospects" who had found their way into Creem's bed.

But that was then. This was now. And *everything* had changed in the meantime.

Josh wasn't just upping his own game anymore, was he? Now he was trying to up Creem's as well. Either that, or he was eager to move things along and get the ball back into his own court. It didn't really matter which. The point was— Bergman knew exactly what Creem liked.

"This is a surprise," Creem said. "I assume she's the right type?"

"Yes, yes, lots of potential," Bergman said breezily. "Almost perfect, in fact. But that's where you come in, isn't it, doctor? How about if we swing by your home office around eight o'clock?"

And there it was. The *tour de salaud*. Josh's dirty little twist.

"I see," Creem said. "You want to be here when it happens. What is that, your commission?"

Bergman laughed. "This is why I like working with you, Elijah. You know me so well." He seemed to put his hand over the phone then, and addressed the girl. "Dr. Creem says he can't wait to meet you, sweetie."

It was a brilliant performance, really. There were few people as well trusted in the modeling world as gay men—and who else but Josh Bergman could play sister-friend with these Twiggies in one breath and offer them up for sport in the next?

Creem looked at his watch. It was just after seven.

"Make it eight thirty," he said. "And don't park in the street. I'll leave the garage open. And, Josh?"

"Yes?"

"If you're going to bring her here, you're going to have to get rid of her. I'm not taking that on," Creem said. "Are we clear?"

"Crystal," Bergman said. "Nice chatting, doctor. We'll see you soon."

AT EIGHT THIRTY EXACTLY, THE ELECTRIC CHIME OUTSIDE DR. CREEM'S LOWER-level waiting room rang. Bergman was almost always hyper-punctual, and tonight was no exception. When Creem opened the door, Bergman was standing there with a statuesque blond beauty on his arm.

He wore a simple two-button blazer over a white shirt, open at the collar. His "uniform," he called it. The young woman wore an LBD—the sort of little black dress that said, I'm a serious model, but I'm not opposed to giving a hand job or two on my way to the top.

"Was I right, or was I right?" Josh said.

"You were right," Creem said, gesturing them both inside. "You're a lovely girl, Miss...?"

"Larissa Swenson, Dr. Elijah Creem," Bergman said, making the introductions, even as his eyes darted around the room. "I don't suppose you have anything to drink down here, Elijah?"

"Thank you so much for seeing me," the girl said. Her hand was warm in his, her skin perfectly soft. "Mr. Bergman tells me you're the best there is."

"Mr. Bergman is a smart man," Creem said, his eyes locked on hers. "Joshua, try the console in the media room down the hall."

He'd already forgotten the girl's name, but she was, in fact, perfect. He could feel that creeping sense of adrenaline up his spine, and in the tension of his jaw. It was the feeling of coming back to life, he now knew. He'd felt the same way on the night of Darcy Vickers.

"My receptionist is off this week," he told the girl. "We'll worry about paperwork later, if it's all the same."

"Fine, fine," Bergman answered for her, coming back into the room with three glasses clutched in one hand and a cut crystal decanter in the other. "Larissa? Elijah? A little drink?"

"No, thank you," the girl answered politely.

"Maybe afterward," Creem said.

"Suit yourself." Bergman poured himself a two-finger shot and turned toward the examination room door. "In here, I assume?" He wasn't even trying to contain his excitement anymore. It was a little funny, and a little infectious, too.

"Are you...both coming in?" the girl asked. She seemed suddenly wary, but Creem gave her his best professional smile. Worked every time.

"It's really in your own best interest," he said. "Josh will be handling the cost of any procedures, as I'm sure he told you. But if you'd rather decline the consult, now would be a good time to say so."

"No," the girl said quickly. "It's fine." She sounded as if she were convincing herself as much as anything. Talk about blind ambition!

"You're sure?" Creem asked, more for fun than anything. He knew he had her now.

Within a few minutes, all three of them were inside the examination room. Creem stood waiting with a clipboard in hand, as the girl stepped out from the changing cubicle in a thin blue hospital gown, while Josh watched expectantly from the rolling chair in the corner.

"So," Creem said, looking down at the blank intake form in front of him. "What are we thinking about here?"

"Breast augmentation, for sure," Bergman piped up. "We want to be able to book Larissa for print, runway, editorial—all of it. Isn't that right, sweetie?"

"Sure," the girl answered, with another determined smile.

Creem set the clipboard down behind her and took the stainless-steel pointer out of his pocket.

"All right, stand up nice and tall for me, with your hands on your hips," he said. He untied the gown in front and stepped back to take a look, playing out the charade to its fullest.

"Nice symmetry. Good elasticity of the skin," he said. "All I'd really need to do is make a small incision, right along here."

He used the pointer to indicate a line under the girl's breast to illustrate. Not for the girl, though. For Bergman. Josh had been nice enough to arrange this little home delivery. Might as well give him a good show.

"That's where I'd like to cut. Do you see?" Creem said.

"I see," Bergman said. The girl only nodded.

"But let's not limit ourselves," Creem went on. "Should I keep going?"

"Definitely," Bergman said, pouring himself another drink. "Tell me what you're thinking about, Elijah."

Creem stood to the side and used the pointer

again, pressing the tip of it into the girl's well-toned obliques.

"Let's say we wanted to go for a little tummy tuck, while we were at it," he said. "In that case, I might try coming in right here, or maybe even here...." Now he plied the lower abdominals under her navel. There was more resistance there, but that meant more payoff—more purchase for his blade when it went in.

"Something like that?" Creem said, ostensibly for the girl, but again it was Bergman who answered.

"Yes," he said, his voice a little smaller than before. "Something like that."

"And how about the thighs?" Creem went on, turning his attention south. "It wouldn't be much to take those down a little." He drew another line, along the psoas, and came to a stop just over the femoral artery. His favorite. "That's where I'd like to cut. Right there."

"Mm-hm," Bergman said. The girl blinked a few times. She seemed confused by now, which was fine.

"I'm just going to make some notes," Creem said, and indicated the gown again. "You can close up there, Justine."

"It's Larissa," she said.

"Right. Sorry. It's just that...you look so much like my daughter. Almost exactly, really."

He put away his pointer and stepped over to the clipboard on the counter behind her. There, he opened a drawer and took out a number eighteen blade. It was perfect for deep cutting, and the custom handle made it feel like an extension of his own arm.

He probably should have stuck with the same cheap steak knife as before, he knew. In fact, it was right there in the drawer where he'd left it half an hour ago. But with skin like this girl had, that would have been like taking a chain saw to porcelain.

He'd just have to go back and rough up his work a bit afterward, to cover his tracks.

"So, what do you think, Josh?" Creem turned to face his friend. "Have you heard enough, or should I keep going?"

"Keep going," Bergman said right away. His eyes were focused on the scalpel in Dr. Creem's hand. He was sitting perfectly still by now, and his voice was little more than a hoarse whisper. "By all means, Elijah. Keep going. Please."

"Are you okay to keep going, too, Justine?" Creem asked.

"Um...Larissa," the girl said again.

"Shh," Creem told her. "It doesn't matter, Justine. Just stand nice and still for me like a good girl. We'll be done here before you know it."

CHAPTER
28

WHEN IT WAS OVER, CREEM AND BERGMAN HAD NO TROUBLE GETTING THE GIRL wrapped up and ready to go. They used latex gloves and a white nylon disaster bag to move her down the hall, a straight shot into the garage and then Bergman's waiting trunk.

It really was like spring break, 1988, all over again, Creem thought. One of those sweet little fillips of time, where the normal rules of the world didn't apply.

Not that they'd been better off with their piece of shit cars and four-digit bank accounts, trawling Fort Lauderdale for thrills. But it had, in fact, been a golden time.

"What's better than gold?" Creem said.

"Platinum, I guess," Bergman said. "Why?"

"That's what this is, Josh. These are our platinum days."

He held up his glass in a toast. They were leaning against the hood of Bergman's Audi now, drinking sixteen-year-old Hirsch Reserve, while Creem enjoyed a cigar.

"I'll drink to that," Bergman said.

"You'll drink to anything," Creem said, and his friend shrugged at the truth of it. "What are you going to do with her, anyway?"

"Rock Creek Park," he said. "I know a place."

Creem tapped the ash of his Romeo y Julieta, watching it float down like snow onto the concrete garage floor. He felt calm and contemplative, not at all worked up the way Josh was. It pleased him to see Bergman so happy, but it made him a bit nervous, too, the way he seemed to enjoy this. Almost too much, if there were such a thing.

"Just be careful," Creem said. "We're not twenty-two anymore, Josh. We're better than that."

"I'm always careful," Bergman said.

"No," Creem said. "In fact, you're not."

"That's true," Bergman said, and they both laughed. "But I will be, Elijah. Cross my heart. We started this together, and when it's time, we'll end it together. That's a promise."

Creem wasn't entirely sure what Bergman meant. Maybe it was the bourbon talking. Or maybe it meant nothing at all. But for reasons of his own, he let it lie where it was. When the time was right, he'd pick it back up again.

In the meantime, he finished his drink and stood up, indicating it was time for Josh to leave. He was tired. He wanted to go to bed.

And tonight, he was going to sleep like a baby.

CHAPTER
29

WHEN THE PHONE RINGS AT TWO IN THE MORNING IN MY HOUSE, THERE'S a better than average chance that someone's dead. The only question is whose phone—mine or Bree's. She's with the Violent Crimes Branch at MPD, and I'm with Major Case Squad.

On this particular night, the wake-up call came from my side of the bed. I got the details from Sergeant Huizenga before I was even fully awake. Another body had turned up, in Rock Creek Park this time. White. Female. Multiple stab wounds. Hair all cut off.

Another Darcy Vickers.

"I'll be right there," I told Huizenga, and stood up with a Gordian knot in my stomach. If this homicide was what it sounded like, we'd just opened up a whole new dimension on an already-complicated case.

As I headed down the stairs a few minutes later, I was surprised to see the light of the TV, flashing into the hall from the living room. Nana had her own set in her room, and as far as I knew, the kids were all tucked in.

What I found was Ava, asleep on the couch. She was slumped in a sitting position, with the remote in her hand, and her chin on her chest.

The TV was muted while an episode of *Hoarders* played silently on the screen. She was still dressed, too, including the new suede boots Bree had just bought her.

Or maybe she was dressed again. Had she snuck out in the night?

"Ava, you need to go to bed," I said, with a hand on her shoulder from behind.

She didn't move.

"Ava?" I came around and gave her a shake. "Ava!" She stirred then, but barely. Her eyes opened halfway, and she looked at me like I was some kind of stranger.

"Wassup?" she said in a half slur that sent my heart sinking.

"Ava, are you high?" I said. When I turned on the lamp next to the couch, she put a hand up to shield her face. "Let me see your eyes."

"I ain't high," she said, and turned farther away.

But I wasn't messing around now. I sat down and squared her off by the shoulders to face me. "Look at me," I said. "Right now."

Her eyes weren't bloodshot, like I expected, but her pupils looked small, which was maybe even worse.

"Ava, what did you take?" I said.

"Nothin'."

"Was it Oxy? Something else?"

OxyContin is expensive, but there are also plenty of cheap, and more dangerous, knockoff drugs floating around out there. Ava was fourteen now, more than old enough to cross paths with any number of controlled substances on the street, especially considering her background. The few friends I knew about were street kids, who she used to crash with around Seward Square. Was that where she'd been tonight?

"What's going on in here?" Nana said, suddenly appearing in the archway from the hall. Her room is on the first floor of the house, and she's also the world's lightest sleeper.

Ava scooted away from me, to the far end of the couch. "He's saying I done something I didn't do. Why he's always gotta think I'm doing something bad? Damn!"

"Watch your mouth," Nana said. She parked herself on the cushion between us and turned to face Ava. "What is it you didn't do, honey?"

"He's saying I'm high, but I ain't."

"I'm *not,*" Nana corrected her, probably because she couldn't help herself.

"And why are you up this late?" I asked. "Did you sneak out?"

"See?" Ava said, pointing at me. "I can't do nothing right for him."

I looked at Nana, feeling more than a little frustrated. I had a crime scene to get to, and it couldn't wait.

"I'm going to get Bree," I said.

"No. Let her sleep. I'll put Ava to bed in my room and keep an eye on her," she said, eyeballing the keys and necktie in my hand. "You obviously have somewhere to be."

Nana hates my job, a lot of the time. But why was I suddenly feeling like the bad guy here?

"Nana," I said.

"Just go."

I looked Ava over one more time. Was she just sleepy—or something else?

"I'll be back first thing in the morning," I said. "We'll talk about this then."

She rolled her eyes at me but didn't answer. It wasn't until I was almost all the way out of the house that I heard her speak up at all, somewhere behind me.

"It *is* first thing in the morning," she said.

CHAPTER
30

I WASN'T THE FIRST ONE ON THE SCENE THIS TIME. BESIDES THE CRUISERS parked at the picnic area just off Beach Drive in Rock Creek Park, there were several unmarked cars in the lot when I got there.

The action was across the grass, at the edge of the woods, where Rock Creek itself runs through the park's seventeen hundred acres. We'd have kliegs up soon, but for now everyone was working with flashlights and headlamps.

I found Sergeant Huizenga leaning against the edge of a picnic table, signing off on something for a uniformed officer and talking on the phone at the same time.

"Yes, sir, I know. Yes, yes, we're all over it. We will."

I figured it was either the chief or the mayor himself on the line. Not too many people get a willing "sir" out of Marti Huizenga. She's a good cop, but her temper gets in her way sometimes.

"We're screwed, Alex," she said, just as she hung up. "We could solve this tonight, and we're still screwed. I've got the mayor's command center so far up my ass, I can't even breathe. How did they even know about this yet?"

It was a rhetorical question more than anything. Not all mayoral administrations are created equally, and this one had a strong tendency to step in sooner rather than later. The fact that we were now getting a substantial boost in resources from the city only exacerbated the situation. Increased resources meant increased oversight, accountability, and yes, sometimes meddling. Just one of the reasons I tend to avoid upward mobility at the police department as much as I can. I like working the cases, not the politics, where I can help it.

I followed Huizenga into the woods and down to the creek bed where the body had been left.

Errico Valente was already there, along with Tom D'Auria. Valente was the lead investigator on the Darcy Vickers case, and D'Auria is MPD's Homicide Division captain. It didn't look like anyone was sitting this one out.

At their feet was a nude victim, facedown along the edge of the water. She'd been there long enough for postmortem lividity to set in, with a line of bright red coloration along the lower parts of the body, where her blood had settled by gravity since the time of death.

If the previous case was any indication, she would have also lost quite a bit of blood in the attack, but a quick scan of the ground around her didn't show any signs of it. No loose hair, either, even though she'd obviously been sheared nearly down to the scalp. That told me she'd been brought here from somewhere else.

"Do we have an ID?" I asked.

Valente shook his head. "Jane Doe, so far. Stab wounds are in the chest, abdomen, and upper thigh."

"Just like Darcy Vickers," I said.

"Yeah."

"Shit."

Psychologically speaking, we were looking at a whole new kind of perpetrator now. This was my worst nightmare—someone who seemed to be getting a taste for his craft. The first murder had gone sufficiently well, which meant there was no motivation to stop. Just the opposite. The resting period between Darcy Vickers and this young woman had been statistically very short. If he wasn't already thinking about what he wanted to do next, he would be soon.

Also, it seemed pretty clear now that our killer had a type. The nudity was a departure from the Vickers case, but the physical similarity between the two victims was striking. This girl looked like she could have been Ms. Vickers's daughter, with her pale white skin, remnants of blond hair, and well-proportioned, athletic body.

I thought about the old man we'd seen on the security video from the parking garage where Vickers was found. Could someone like him have gotten her all the way out here? Maybe. Was that what happened?

The girl's back and legs were streaked with mud. By all appearances, she'd been brought to the top of the bank, rolled down, and left behind. But there was something about the way her right arm was cocked over her head that I didn't quite buy.

"Does that positioning look natural to you?" I asked the others.

"Why?" Huizenga said. "What are you thinking?"

I came around to get a better look, and shined my light down. The girl's hand on that side was closed in a loose fist, except for the index finger, which was extended. Or pointing, maybe, straight downstream.

"How wide's our perimeter so far?" I asked.

"Just what you see," Valente said. There were a handful of crime-scene techs scanning the banks around us, but it didn't look like any of them had gotten more than thirty feet from the body so far.

"What are you thinking, Alex?" Huizenga asked me.

"I'm not sure." Maybe I was thinking too much. Maybe not. "I'm just curious. Walk with me?"

Huizenga and I left Valente and D'Auria with the girl and started picking our way downstream.

It didn't take long, either. After a hundred feet or so, we came around a shallow bend and my light landed on something straight ahead.

It was another body, I realized all at once. It sent a fresh wave of dread straight through me. What the hell were we up against here?

"Oh . . . God," Huizenga said, and then shouted over her shoulder. "Let's get some backup over here! Now!"

I ran over to check vitals, but even before I knelt down I could see there was no chance. It was a young man this time. White. Fully clothed. He'd taken a single gunshot to the face, and there were several fresh stab wounds, all around the groin.

Another Cory Smithe.

He'd been left at the water's edge, like our Jane Doe, with one arm extended out over his head. His hand on that side was clenched into a loose fist, and his index finger was pointed back upstream, the way we'd just come.

CHAPTER
31

BEFORE ANYONE REACHED US, HUIZENGA SWUNG AROUND AND SHINED HER light up into the woods on the opposite bank.

"What is it?" I said.

"Shh!"

She put a hand on my arm and pointed. That's when I heard it. Someone was moving through the woods, breaking twigs and going at a good clip over dead leaves and soft ground.

Huizenga started up that way a beat before I did.

"Whoever you are, this is the police. Stop right there! Don't *make* me chase you!"

I've got legs almost twice as long as hers, and by the time I was up the bank and past the tree line, I'd already left her behind. My Glock was out in one hand, my Maglite in the other. Maybe this was just some homeless person we were chasing, or a curious kid, but if not—I wanted this guy, bad.

About twenty yards in, I stopped and listened. Whoever it was, they'd been heading toward the Sixteenth Street side of the park, but now he— she? he?—had turned and was running parallel to the creek instead.

Meanwhile, I could hear Huizenga on the radio, somewhere behind me.

"—any available units to Sixteenth Street, north of Sherrill Drive. We've got an unsub, on foot, possibly headed out of Rock Creek Park—"

I took off at a sprint again, catching a few low branches in the face as I went. The adrenaline was driving me as much as anything right now.

Again, the footfalls ahead of me changed direction—but this time I caught him with the beam of my light. It was a man, anyway, in dark clothes. That's all I saw. He'd just disappeared up and over a small rise, straight ahead.

I was right behind him, and a few seconds later I spilled out onto the pavement of Sherrill Drive. The road curved here, in a hairpin turn on its way out of the park. There was no sign of the guy, though. Had he kept going, back into the woods? Turned and run up the road?

If I'd had another half second, I would have realized why I didn't hear him running anymore. But the next thing I felt was something hard, slamming into the back of my head. My knees buckled, and what little vision I had in the dark blurred out completely. Pain shot down my neck and back as I hit the pavement.

I tried to jump right up, but it was no good. Everything spun. The ground turned sideways, and I was down again.

"Alex?"

I heard Huizenga now, moving through the woods behind me.

"Sixteenth Street!" I shouted back. "Keep going!"

I wasn't even sure about that, but a guess was

better than nothing at this point. All I could do was kneel there waiting for some sense of equilibrium to come back while the seconds ticked away—when seconds mattered.

By the time I finally caught up to Huizenga, our guy was gone, gone, gone.

CHAPTER
32

I MISSED A GOOD HALF HOUR WITH THE PARAMEDICS BEFORE HUIZENGA would let me get back to work. There was no concussion, just a gash and a bad headache. Even then she wanted me to go home, but she didn't insist.

By the time I was back in the loop, Chief Perkins was on-site, along with Jessica Jacobs as well. Jacobs was the primary investigator on the Cory Smithe murder. By all indications, we either had one very busy psychopath on our hands, or more likely, two cases that had more to do with each other than we'd previously imagined.

Neither of the latest victims had been identified yet, but it had already been decided that MPD was going to hold a major press conference later that morning, to report out on the situation.

"Are we sure that's a good idea?" I said. "I know I'm coming late to the conversation, but—"

"You also weren't on the receiving end of the mayor's calls," Huizenga told me. "It's done, Alex. This is our reality now. Let's move on. Tell us what you're thinking here."

For better or worse, I'm the go-to profiler in the Homicide Division, not that there's any official title to that effect. Either way, I'd already started working up a few new ideas.

"Assuming we're talking about two killers," I said, "I'd say they're both white, like their victims, just going by statistics. Also bright, and well organized—but angry, too. Not necessarily about the same thing."

It wasn't such a stretch that murder and anger would go hand in hand, but that was the quality that struck me the most about all four of these homicides. None of them were simple or straightforward, in terms of methods. The knife work in particular had gone above and beyond the necessary, in terms of strictly taking lives.

That meant there was some emotion to it. Maybe some level of fantasy playing out here as well. And almost certainly some kind of high-functioning psychosis, which is the slipperiest aspect of all when it comes to pinning down any perpetrator.

Much less two of them.

I gave the others my spiel, and then shut up and listened again while D'Auria divvied the work to be done in the coming hours. If nothing else, we had a pretty good investigative machine up and running.

Valente was going to work IDs on both victims. Jacobs would run the 6 a.m. briefing at headquarters. Chief Perkins was going to be with the mayor's people for the next few hours, and then D'Auria would be the face of the department for our press conference, while the rest of us stood behind him in a show of force. Sometimes, it is about appearances, and Washington was going to need some reassurance that MPD was on this.

Huizenga and I were both going to start pulling teams together, to go back through every report and witness account, and reinterview every first responder on all four of these murders. We'd also need to start from scratch on our victims' profiles. Maybe there was some connection, some cross-reference we'd missed. There had to be.

Something was attaching these cases to each other. We just had to figure out what it was.

CHAPTER
33

JUST AFTER THE SUN CAME UP, I STOLE AN HOUR I DIDN'T HAVE AND SWUNG back by the house before Ava left for school. Jannie and Ali were already gone when I got there, but Bree had told Ava she'd write her a note for being late. We had to talk.

There were plenty of reasons to be concerned. The smiling, happy Ava from Kinkead's the other night had turned out to be a momentary bit of sunshine. Most of the time these days she was sullen, withdrawn, and almost impossible for me to get through to. What I'd just seen the night before only added another layer.

"I wasn't high," she insisted, almost as soon as we sat her down in the living room. "I wasn't! Serious."

"You were pretty out of it, Ava," I said.

"Whatcha want me to say? Swear to God, okay?"

I didn't know whether to believe her or not. I wanted to, desperately, if only to establish some kind of mutual trust. But Ava was also an easy liar, and that wasn't a pattern I wanted to reinforce. I wanted her to use those smarts of hers for something more than a quick lie and squirming out of trouble.

"Why were you still dressed, in the middle of the night? Did you sneak out?" Nana asked.

For the first time, some of the fire went out of Ava's eyes. She jutted out her jaw and looked at the floor, answering and not answering at the same time.

"We can't have that, Ava," Bree told her. "Not even a little."

"I know," Ava said. "But I wasn't on anything, if that's what you're thinking."

"Either way," Nana said, "things are going to change around here. No more running out to the store, or whatever it is you're doing with your friends around Seward Square. No more dawdling on the way home from school like you've been doing. And *absolutely* no leaving the house by yourself at night. Don't test me on that, Miss Ava."

"Whatever," she said, and started up. "Can I go now?"

"No, you can't go," Bree told her. "Sit down."

Ava sat back again and folded her long arms over her chest. She was two years younger than Damon but just as tall and lanky.

"Ava, do you understand where all this is coming from?" Bree said. "We love you. We don't want anything bad to happen to you. If it did, that would be like something bad happening to us. Does that make any sense?"

Ava tossed off another shrug, but I could see her getting smaller, the longer this went on. She was breathing through her nose, and if I wasn't mistaken, trying not to cry.

So far, I'd been holding back. The truth was, Ava responded better to Nana and Bree than she did to me. But I didn't want to stay silent anymore. I pulled the hassock around and sat down right in front of her. She *was* going to hear me.

"Do you *want* to be part of this family?" I asked her.

"Huh?"

"I'm not saying you have a choice about where you live right now. You're kind of stuck with us for the time being," I went on. "But what I am saying is that there's a *family* in this house, if you want one. Do you?"

Nana, Bree, and I had all agreed that we'd wait until the end of the school year to think seriously about adoption, either way. The foster system was still overseeing Ava's case, and maybe I shouldn't have said anything yet. But then again, I was the one who'd been dragging his feet.

Ava seemed to fold in on herself a little more, pulling her arms tight around her own thin frame. When I saw the first tear start down her cheek, I didn't think about it. I just wrapped her up in a hug and held on tight.

At first, she stiffened up. But then, all at once, she broke. It was like she'd turned into a rag doll in my arms, and she started sobbing like I'd never heard her before. Nana reached over and put a hand on Ava's back. Bree did the same from the other side, and none of us said anything for a long time.

In fact, Ava was the first one to speak.

"I miss my mom," she said against my chest. That was all she got out before she started crying, even harder, as if just saying it was its own kind of pain.

"Of course you do," I said, rocking her gently. "I would, too."

It was heartbreaking. Nobody had ever shown Ava what it meant to really be there for her. She'd had a nonexistent father, and a mother whose drug addiction was stronger than their own relationship had been. But she was also the only mother Ava had ever known. I would have been more concerned if she *didn't* miss her.

We still had a lot of talking to do, and a lot of issues to address together—eventually. For the moment, though, it seemed like what Ava needed more than anything was to cry.

Maybe it was even a step in the right direction.

CHAPTER
34

OUR PRESS CONFERENCE WAS SCHEDULED TO START AT TEN THAT MORNING.
For something as big as this, we use the largest all-purpose space at headquarters, which also happens to be the lineup room. The only difference was that we were the ones lining up this time.

Everything was hopping when I got there. We had at least eighty reporters in chairs, and maybe twenty news cameras across the back wall. Channels Four, Five, Seven, and Nine were all going live, I was pretty sure. The nationals were probably here to test the waters, and see what might be worth putting on the teleprompter for Diane Sawyer or Brian Williams that night.

At the front, on a small, low stage, the podium was already covered with a sloppy bouquet of microphones. A heavy blue curtain had been drawn across the one-way glass.

It looked like D'Auria was getting ready to start, so I went and took my place behind him with the other primaries—Huizenga, Jacobs, Valente, and Chief Perkins. It was a deliberate image for the cameras, to be sure. Washington was going to need to know—and see—that MPD was on top of these murders.

At ten o'clock exactly, our public information

officer, Joyce Catalone, closed the secure door to the hall and nodded at D'Auria to go ahead. He stepped up to the mikes and started right in.

"Good morning, everyone. I'm Commander Tom D'Auria with the Metropolitan Police Department. I've got a prepared statement regarding the events of the last twelve hours, and then we'll have some time for questions."

D'Auria quickly covered the basics, without getting too specific about methods, weapons, or the exact location where the bodies had been found. It was too early to make any of that publicly available. He did indicate both victims by name, though—Larissa Swenson and Ricky Samuels. That part was news to me. They'd been Jane and John Doe, the last I'd heard.

D'Auria also indicated that Mr. Samuels was a known sex worker, like Cory Smithe before him; but he didn't make any mention of the physical similarity between Ms. Swenson and her equivalent "partner victim," Darcy Vickers.

I would have made the same call. Gay hustlers are a specific group of people who might be able to use information like this to protect themselves. By the same token, there's no effective way to warn and protect a city's worth of attractive blond women. Protect them against doing what, exactly? It's a fine line between what's useful at this point, and what just stirs up panic. Sometimes you have to make your best guess and roll the dice.

As soon as D'Auria reached the end of his statement, the questions started flying. At first they were the usual logistical kind of inquiries. Were the bodies found near each other? Yes. How near? No comment. Did we have any evidence of a connection between the two victims? No comment. Would MPD be updating the press that afternoon? Yes, if there was anything to tell.

But then, after about five minutes, D'Auria called on Bev Sherman from the *Post,* and things took a turn.

"Commander, you mention two possible serial cases associated with these murders—"

"I didn't say serial," D'Auria cut in. "Let me be clear. We have what appear to be second homicides by the same perpetrators, in two previously unrelated cases."

"Fair enough," Bev went on. "My question is about a third incident. The Elizabeth Reilly murder?"

My ears pricked up at that one. Technically, all these cases were on my plate, but I'd just been down to Shellman Bluff. I'd met the Reillys. I'd held that baby girl.

"What about it?" D'Auria asked.

"A new blog by the name of *The Real Deal* has been quite critical of MPD lately, and the Elizabeth Reilly investigation in particular. Most specifically, *The Real Deal* has been focusing on Detective Cross, who I know is coordinating on all three of these cases. I was wondering if the detective himself would care to comment?"

All around the room, people started tapping away on phones and iPads, presumably looking up *The Real Deal.* I also felt a good number of eyes turning my way.

D'Auria held the floor, though. "Bev, I'm not going to respond to rumors on a blog I've never heard of," he answered. "That's something we'll have to look into."

"Let me be more specific," Bev jumped in before he could move on. "Detective Cross, would you be willing to comment on some of the allegations—for instance, that you violated department policy by moving Ms. Reilly's body before a proper examination? Or that you were out socializing on Saturday night while the investigation, arguably, should have been gearing up?"

I was stunned, and thrown off guard, and most of all, steaming goddamn mad. Where was this coming from? What was this blog I'd never heard about before? And who the hell had been watching me and my family go out to dinner?

I had about eighteen responses for Bev, none of them fit to print in her paper. Chief Perkins didn't look too pleased, either. He was giving Joyce Catalone a signal to wrap this thing up.

"I can only repeat what Commander D'Auria already said," I finally answered. "Until we get a look at the material in question—"

"So, you're not familiar with *The Real Deal*?" someone else asked.

"Believe me, I will be in about ten minutes," I said. It got a few chuckles around the room, and then Joyce was there at the podium.

"Ladies and gentlemen, that's all we have time for this morning. The investigative team has other business to attend to, but we will be updating you throughout the day, if there's anything to tell."

It's a thin charade, but absolutely preferable to letting the press conference spiral out of control. We'd come in trying to play offense, and already we were back on our heels.

Things weren't looking so good for the department right now. And maybe even worse for me.

CHAPTER 35

FIVE MINUTES AFTER THE PRESS CONFERENCE LET OUT, OUR CORE TEAM WAS up in Chief Perkins's office on the fifth floor.

"What the hell just happened down there?" Perkins wanted to know.

"We got coldcocked by some random blogger," D'Auria said. "A million nobodies tapping away out there, and you never know which one's going to blow up until you're picking shrapnel out of your ass."

Perkins didn't keep a computer in his office, so Huizenga opened her laptop on the big round conference table. After a quick Google, she had *The Real Deal* up in front of her, and we all gathered around.

"Oh God," she said. "One of these."

The blog had a simple masthead—THE REAL DEAL, in a plain black font. Beneath that was a subheading, "Who's Policing the Police?"

In the margin, there was a numbered list of twenty-three MPD officers, each one clickable to some other page. I recognized several names right away. They were all cops who had been arrested in the last year, for anything from petty theft to domestic abuse, and even one murder. There was also a small map of the city's police districts, with different colored dots, presumably corresponding to various types of crimes.

The most recent blog entry was dated that morning. Its title was "America's Most Dangerous City?" Beneath that, "Murder Season in DC." And then, "Detective Cross: Asleep at the Wheel?"

"Looks like this guy's got a crush on you," Huizenga said. My name was clickable, like the others, and she hovered her pointer over it. "You mind?"

"I can hardly wait," I said.

What opened up then was a whole page dedicated to yours truly. It included my CV with the department, an old ID photo, a list of current and previous cases, and several other small images.

The first of those was a picture that had been taken from below, on Vernon Street, just as I'd gone to pull Elizabeth Reilly's body out of the window where she'd been hanging. Her face was even fuzzed out, in some kind of twisted nod to journalistic propriety.

The other picture showed Kinkead's restaurant from the outside. Beneath that was a screen capture of a tweet that had apparently been sent to go with it:

Three dead, and where's DC's favorite cop? Out to dinner. More like out to lunch! Priorities, anyone? #incompetentcops.

Finally, there was a long screed at the bottom, all about how I was the wrong one to be coordinating on these cases, and blowing it at every turn, apparently.

"Who the hell is this guy?" Valente asked.

The blog did have a contact page, but when Huizenga pulled it up, it gave us everything *but* a name. You could e-mail *The Real Deal* with questions, tips, or other thoughts about the job MPD was doing. There were invitations to follow *The Real Deal* on Twitter, or like it on Facebook, or "join the conversation" on something called NewsNet. For someone who had just gotten started, this so-called reporter was clearly going all in.

And I was starting to think I knew who he was. Or at least that we'd met.

"We need to get him out in the open," I said to Perkins. "Let me run a subpoena on the blog's ISP records, and see who's attached to the account."

I was remembering the bearded jag-off from the morning Cory Smithe's body had been found. This was the guy with no press credentials who had refused to give me his name.

Perkins shoved back in his chair.

"Alex, I've got to ask you. Did you pull Elizabeth Reilly's body before the ME reached that scene?"

"I did," I told him. I wasn't going to start tap dancing for the chief right now. It was all in the report, anyway.

"And, were you out to dinner that night, like it says?"

I could feel the heat coming up into my face. "I'm sorry, Chief, but what the hell does it matter?"

"In and of itself? It doesn't. But if he's telling the truth, he can say whatever he wants," Perkins told me. "The last thing I need is a questionable subpoena on a guy like this, especially if he's got any kind of audience."

"If he doesn't now, he will after that press conference," Huizenga said, closing her laptop. "Stand by for the shit storm, everyone."

"See what you can find out on your own," Perkins said. "Pull whoever you need for this, but please, Alex—step lightly. We're fighting a war of public perception right now. Approval of the department's at an all-time low."

Chief Perkins is no hysteric. He usually doesn't give a hoot about public perception, especially not at the expense of an investigation. But the reality was, we were operating at expanded levels these days, and that hinged on a good relationship with the mayor, who had his own political angles to consider. The fact that he and his people had stayed away from the press conference meant they were already feeling skittish about this.

"I'm sorry, Alex," Perkins said. "It is what it is."

"Not a problem," I told him. "I'll find him anyway."

That was the answer the chief needed right now, and hopefully the one that was going to keep me as far from under his thumb as possible.

I just hoped it was also true.

CHAPTER
36

PULL WHOEVER YOU WANT. THAT'S WHAT THE CHIEF HAD SAID. SO I STARTED close to home.

Even on my way down the stairs, I was on the phone with Bree, asking her to take a look at *The Real Deal,* and meanwhile, to keep digging on the Elizabeth Reilly case.

When I hit the third-floor hall, I called Sampson. He was in court that day, but I left a long message and asked him to swing by the house later on if he could. Both of them were already invested in Elizabeth's murder. I didn't see any reason not to make it official.

As soon as I was back at my desk, I pulled up *The Real Deal*'s contact page again and fired off a quick e-mail.

> To whom it may concern: Please contact me at your earliest convenience. Thank you, Detective Alex Cross, MPD.

I was going to play it civil for the time being. I'd even play it nice if I had to, but only as a means to an end. This guy had been putting eyes on me and my family, and that's a line you don't cross.

Next up, I wound my way around the little

warren of cubicles in our office to find Jarret
Krause at his desk. Krause was one of Major Case
Squad's newbies, a Flatbush, Brooklyn, boy whose
wife had taken a job working in their congress-
man's DC office the previous fall. Already he'd
made a name for himself, tracking down two very
slippery violent offenders online—one serial rapist
who connected with his victims on Facebook, and
an eighteen-year-old thug from Shaw who had
robbed and killed a seventy-year-old liquor store
owner, then tried to sell a case of Cristal on
Craigslist. Someday, these punks are going to wise
up to their own virtual footprints. In the meantime, we've got guys like Krause to go around and
scoop them up.

"'Sup, Alex?" he said, when I showed up over
the wall of his ridiculously tidy cubicle. For that, I
was giving him another six months.

"Have you heard of this blog, *The Real Deal*?"
I asked.

"Yeah." His fingers hit the keyboard in front of
him and he brought it up. "This guy sucks," he
said. "And he's seriously hating on you, too. How
can I help?"

I was a little surprised at how much Krause already knew, but maybe I shouldn't have been. Bad
news travels about as fast as sound around that
department.

"I need a name," I said. "The blog's hosted at
DC Access, but Perkins doesn't want to do an ad-
min subpoena if we can avoid it. I was hoping—"

Already, Krause was scanning pages. "Yeah,"
he said. "He's hitting all the major platforms.
Shouldn't be too hard."

"I'd appreciate it," I said.

"You want me to stop there, or keep going?" he asked.

I wasn't going to say no. "Define 'keep going,'" I said.

"Well, for instance—this." He came back to the latest blog entry, and pointed at the screen. "Twenty-six comments since seven this morning. These are the people you want to keep an eye on. Ninety-nine percent of the time, they're going to be nobodies. But then once in a while, one of them will know something they shouldn't, like a bullet caliber, or time of death, or whatever. That can be gold."

"I'll take it," I said. "Anything you can do. But first—get me a name."

"A name, to the face, to the asshole," he said. "No prob. I'll get back to you by the end of the day."

CHAPTER
37

BY 9 P.M. I'D PUT IN A FULL WORKDAY, FOLLOWED BY A LATE DINNER WITH the family, homework with Ava, more homework with Jannie, and a chapter of *Percy Jackson* with Ali before bed.

I wasn't going to say no to the six-pack of Cigar City Brown Ale that Sampson showed up with, just as Nana Mama and the girls were settling in for an episode of *Once Upon A Time*. John, Bree, and I took the beer up to my office in the attic and got back to work.

"Catch me up," John said, twisting off a cap. "Where are we?"

Bree unwrapped the red figure-eight string from a big manila envelope and took out the case materials she'd picked up that afternoon. A tan clip folder and several black-and-white crime-scene photos spilled onto her lap.

"I've been cross-referencing cases all day, and I found this. I can't say it's definitively tied to Elizabeth Reilly, but it seems like a red flag, anyway."

She picked up the crime report and looked it over as she kept talking.

"The name's Amanda Simms. Ran away from an abusive home in West Virginia at age fifteen. Then no sign of her at all for eleven months, until

a maid found her body in the tub at an Econo
Lodge in Takoma Park. That was four and a half
years ago."

"Four and a half years?" Sampson said.
"What's the supposed connection to Elizabeth
Reilly?"

Bree turned one of the crime-scene photos
around to show him. John looked like he felt sick
to his stomach.

"She was pregnant," Bree said. "The autopsy
showed heavy doses of Rohypnol and morphine.
All indications are that she was drugged, cut open,
and left for dead."

"And the baby?"

"Never found."

"Jesus." John scrubbed at his eyes with a thumb
and forefinger. We'd all had long days.

"So basically," I said, "we've got a young girl,
away from home for the first time, and pregnant.
All of that's in line with Elizabeth Reilly."

"What about this phantom boyfriend, Russell?" John asked.

Bree shook her head. "I've got nothing. Presumably, that's not his real name."

"But let's assume he's part of the picture," I
went on. "Maybe Elizabeth finds out about
Amanda somehow. She figures out her boyfriend
is a monster, and she's carrying his baby. That
could go a long way to explain why she'd go all
the way to Georgia to induce labor."

"For that matter, maybe Amanda's not the only
other one," Bree said. "I'm still looking."

After a long stretch of silence, Sampson spoke
up again.

"You said something else on the phone this

morning. This blogger. What's his deal? And why's he hating on you?"

"Good question," I said, and pulled up *The Real Deal* on my desktop. There was a new entry now, "MPD Whiffs Its Own Press Conference." It had been posted at four that afternoon, and it already had ninety-two comments. Word was definitely getting out on this thing.

"He's either got a vested interest in Elizabeth Reilly, or against me," I said. "Or both."

"Or," Sampson said, "maybe he's just looking to make a name for himself—trying to establish the blog and get some attention with a couple of big stories."

"Yeah, well, he's got my attention," Bree said. She was at least as put out by the whole thing as I was—most especially by that picture of Kinkead's from the night we were there.

"Alex, let me take a run at this guy," John said. "You've got five homicides on the line. Six now, if we're counting Amanda Simms."

"Thanks. I'd welcome the help, actually," I said. "Not to mention, you can be damn scary when you want to be."

Sampson just grinned. "What's the name on the account?" he asked.

"Still waiting on that."

It wasn't until close to eleven, when John was just getting up to leave, that I finally heard from Krause. It was perfect timing, actually.

"Sorry to take so long," he said. "But I tracked a couple of tweets back to a phone number with a DC exchange. No real address on the account, just a PO box, but I do have a name for you."

I grabbed a pencil off my desk and the nearest

piece of paper—a takeout menu from Fusion Grill.

"Go ahead."

"The name is Ron Guidice," he said, and spelled it for me, then gave me the number. "You want me to bring him in?"

"No, but thanks," I said. It seemed like everyone wanted a piece of this guy, which was fine with me. I tore off the corner of the menu and put it into Sampson's very large outstretched hand. "We've got it from here."

CHAPTER
38

HOURS AFTER SAMPSON LEFT, I WAS STILL AWAKE. SOMETHING WAS BUGGING me, and I couldn't figure out what it was. That name, Ron Guidice, was sticking in my head for some reason. Was it familiar? Or did I just want to think so?

Finally, I got out of bed and headed back up to the office.

"Where are you going?" Bree asked me, still half asleep.

"I just want to check something," I said. "I'll be right back."

Up at my desk, I got online and logged into the MPD case files. Members of Homicide have the highest level of clearance on investigative reports, which meant I could access the system from any departmental computer, including the laptop I had at home.

After a quick search, the only place I found Guidice's name was in a police report from six years earlier. And in fact, he hadn't committed any crime. He was the named next of kin for a woman who had died during a police action in Chinatown.

I remembered the case now. It came back to me with a creeping sort of dread. This one was not a good memory.

I'd been heading up an investigation on a mid-level arms runner who'd been playing both sides of the fence, providing automatic weapons to rival gangs in Southeast and Northwest DC. Word had been coming down from more than one informant that a major brawl was on its way. When you're talking about automatic weapons, crossed with two crews who had a history of disregard not just for each other but for innocent bystanders as well, it's best not to take too many chances. Even though we were still hoping to ID this guy's upper-level contacts, I made the call to bring him in, ASAP.

Now, sitting there at my desk, I didn't need to reread the report in front of me to remember what happened next.

The thug's name was Marco Bruillo, with a last known address at an expensive studio apartment on H Street. On the night in question, Bruillo had been tracked there, and the plan was to make the arrest inside, as quietly as possible.

When we arrived, though, Bruillo was just on his way back out. We had no choice but to take him right there on the sidewalk, or risk losing him altogether.

What we couldn't know was that two of his own people were parked and waiting for him across the street. As soon as we had Bruillo up against the wall, they opened fire from their vehicle.

It was the fastest-moving shootout I've ever found myself in. Within fifteen seconds, it was over. Bruillo was dead, but so were three other bystanders, all of them waiting in line to buy movie tickets at the theater next to his building.

In the end, forensics had shown that two of those bystanders had been killed with automatic weapon fire. But the third—a woman by the name of Theresa Filmore—was accidentally shot and killed by one of my fellow MPD detectives. It was a tragedy, no two ways about it.

The city had taken full responsibility, and settled out of court with Ms. Filmore's named next of kin—her fiancé, a man by the name of Ronald F. Guidice.

I'd never forgotten about Theresa Filmore, but it wasn't until I looked back at that file that I realized why Guidice's name had rung a bell.

Now I knew. And everything was starting to make a little more sense.

Part Two

TIPPING POINT

NIGHT FISHING WAS ALL THE COVER RON GUIDICE NEEDED TONIGHT. THERE WAS
no necessity for a pseudonym, or physical camou-
flage, or even keeping out of sight, for that matter.
From the middle of the wide saltwater channel where
he sat, he could watch the little stilt house on the
shore all he liked. Even if the cop in the driveway
happened to look over and notice him, all he'd see
was some goober out trying to hook a few snapper in
the dark.

It was a good time to be away from DC, too.
Guidice had started to pull back the covers now,
and chances were high that Alex Cross had begun
to figure out who he was. Which was fine. As
long as Guidice controlled the flow of information, then he controlled Alex, too.

In the meantime, he kept his rod in the water
and his eyes on the house at the shoreline, waiting
for his gut to tell him it was time to move.

The fishing gear was the cheapest he'd been
able to find, at an Outdoor World near Savannah.
The boat had been even easier to procure. Shellman Bluff wasn't the kind of place where folks
locked up their stuff at night, much less a dinged-
up old aluminum dory like this one.

On the floor of the boat was a black-market

M16. The detachable night scope sat on Guidice's lap. In the pouch pocket of his gray hoodie pullover, he also had a small Kahr 9mm with six rounds in the magazine. If everything went to plan, that was four more rounds than he'd need.

The only real variable here was time. The lights in the house had gone out at eleven o'clock. They'd come back on briefly at twelve thirty, and then again just after two. Such was life with a newborn baby.

Finally, when the house went dark a third time, Guidice set down the rod and pulled the M16 onto his lap. He could feel the adrenaline sharpening his focus as he raised the rifle to his shoulder and pressed his cheek against the hollowed-out stock.

Through the green and black night-vision lens, the cop's face came clear. He was sitting behind the wheel of his McIntosh County cruiser, looking bored and drumming his fingers on his jaw while he watched the house.

Guidice took a deep breath. He centered his main targeting chevron over the man's forehead. Then he squeezed off one fast round.

The rifle's suppressor allowed a small pop of sound, nothing more. Simultaneously, to the eye, a snowflake-shaped hole opened in the cruiser's windshield. The man inside stiffened for a fraction of a second, before his head lolled softly to the side. It looked like he'd fallen asleep as much as anything else.

For another count of thirty, Guidice kept his eye pressed to the scope. When the cop didn't move, he lowered the rifle and let it slip over the side of the boat, into the water. Finally, he took up his oars and started in toward shore.

It wasn't far to row. Within a minute, maybe two, the little dory was scraping across soft sand and gravel at the water's edge. Guidice stepped over the bow and onto the property, keeping his boots dry as he pulled the 9mm out of his pocket.

He went straight for the police cruiser first. The cop inside was no issue, that much was clear. Instead, he went to the passenger side and took the man's hat off the seat, as well as the uniform jacket folded neatly over the headrest.

He slipped both of them on as he rounded the house toward the back. The front door had a line of sight to the neighbors, but the only view from the rear deck was out toward the yard, and the dark tidal marsh beyond that.

Guidice paused at the back kitchen door, just long enough to pull the cop's hat a little lower over his eyes, and to check the pistol's magazine— a quick tap with the butt of his hand. Then he rapped hard, several times on one of the door's small glass panes.

Almost right away, a light went on from somewhere inside. The Reillys were sleeping light these days, no doubt.

A moment later, another light came on, in the kitchen this time. Through the sheer curtain hanging over the glass, Guidice could see Tommy Reilly tying the belt of a plaid bathrobe around his considerable middle as he came around the corner.

"Mr. Reilly?" he called through. "Sorry to disturb you, but we've got a bit of a problem out here. Would you mind opening up for a second?"

CHAPTER
40

JOSH BERGMAN KEPT IT SIMPLE TONIGHT. JUST A DARK PAIR OF JEANS, a long-sleeved tee, and an excruciatingly boring Gap blazer. It was important to look presentable, but there was no sense in spending major cash to get it done. It was all going in the incinerator by the end of the night, anyway.

He kept his change of clothes—his *real* clothes—in the trunk. Ian Velardi dot-print shirt, Armani trousers, and the custom Italian slip-ons from Vicenza, along with a change of underwear, and his Rolex Submariner.

For after.

Just before ten o'clock, he pulled his silver Audi A7 off Water Street and into the fenced waterfront parking lot. As he came around to the back, he spotted a single silhouetted male figure standing against the chain link and looking out at the Potomac.

Bergman came to a stop and lowered the passenger window.

"Travis?" he said.

The boy turned around and came closer. "Are you Bill?" he asked.

"I sure am," Bergman said. "Get in."

He pointed at the bank envelope on the seat

as the young hustler opened the door. There were two one hundred dollar bills inside, but the kid didn't check. He just stuck it in his back pocket and sat down.

"Nice car," he said.

"Isn't it?" Bergman said.

He was thin. Maybe a little too thin, but cute, with a sexy little gap in his smile. His clothes were preppy-slouchy, a half-tucked oxford in ripped jeans. But it was the bright green limited edition Nike kicks that gave him away. This boy was obviously pulling down more cash than his friends with their little jobs at Abercrombie and Pizzeria Paradiso.

Bergman pulled out of the lot and headed north, toward MacArthur. He had Elvis Costello on the stereo. "Pills and Soap." A bit of vintage gold to go with his great mood.

For a while, he drove upriver and they played small talk. The boy was from Maine. He hadn't seen any good movies lately. He thought Mumford and Sons were just *awesome*.

Eventually, the kid took a breath and looked around.

"Where are we going?" he said. "This is like, practically Maryland."

"It is Maryland," Bergman said. "I know a place. How do you feel about outside? Your profile didn't really say either way."

The kid shrugged. "I like outside," he said. He put a hand on Bergman's knee as he leaned in to bump up the stereo's volume. "Whatever you're into."

"Awesome," Bergman said.

At the little one-lane stone bridge, he took a left

off MacArthur, crossed over, and doubled back, half a mile down Clara Barton Parkway. The parking lot was just off the road, but low enough to offer some privacy. The only time anyone used it was during the day, and not even that much then.

"Here we are," he said, killing the engine. "Let's go for a walk."

If the kid had any second thoughts, he was keeping them to himself. Probably thinking about his next pair of kicks instead.

They got out and headed down into the woods. Bergman walked just behind him on the little footpath, his hand in his pocket, touching himself through the cloth.

"Down here?" the boy asked.

"Actually, stop right there," Bergman said. They were at the midpoint in the woods, between the lot and the canal down the hill. "This is good."

The boy turned around in the dark and stepped up toward him. He reached out and ran a hand over Bergman's crotch.

"Dude. You're ready to go, aren't you?" the kid asked.

"I am," Bergman said. "I really am."

It was likely the boy never even saw the gun. Bergman took one quick step back to avoid any splatter, and pulled the trigger.

The kid's shadow dropped to the ground unceremoniously, like a sack of whatever. Bergman dropped, too, onto his knees.

The knife was out next. He drove it in—once, twice, three times, fast...then again—four, five, six...seven...eight...

He lost count somewhere after that, as the rising swirl of it all caught him up, and then seemed to reverse direction, funneling back down into a final, excruciating explosion of pleasure—literal and figurative.

It was done. Again.

Bergman fell back onto his elbows. His breath was ragged. The inside of his pants was wet.

One by one, his senses seemed to float back into place. There was the boy on the ground. The sound of traffic on the highway. A slight metallic taste in his mouth.

As his head cleared, logic moved back in. He couldn't stay here, of course. He had to keep moving.

It was just a quick drag down to the canal, where he emptied the boy's pockets and rolled him into the water.

Then he made his way back up to the parking lot, popped his trunk, and changed quickly, bagging everything else for disposal.

By the time he was behind the wheel of his car again, heading south into the city, Bergman had come full circle and then some. He felt better now than he could remember feeling, ever.

And the night was young. It was time to take this party somewhere else.

CHAPTER
41

BY MIDNIGHT, BERGMAN WAS BACK DOWNTOWN AND READY FOR THE NEXT PART of his evening. He got out at the corner of Seventh and D, handed his keys to the valet, and headed inside.

The three-tiered lobby of the Woolly Mammoth Theatre was jumping, with the annual Fashion Fights Hunger fundraiser. They had the whole place awash in yellow light, with bright pink theatrical spots throwing shards of magenta around the room. It wasn't exactly flattering, but it was festive, anyway. The deejay booth at the far end was spinning salsa, and it was a hoot to see some of these industry suits trying to shake the sticks out of their asses on the dance floor.

Bergman hit the bar first, then worked his way up to the third level, the better to take in the scene.

"Joshua!" a voice screamed out as soon as he hit the landing. He turned around and saw a big pair of red lips coming at him, with his friend Kiki attached.

"Incoming!" she said, and kissed him full on the mouth. "How's my darling boy doing? It's been forever and a half!"

Bergman nodded at the mostly finished pink

concoction in her hand. "I think I have some catching up to do," he said.

"Oh, you do," she said. "You totally do. Garth and Tina are going to want to know you're here, too."

Unlike with Elijah, Joshua Bergman's recent troubles in the press had only upped his stock. He was now Washington's bad boy of style and fashion, it seemed. Well, if the shoe fit, why not?

He downed the rest of his watered half-rate Scotch and wagged the glass at Kiki. "Would you?" he said. "I have to make a call."

"I would," she said. "And stand by for Garth and Tina. I'm going to bring them back up here. I think Tina has coke, which is so freaking retro, I can't stand it."

As soon as she was gone, Bergman took out his phone and hit speed-dial one. He stood at the rail, watching the party and waiting for Elijah to answer.

"Josh?"

"Why do you always say my name like it's a question?" Bergman said. "Don't you trust caller ID?"

"I don't trust my mother, Josh. Why would I trust my phone?"

Bergman loved the way they could just fall into it. Elijah acted like he didn't care, Josh acted like he did, and both of them knew where the other was coming from. It was comfortable.

"Well, guess where I am," he said.

"Someplace loud."

"It's the Fashion Fights Hunger thing. You should come down and have a drink with me. It's been a big night."

"Rain check," Creem said. "I'm working at my

desk, and I don't want to put all of this away right now."

Bergman felt a bubble of excitement rise up from his belly, and into his throat. It came out as a giggle.

"Let me try that again," he said. "It's been a *very* big night, Elijah, and I mean that in a way that only you could appreciate. I thought it would be nice to have a drink together."

Elijah didn't answer, or say anything at all for a very long time. Kiki, Garth, and Tina were on their way up the stairs now, and Bergman gave them a just-a-minute finger before he walked farther up the mezzanine.

"Elijah?" he said. "Are you still there?"

"I'm here," Creem said. "And you need to slow down, my friend. This isn't a race."

"It's not an *anything,*" Bergman said. "Isn't that part of the beauty? It's whatever we want it to be. Just like life."

He could feel the adrenaline, or endorphins, or whatever it was running through his veins as hot as that salsa music down below. He even did a few giddy steps while they talked. Back, forth, cha-cha-cha.

"Well, enjoy yourself," Creem said. "I'll catch up with you soon."

Bergman smiled. "I hope that's a double entendre," he said. "Because just for the record, Elijah—if this *were* a race? I'd be winning."

"Good night, Josh."

"Love you, Elijah. Talk soon."

CHAPTER
42

THE NEXT DAY WAS ONE OF THE WORST I'VE EVER HAD ON THE FORCE.

It started just before the 6 a.m. briefing at headquarters. With all three of these cases in full go mode, the brass had shifted our morning meetings up to the Joint Operations Command Center on the fifth floor. Everything to do with these homicides was now tracked in real time through the JOCC, so we would always know who was working which leads, and if anyone had made any progress. The briefings were a chance to cross-reference any police action from the overnight shift against our open investigations, to see if anything might prove relevant.

When I got there that morning, Tom D'Auria was waiting in the fifth-floor hall to head me off with some very bad news. Word had just come in that Jeannette and Tommy Reilly, as well as the sheriff's deputy assigned to their house in Shellman Bluff, had all been killed sometime in the last eight hours.

"All three of them were shot," D'Auria told me. "But they're reporting two different calibers, so some of this is a little up in the air. CIC just got it a few minutes ago."

I nodded, but I wasn't hearing much. My chest

had gone tight, and I felt like I couldn't breathe until I got an answer to my next question.

"What about the baby?" I said.

"Missing," Tom told me.

It was a one-word punch in the stomach. D'Auria ducked his chin, just to give me a moment of space. He knew I was invested here.

"What can I do?" I said.

"Not much," he said. "FBI's already on it. They're working with McIntosh County, and the state troopers. The AMBER Alerts are up. Transportation hubs in all contiguous states are already covered."

"There has to be something," I said.

"You can give a call down to the Atlanta field office if you want, or the Savannah satellite office, if anyone's there. They may want to talk to you. But other than that, it's going to be a waiting game at this point."

They were coming at it aggressively. That was good. If and when they determined Rebecca had been taken across any state lines, it would automatically go federal, and they were already set up for that.

I just hoped it was all enough. Without knowing how long ago she'd been taken, it was hard to say.

Meanwhile, the shift change was filing past us into the JOCC. I saw a lot of bleary-eyed cops, either because they were just finishing for the night, or just getting started for the day.

"I'm going to cover all of this inside," D'Auria told me. "I figured you'd want a heads-up."

"I appreciate it, Tom."

"If you need to talk—"

"I'm good," I said. "I'll be right in."

Every cop I know gets overwhelmed sometimes. It's nothing to be ashamed of. I always encourage my people to talk it out when they need to. We've got an employee assistance program for that, but there's also supervisors, coworkers, shrinks, clergy, whatever. You just have to choose someone, is what I tell people.

Sometimes I take my own advice, and sometimes I don't.

I walked down the hall and locked myself in the handicapped bathroom by the stairs. I just needed a minute to breathe.

This wasn't my fault. Not technically. I knew that. But it was also true that I'd had more of a chance to stop it from happening than just about anyone else. I could have pushed harder to get Rebecca into protective services. I could have worked more closely with McIntosh County.

But I didn't. I'd made a perfectly justifiable call, on paper. Now three more people were dead, and one very little girl was missing. Again.

I turned on the sink and splashed some water on my face, as cold as I could make it. When I looked up again, I guess I caught sight of myself too fast or something. I couldn't help it—my fist came up and smashed the mirror into shards. It was a dumbass move, the kind of thing I'd yell at anyone else for pulling. All it got me was a bunch of broken glass and some bloody knuckles.

And the kicker was—my crap day had only just begun.

CHAPTER
43

I SPENT THE MORNING PULLING TOGETHER EVERYTHING I HAD ON THE REILLY family and faxing it down to the FBI in Atlanta. I gave them what we had on Amanda Simms as well, for whatever that was worth. We still didn't know if both of these "pregnant girl" cases were linked or not.

Beyond that, I spent way too much time trying to get someone to answer at the Bureau's Savannah satellite office, but that was just an exercise in frustration. Hopefully, they were all out in the field, getting the job done.

The one piece of relative good news was that Rebecca had been taken at all. Given the three homicides, it meant that the kidnapper—or someone—wanted to keep her. That was better than the alternative. At least it left open the possibility that she could still be found.

Then, while I was sitting on hold with Savannah for the third time that morning, I heard my name called out from somewhere else in the squad room.

I stood up and looked around. Across the cubicles, Huizenga was standing in the door of her office with Jessica Jacobs. When she motioned me over to join them, I pointed at the phone in my hand.

"Hang up!" she yelled back, and headed inside.

I didn't have to think hard about what this might be. Jacobs was the lead investigator assigned to Cory Smithe and Ricky Samuels, the two young hustlers who had been killed. I felt numb walking over to Huizenga's office, like there wasn't room for anything else right now. Not that it mattered.

Huizenga had her head in her hands when I came in. Jacobs was on the phone, scribbling notes on a yellow legal pad.

"Marti?" I said.

"Number three," she said, without looking up. "Young white male, single gunshot, multiple stab wounds, no ID."

"A jogger found the kid," Jacobs said, with a hand over her phone. "Way up at Lock Seven on the C and O Canal."

"Lock Seven," I said. "That's Maryland, isn't it?"

Huizenga nodded. "Montgomery County's already on the scene. You may see the Bureau before the day's over, too. I'll talk to D'Auria. This is the chief's call, but I'd rather not open this up if we don't have to."

Three murders committed in a similar fashion put this case squarely into serial territory. That's usually when the FBI starts asking questions. They can be hugely useful, given the resources the Feds have, but they can also be an impediment, especially if anyone starts getting turfy about this stuff. I've been on both sides of that fence, and I know.

In the meantime, before I headed up to Lock Seven, what I needed was a vending machine, a cup of coffee, and a reset button for my brain.

I got two out of three, anyway.

CHAPTER
44

RON GUIDICE STOOD IN THE FRONT HALL OF THE OLD PLACE AND LOOKED around. The house was like some kind of time capsule from 1979. There was gray shag carpet on the floor. A powder-blue toilet in the bathroom.

Still, it was solid, with three bedrooms, a back-yard, and plenty of privacy. Also just ninety minutes from the city. The perfect hiding place for his growing family.

"Don't mind all these boxes," the rental lady said. "I have one of those Got Junk trucks coming this afternoon. Unless you see anything you'd like to keep."

"Just the furniture. Everything else can go," Guidice told her.

The woman, Mrs. Patten, stopped to look down into the Snugli, where Grace was fast asleep against his chest. She'd been fussy in the car but had tired herself out by the time they got to Virginia.

And it was Grace now. Not Rebecca. Not ever again.

"They're just little gifts from God, aren't they?" Mrs. Patten said. "How old?"

"She's three weeks today," Guidice said. "And yes, they really are. I fell in love the second I laid eyes on her."

That much was true. Mrs. Patten smiled, the way women always did when men showed even a hint of softness. Like he'd just done her some kind of favor.

"Would you like to see the back?" she asked.

"Please."

He followed her into a large eat-in kitchen, with a picture window over the formica table. Outside there was a wooden swing set at the back of the overgrown yard. It didn't look fit to use, but he could fix it up. Beyond that, Guidice could see a horse paddock through the trees. Half a dozen brown mares were munching on the spring grass.

Emma Lee was going to love it here. They all were, even Lydia, once she got used to it.

"I hope you don't mind vintage," Mrs. Patten said, "if that's what you call all this. Mr. Schiavo seemed to have stopped shopping quite a while ago."

"It's fine."

"A pity, really, how he died so suddenly. But I think he'd be happy to know there was a young family moving in. What do you do, Mr. Henderson?"

"I'm a journalist," Guidice said. "But I'm looking to take some time off."

Like Grace, he had a new name here, too. He'd used pseudonyms before, never as a byline, but sometimes to cover his tracks when he was chasing down a story. Paul Henderson was the one he'd used the most often, and the one for which he had passable identification, including a rarely used credit card. It was enough to secure the house, in any case.

"How about your wife?" the rental agent asked brightly. "Will she be staying home as well?"

"My wife isn't with us anymore," Guidice said. "We lost her on the night Grace was born."

Mrs. Patten stopped and put a hand to her mouth, covering the little O that had just formed there. "Oh my lord. I'm so sorry. I had no idea."

"Of course," Guidice said. "I'm just looking for somewhere quiet where my mother, my daughters, and I can put our lives back together in private."

She looked like she might actually cry. Guidice hoped not.

"How old is your other daughter?" she asked.

"Emma Lee's four and a half. She misses her mama, but she's very excited about being a big sister."

"And you have your mother as well. That's a blessing. I'm sure she's wonderful with the girls."

"Yes," Guidice said. He glanced down at the soft little angel curls on the top of his daughter's head. "Because there's nothing more important than family. Isn't that right, Grace?"

CHAPTER
45

LOCK SEVEN ON THE CHESAPEAKE AND OHIO CANAL IS ORDINARILY A LITTLE recreational area just off the Clara Barton Parkway. Today, it had a yellow tape fence around the entrance. Later on, this quiet spot was going to be all over the news.

Our latest victim had been found just before noon. His body was entangled in the old drop gate mechanism of what used to be an operating lock. The original purpose of the canal was to run material goods over a 184-mile stretch between Georgetown and Cumberland Park, Maryland. Now, it was mostly something to run, bike, or walk along, though very few people got this far up the tow path anymore. My guess was that the killer didn't expect the body to be discovered so soon.

The Montgomery County detective assigned to the case was an older guy I knew and liked, Bob Semillon. He met Jacobs and me in the parking lot and walked us down through the woods.

"Our ME's already gone, but I assumed you'd want one of your folks to take a look," Bob said. "It all sounds like the same character you've been dealing with down there in the city. Pretty awful stuff."

That was one way of putting it.

All indications were that the murder itself had taken place up here on the trail. A dark patch of dried blood in the dirt had been found about halfway down the hill, and there were some pretty clear drag marks between that spot and the canal.

They had the body laid out on the grass when we got there, giving me a sickening sense of déjà vu. There was the one gunshot wound to the face, and then multiple stab wounds around the hips and genitals.

Also, there was a water factor. Cory Smithe had been found in the Potomac, Ricky Samuels in Rock Creek, and now this.

The only real difference I could see, besides location, was in the knife work. Each victim seemed to have been stabbed quite a few more times than the one before him. This boy's jeans were blood-stained all the way down to his neon green shoes.

Jacobs knelt next to the body. I could tell she was doing what I did sometimes—forcing herself to get close and absorb as much as she could, subconsciously or otherwise.

"What's this guy so pissed off about?" she said. "What's he trying to work out here, do you suppose?"

She seemed to be homing in on some of the same anger I'd been seeing in all these cases. That word kept coming up.

"I don't know," I said. "But it can be a vicious cycle. The harder he tries to scratch that itch, the more he's going to find out it can't be done, and the more desperate he's going to get."

"Or enthusiastic," she said, fingering one of the

perforations in the kid's pants with a gloved finger. "Or both."

The gunshot was a means to an end, I felt pretty sure. It was the knife work where his emotions took over. In every other respect, he seemed to be extremely well disciplined about the whole thing. These weren't spontaneous murders. Each one of them required some forethought and planning.

And that brought up the other big question here.

The last time around, in Rock Creek, our victim hadn't been alone. There were two bodies that night, most likely from two different killers.

The Montgomery County CSI unit had already made a first pass up and down the canal, and they were still dragging the woods, but it seemed clear to me by now that this was another solo job.

But why? What had changed? Or changed back?

I had no idea, but even as I stood there taking it all in, some part of me was already bracing for what came next. Whatever game these people were playing, it wasn't over yet.

And the score was three to two.

CHAPTER
46

IT WAS JUST BEFORE DARK WHEN I FINALLY WRAPPED UP AT THE CRIME SCENE. I'd been there longer than I meant to be, but then again, I always am. I walked back up through the woods to the parking lot and toward my car.

When I got there, someone was waiting for me. It was dusk, and I couldn't see who it was at first, but then I recognized the beard. Even the hoodie and cargo shorts were the same as the last time.

"Ron Guidice?" I said.

Sure enough, he turned around. I'd been right all along. It was him.

"I've been trying to reach you," I said. "We need to talk."

"Oh, now you want to talk?" he said, immediately aggressive. "Last time I got the brush off."

I took a deep breath. Part of me wanted to cuff him and throw him in the back of the car. But that wasn't going to get me anywhere. I pressed on instead.

"Listen, I'm not going to pretend that I understand exactly what you went through six years ago. But what you're doing now? It's not helping anyone."

"I guess that's a matter of opinion," he said.

"I want you to know that I'm sorry for your loss," I told him. "I really am, but—"

"But what, Alex? I should just shut up and go away? I already tried that, but it didn't help. You and your department are just as incompetent as you were six years ago."

I looked him in the eye, trying to gauge how put together this guy was—or wasn't. Were there emerging paranoia issues here? Was Guidice one hundred percent? I wasn't convinced.

"It's not just my life you're making difficult," I said. "You're potentially putting future victims' lives at risk here. Do you understand that?"

"That's funny," he said. "Because I write what I do to protect the people *you're* putting at risk."

"You've got the wrong idea," I said.

"Do I?" he said. "What about Rebecca Reilly, detective? Can you tell me where she is? Because as far as I know, she disappeared on your watch."

He was just baiting me now. That much was obvious. I wasn't going to be able to placate this guy, and I wasn't sure it was worth trying anymore.

But I did have one other thing to say.

"All right, fine," I told him. "You want to blog your bullshit, that's your right. But I'll tell you something else. If I find you tailing me when I'm with my family again, we're going to have a very different kind of problem. Do you understand?"

He stepped a little closer. Guidice was a big dude, and obviously not intimidated by much. But neither am I.

"Are you threatening me, Detective Cross?" he asked. "Is that what's going on here?"

I hadn't even noticed the recorder in his hand

until now. He'd been palming it, just out of sight. Before I thought too much about it, I snatched it out of his hand and threw it as far as I could into the woods. Probably a mistake. Another one for my resume.

"You think that's going to stop me?" he said. He laughed without smiling before he went on. "This is your other problem. You've started to believe your own publicity. Alex Cross, the Dragonslayer. Alex Cross, the Sherlock Holmes of MPD. Alex Cross, the second goddamn coming of Christ! You're a paper tiger, Alex. A phony! And people need to know about it."

I was already walking away.

"This isn't over," he called after me. "Not even close!"

"That's one place where we agree, Guidice," I said as I got into my car. "It definitely isn't."

It was time to hit this guy from another angle.

CHAPTER
47

IT'S NOT LIKE I WAS COMPLETELY UNSYMPATHETIC TO GUIDICE. I LOST MY OWN first wife to senseless violence. It was the worst day of my life, and in a strange way it connected the two of us.

But that didn't mean I was going to let him keep going unchecked. If he wouldn't talk to me, in a real way, then I had to do whatever else I could to stop him.

I spent the evening pulling everything we had on Guidice, and digging for anything else I could find. Commander D'Auria let me piggyback onto his LexisNexis access, and that turned up what was basically a bibliography of Guidice's past work. It gave me a whole new lens on him.

What I already knew was that he'd been with the US Army for several years before receiving an honorable discharge in 2005. That was where he'd cut his teeth, journalistically speaking.

Most of his work in the army had been with administrative and communications units, first at Fort Bragg, then in Newark, New Jersey, with one six-month deployment to Baghdad for the *Army Times*. Overseas, he'd written a series of PR pieces highlighting US humanitarian efforts and infrastructure projects in Iraq. All of that was a matter of public record.

Then there was everything that came after his discharge. I don't know what happened to Guidice in the army, but by the time he started writing freelance—and well before Theresa Filmore died—it was like he'd turned a one eighty. His focus at that point was almost entirely on the overreach of the US government, both at home and abroad.

He'd traveled back to the Middle East a few times for some small presses, and he even won a few obscure awards for his work. At the same time, he wrote pieces on everything from police brutality to time-card falsification in law enforcement, and several scathing articles about MPD's supposed mishandling of the Al Ayla terrorist attacks in DC in the fall.

The one thing he seemed to have never written about directly was the death of his fiancée. For whatever reasons of his own, he'd left that incident off the table, but I could only imagine the kind of fuel it would have poured onto the fire he already had burning.

Now, all of it seemed to be bubbling up to the surface, including the blame he was laying so squarely at my feet.

I didn't know what exactly to expect from him next, but it was clear to me that I hadn't seen the last—or the worst—of Ron Guidice yet.

CHAPTER
48

BY TWO O'CLOCK THE NEXT AFTERNOON, I'D GRABBED THE FIRST APPOINTMENT I could get with the US Attorney's Office. It's not always the fastest-moving machine over there, and if they could do anything for me about Guidice, I wanted to find out sooner rather than later.

At one forty-five, I left my office and made the quick walk from headquarters, up Fourth Street to the Judiciary Center Building. My meeting was with one of their line assistants, Larry Kim, in his third-floor office.

Kim and I knew each other more by reputation than from actually working together. He was known as a solid prosecutor, with a good grasp of case law and a willingness to go to bat for something he believed in. We'd already spoken on the phone, and he knew the basics of why I was there.

"Honestly, I'm not sure there's much you can do," he told me. "The fact is, citizens have every right to investigate government affairs and share what they learn with other people."

"What about the invasion of my own privacy? Or a public good mandate, for that matter? At some point he's going to represent a threat to the investigation. I'm not just talking about murders already committed. I'm talking about a missing baby, and more than one killer still active out there."

Kim shook his head. "First Amendment, man. Freedom of the press. It's a tough nut to crack—for good reason. And getting tougher all the time."

"He's not the press," I said. "He's some guy with a computer, a cell phone, and a grudge."

"This is my point." Kim set down the extra-large Starbucks he'd been drinking and leaned toward me, warming to the conversation. "It used to be major stories broke in the mainstream press first, and filtered down. Now, you're just as likely to see some guy with a smartphone or a blog out in front of this stuff. The courts are recognizing that.

"There was a national security blog out of Oregon last year. Same thing—just some guy operating off a laptop, with questionable sources. Well, guess what? His rights to privacy were upheld all the way to the state supreme court. If Oregon thought they had a case, they would have appealed to the Feds, but they let it drop." Kim sat back and picked up his coffee. "That's the new reality."

"That's one case," I said.

"No," he said. "One of several. I'm guessing this Guidice person knows it, and he's taking full advantage. And frankly, the fact that he's been coming after you personally doesn't bolster your case. If anything, it muddies the water."

"I'm just asking you to run this up the flagpole," I told him. The US Attorney's Office had a full staff of legal research lawyers. I trusted Kim's expertise, but maybe there was some alternate precedent out there. "If I could get as far as filing a motion in court, it might get Guidice to back off."

Larry nodded several times and started shuffling the files on his desk. It was a not-so-subtle indication that he was out of time for me.

"I can do that," he told me. "But it's not much to work with. If you can find anything more specific on Guidice—if he's broken any laws—you might have a better chance at getting some traction here."

"Believe me," I said. "I'm working on it."

I just hoped nobody else wound up dead in the meantime.

CHAPTER
49

I LEFT THE MEETING WITH KIM AND WENT STRAIGHT BACK TO MY CAR, IN the parking garage under the Daly Building. Sometimes there's no better place to get some work done in private. Bree calls it my mobile office.

Mostly, I had calls to make. I flipped open a pad on my knee and dialed the first of several names on my list—Ned Mahoney.

Ned's a good friend, a great FBI agent, and the person over at the Bureau who I most trust to give me a straight answer. He ran the Hostage and Rescue Team out of Quantico, but I'd also been hearing murmurs that Mahoney was on his way up at the Bureau. I'd believe it when I saw it.

"Alex," he answered. "How's the hardest-working man in show business? Wait, don't tell me. Up to your ass, am I right?"

Ned also has a mouth that won't quit. He comes across as sarcastic a lot of the time, but the truth is, there just aren't many sacred cows in Ned's world. It's one of the things I like about him.

"I need some info," I told him. "It's about a kidnapping down in Georgia," I said. "The name's Rebecca Reilly."

"Reilly," he said. "Anything to do with that

nasty windowsill action over on Vernon a few weeks ago?"

"Off the record? Yeah," I said. "Rebecca's the vic's baby. She was in her grandparents' custody down south when she was taken. The grandparents were killed, too. I can't get anyone in Atlanta or Savannah to talk to me about it."

Ned made a sound like he was sucking air through his teeth. "This business stinks, doesn't it? Why didn't we become accountants or something?"

"'Cause we care, Ned."

"Oh, right. That," he said. "Let me see what I can do. I'll get you back as soon as I can."

It didn't take him long, either. By the time I'd put in calls to Jarret Krause, Sampson, and Sergeant Huizenga, I had a voice mail waiting from Ned. He didn't want to leave any specific information on my phone, so I called him back right away.

"Not much to tell," he said. "The Bureau's still active with the case, so they probably have good reason to believe Rebecca was taken out of Georgia. But that's as far as I got. They're holding their cards pretty close."

"Thanks for trying," I said. It was more than I'd had before.

"How're you doing, anyway?" Ned asked. "Seems like you've been getting spanked pretty bad in the press lately."

This was the one thing I didn't want to talk about, but curiosity got the best of me. It often does.

"Why?" I said. "What have you heard?"

"That whole *Real Deal* thing," Ned said.

"Seems like I can't turn around without reading about it these days. Or you. Is it true you threw that guy's tape recorder into the woods?"

"I'll take the fifth," I told him. It wasn't like I thought Guidice's blog was a secret anymore, but it was no fun to be reminded of the fact. The longer this went on, the more I'd become a part of the story myself—and that's nowhere a self-respecting cop wants to be. "Bottom line, the guy's a major tool," I said.

"Don't sweat it too much," Ned told me. "This stuff's like herpes. It pops up, it goes away for a while, then it comes back. There's nothing you can do but keep your head down and stick to what's important."

I had to laugh. "Herpes, huh? Remind me to call you back the next time I need cheering up."

"Anytime, Alex. Meanwhile, just don't read that crap. It's only going to piss you off. Especially today."

It was probably good advice, but it was coming a little too late. As soon as I hung up with Ned, I opened the browser on my phone and went straight to *The Real Deal*.

For better or worse.

CHAPTER
50

A NEW LOW
Posted by RG at 11:52 p.m.

Sometimes I'm surprised at the depths to which the Metropolitan Police Department will sink. Yesterday evening was a good example. My own criticisms of Detective Alex Cross (see sidebar, *here*) are well known. Despite his reputation as a superior investigator—which he may well be—Dr. Cross is also a prime example of the kind of wolf in sheep's clothing that pervades that department.

Click *here* for an audio recording of my encounter with Detective Cross just yesterday. See what you think for yourself. I was attempting to report on the latest in a series of murders, of young hustlers in and around Georgetown—the so-called River Killer case (for which the MPD has no reported progress, by the way). At the time of the incident, I was in the parking lot at Lock Seven of the C&O Canal, off of Clara Barton Parkway. I've Google mapped it *here,* and marked the police perimeter as it was established, along with the spot where my encounter with Detective Cross took place. As you'll see, I was well within the allowable area for press and other onlookers. There is no question of trespass in this case.

I will, however, admit to having a concealed recording device during our conversation. It's something I always do in my dealings with MPD, as a backup, but this was the first time it's ever proven necessary. Click *here* to listen to the encounter. What you'll hear is me interacting with Detective Cross, followed by a brief struggle in which he took the handheld recorder I was carrying and threw it deep into the woods, in the direction I've marked with an arrow on the abovementioned map.

What I hope is coming clear here is a growing—I'd say overwhelming—body of evidence that the MPD is badly in need of a little housecleaning. This is the kind of police behavior I've heard about in places like Egypt, and Libya, and China. Is it really what we want here at home?

As always, I encourage you NOT to take my word on any of this. Look into it for yourself. See what other people are saying. See what you think. If you'd like to share a comment or observation about the work MPD is doing, click *here*.

And remember—the police work for you. Not the other way around.

CHAPTER
51

WHEN I GOT HOME JUST BEFORE SEVEN THAT NIGHT, THE HOUSE WAS disconcertingly quiet. There was no Wii from the living room. No Nikki Minaj playing behind some closed door. No pounding feet on the stairs.

Instead, what I found was Bree sitting in the kitchen with Stephanie Gethmann, our social worker. Stephanie was the one from Child and Family Services assigned to Ava's case. Usually we saw her once a month for home visits, but the last visit had been just a week before.

Something was up.

"Alex, come sit down," Bree said. She looked tense, and touched my hand as I pulled out a chair to join them.

"What's going on? Where are the kids?" I said.

"Jannie and Ali are with Aunt Tia," Bree told me.

"What about Ava?" I said. "Is she okay?"

"A patrol cop brought her home this afternoon," Bree said. "He found her in Seward Square, passed out on a park bench."

The news hit me like a punch in the gut, but one that I was already half expecting.

"Passed out?" I said.

"With pupils like pin dots."

That meant opiates. OxyContin, possibly, although Ava didn't have that kind of money. Maybe fentanyl, which was cheaper and easier to get but also harder to control. My cop's mind couldn't help running down a list of possibilities.

"Nana's upstairs with her now," Bree went on. "She's just sleeping. We'll have to do a urine test in the morning."

I nodded and looked down at the table. All of a sudden, it felt like July 1989 all over again. That was the last time drugs had haunted this house.

My brother Blake had been an addict. He'd shown up on Nana's doorstep one night, dope sick and begging for help. Nana called me in my dorm at Georgetown and asked me to come home, which I did. It was a long, sweaty twelve hours, but we got through it. Nana was like an angel of mercy. I just helped out where I could.

What I didn't know then was that it would be the last time all three of us were together. Blake promised to stick with the rehab program Nana found for him, but he quickly skipped out and disappeared. The next we heard was on the morning of September 2—another cop at the front door. Blake had been found in an Anacostia flophouse, dead from a heroin overdose.

Now, sitting here, I couldn't help feeling terrified for Ava. She wasn't Blake, obviously. But it was also true that Nana and I had done all we could for my brother, and it still wasn't enough.

"So, what now?" I asked Stephanie.

"Counseling, for sure," she said. "Maybe treatment. It depends on what Ava has to say for herself. We need to find out how long this has been going on, and if she's dealing with an addiction here. Also, if you can find out where she's getting her drugs, that could be a good step toward doing something about it."

"We've had her on a short leash," Bree said. "There's been a little trouble lately."

"Drug trouble?" Stephanie asked.

Bree and I looked at each other. "We weren't sure," she said. "But I guess we are now."

"Well, as long as you'll have her, Ava's best off staying right here. I'll let her rest tonight, but I'd like to see her tomorrow. And I'll be making more frequent visits to the house. How are Wednesdays and Saturdays for you?"

"Fine," Bree said.

I felt like I was still trying to catch up. My head was too crowded. When I looked up again, Stephanie and Bree were both looking back at me.

"I'm sorry—what?" I said.

"Wednesdays and Saturdays," Stephanie repeated. "Is that okay for you, Alex?"

"Yes. Of course," I said. "Whatever it takes. We'll make it work."

CHAPTER
52

"YES. OF COURSE. WHATEVER IT TAKES. WE'LL MAKE IT WORK."

Ron Guidice slid the headphones off his ears and sat back. He'd heard all he needed to. The rest of the conversation could go to the hard drive.

In the meantime, it sounded like Alex was getting it coming and going these days. This was exactly what the electronic surveillance was for. There was only so much of a story Guidice could build without some kind of inside line on Alex's home life. It was working out perfectly, in fact.

Guidice marked the time on a legal pad next to his computer and had just started typing up some thoughts when a knock came from the hall.

"Ronald, honey?"

"Come in," he said, flipping the laptop closed.

When his mother opened the door, she had baby Grace held in the crook of one arm. A white cloth diaper was draped over her shoulder. The nipple of a small Evenflo bottle showed over the top of her housecoat pocket.

"Emma Lee says she wants daddy to tuck her in tonight."

"No problem," Guidice said.

When he got to the door, though, Lydia didn't move. She just stood there, filling the frame with her considerable girth. It was her own version of passive-aggressive, putting herself in the way like a cow on the tracks. She obviously had something on her mind.

Guidice steeled his patience. It wasn't clear yet whether his mother was going to need a little stick, or a little carrot. Maybe both.

"What is it, Mom?" he asked.

"Did you call the police yet?"

"No," he said. "Don't worry about it."

"Well, I do worry about it," she said, absently rocking the baby. "I mean..." Now she dropped her voice to a whisper, as if anyone else were listening. "How do you even know she's yours?"

Guidice reached over and stroked his daughter's rosy cheek with one finger. Her little half-lidded eyes made him smile.

"Look at her," he said. "She looks just like me."

"Still. This is the baby's mother we're talking about," Lydia insisted.

"She was just some slut, Mom. A one-night stand."

His mother half turned her head and held up a hand. "Too much information, thank you. I'm just saying, it's not right what she did."

"Exactly," he said. "Think about it, Mom. This is someone who leaves a baby in a car with a note and walks away. Do you really want that kind of person in Grace's life?"

Lydia held the baby a little closer. "Well, no, but—"

"That's why we moved. I didn't want her finding us. And frankly, I don't want to find her, either. I say Grace deserves better than that."

"I suppose," Lydia answered tentatively—

either because she agreed with him, or because her tenth-grade education hadn't armed her for any kind of substantive debate in life.

"Don't *suppose,* Mom. Think about it," he told her. "Do you really want someone like that raising your granddaughter?"

"No," she answered, more resolutely this time.

"No," he said. "You don't. And neither do I."

He let it all sink in for a moment, and then softened his tone as he went on. Time for a little carrot.

"Believe me," he said. "You're a way better mother than she'd ever be. No contest, Mom."

Lydia Guidice was always easily flattered. She smiled as she blushed, and then finally stepped out of the way.

"Go on," she said. "Emma Lee's waiting."

Guidice kissed his mother on the cheek before he headed up the hall.

There were other solutions, of course. Lydia could be eliminated just as easily as anyone else, physically speaking. It would even be a relief to put the ultimate gag order on that incessant nagging.

But it was basically a cost-benefit situation at this point. Lydia played a vital role in the family. Like it or not, he needed her right now. It would be shortsighted to take her out just to shut her up.

No, Guidice thought. He couldn't do that. Couldn't even think about it.

Not unless it became absolutely necessary.

CHAPTER
53

I TRIED TO STAY FOCUSED AT THE NEXT MORNING'S BRIEFING, BUT IT WAS HARD to keep my mind in the room.

I was starting to wonder if I'd overextended myself. It's a question that comes up a lot. I had three cases on the books—plus Ava. She was the fourth case. Later in the day, we had a meeting at Child and Family Services. In the meantime, I had more than enough to keep me busy.

Too much, in fact, but how do you say no to something when the stakes are people's lives? We had nine dead so far, one missing, and, with three unknown suspects at large, the looming promise of more to come.

There's a good amount of disagreement about clusters, as they're called in serial homicide. Some people say they're nothing more than coincidence, and that we're bound to see concurrent activity from time to time. The United States is the world capital of serial murder, with somewhere between twenty-five and fifty active killers at any given time.

The most famous cluster I knew of had been in South LA, from the early eighties through 2007. LAPD had tracked down five separate cases then, including the Grim Sleeper and the Southside

Slayer. By the time all five of those files were closed, a total of fifty-five people had died, all within a fifty-square-mile area.

There had also been some recent coverage about the three killers operating simultaneously in Nassau and Suffolk Counties, on Long Island. The last I'd heard, two suspects were in custody, with one still at large, and the body count was up to thirty.

Now, Washington had the makings of its own cluster. I spent virtually all my time turning over these three cases in my head—thinking about methods, victim profiles, possible motives, and most of all, wondering where one of these guys might strike next.

Killer number one was the man I thought of as "Russell," the supposed boyfriend of Elizabeth Reilly. He was the most unpredictable in a way, with four and a half years between his pregnant victims, and a probable kidnapping on his resume, too.

Number two was the one they'd dubbed the River Killer in the press. Three gay hustlers had been found dead so far, but my fear was that we just hadn't found them all yet. Under normal conditions, it can take weeks for a submerged, decomposing body to build up enough gas to become buoyant and rise to the surface.

Killer number three was the least established, but he already had two different monikers. Some were calling him the Georgetown Ripper. Others were using the Barbie Killer, for the blond hair and perfect bodies on his two known victims. MPD had left those comparisons out of their official statements, but the media had picked up on it anyway.

That was the case that had me most on edge right now. Considering the apparent relationship between the River Killer and this guy, I couldn't help feeling as though our Barbie Killer had some catching up to do. In the plainest possible terms, it felt to me like we were overdue for another dead blonde.

Three days later, it turned out I was half right.

This time, it was two dead blondes.

CHAPTER
54

THE BODIES WERE FOUND BY A HOUSEKEEPER WHEN SHE ARRIVED FOR WORK that Monday morning. Time of death was later determined to be somewhere around ten o'clock on Saturday night, which meant that these women were dead in their house for a full thirty-six hours. More bad news for the investigation. I headed over as soon as I got the call.

The place was a pink brick townhome on Cambridge Place, a well-to-do but tightly packed block of Georgetown. Still, there had been no reports of any screams, or disturbances of any kind.

"We've got no signs of forced entry," Errico Valente told me at the front door. "The alarm system was disabled, too. Seems like he might have been admitted to the house."

"Are there neighborhood cameras?"

"Yeah. It's a private security firm," he said. "We're tracking down the logs right now."

The bulk of DC's municipal crime cameras are normally reserved for our most violent neighborhoods. The irony was that these two homicides had now put Second District, which is Georgetown, on par with anywhere else in the city, body for body.

From the home's center hall, I followed Valente

up to the apparent crime scene, a master suite on the second of three floors. The victims in this case were a mother and daughter, Cecily and Keira Whitley, ages forty-three and nineteen. Mrs. Whitley was divorced, but her ex-husband still lived in DC, where they'd raised two daughters. Keira's twin sister was enrolled at UC Santa Barbara out in California.

Now the Whitley family had been cut in half.

Coming into the bedroom, I saw the mother first. She was laid out on the pale pink sheets of an unmade king-size bed. The covers had been pulled off and left in a heap on the floor.

Her daughter was on an overstuffed chaise longue in the corner, facing her mother. Marks in the carpet told me the chaise had been moved to that position recently.

Both victims were tall, attractive women, with the telltale signs of what had once been long blond hair. In fact, they looked quite a bit alike. Two more Barbies for the Barbie Killer. If there was any doubt on that front, the signature knife work clinched it. Both had incurred stab wounds to the left chest, abdomen, and right thigh, near the femoral artery. Dried blood formed a dark corona around each of their bodies on the mattress and chaise, respectively.

"Evil son of a bitch," Valente said. "Just killing for killing's sake."

That seemed to be the case. There were no signs of sexual assault, or robbery. Mrs. Whitley's blue leather purse sat clasped on a dresser by the window, and the heavy diamond studs in Keira's ears had been left untouched.

Age didn't seem to be a factor for this guy,

either. The only real consistencies were the very clear physical type, the repetitive knife work, and of course, the chopped hair. It was virtually everywhere I looked—matted in with the blood on the furniture, but also lying in loose tufts, and endless random strands all over the room, and all over the victims themselves. It was as bizarre a scene as I'd been to in a long time.

But was one of those elements more important than the other? He was working something out, that was for sure. Maybe reliving a fantasy of some kind—over and over.

It was possible these women were surrogates for someone else, I thought. Someone whom our killer only wished he could get to. His dead mother, maybe. Or an ex of some kind. I didn't really see a clear path to figuring that one out yet, but somewhere in my gut, the question felt like it was pointing me in the right direction.

Who was this guy—and who was he trying to kill, over and over again?

CHAPTER
55

BY THE TIME VALENTE AND I MADE A GOOD PASS THROUGH THE HOUSE, WE heard from the sergeant on the front door that a rep from Baseline Security had arrived. Errico radioed back to keep whoever it was outside, and we made our way out to the street to meet with him.

A black Range Rover was parked halfway between the Whitley home and the barriers at the end of the block. The man waiting for us there introduced himself as John Overbey, the owner of Baseline. His company worked for various neighborhood associations, providing video surveillance and away-from-home coverage where the city's municipal cameras fell short.

It looked to me like business was good. Overbey's green silk tie probably cost more than my entire suit.

"We've got one hundred percent coverage on this block," he told us. "I started scanning the logs as soon as I heard the terrible news. And I'm pretty certain we've got your man."

He kept eyeing the Whitleys' town house while we talked. I'd want to get a look inside, too, if I were him, but Valente motioned for him to open his Toughbook right there on the hood of his car instead.

When the laptop screen flicked on, Overbey already had two side-by-side video images waiting. His time coding looked like a jumble to me, maybe some kind of in-house encryption, but he read it easily enough.

"That's nine forty-six on Saturday night," he said, pointing to the image on the left. "And the other is at ten fifteen. Both from the same unit, right over there."

He turned and pointed up the block, to the corner of Cambridge and Thirtieth Street. In fact, I could see a small black box mounted under the second-floor window of the house on that corner.

"Let's go chronologically," Valente said.

Overbey brought the first image up to full screen and let the video play.

Unlike the city cameras, this one recorded a crisp digital color picture. The limitation was the fact that it had been taken at night. Cambridge Place was only sporadically lit by a handful of old-style street lamps along the brick sidewalk.

After a few seconds of empty footage, a man walked into the frame, heading up the block with his back to the camera.

"That's him," Overbey said.

There wasn't much to see, except that he had a ball cap on, and a dark, knee-length coat. When he reached the Whitley home, he stepped up onto the stoop and appeared to ring the bell.

It was chilling, knowing what was about to happen, and not being able to do anything about it.

The porch light came on. There seemed to be a brief exchange at the door, while the man pointed up the street several times. Finally, a blond woman stepped outside. It was too far away to tell if it was Mrs. Whitley or her daughter, but she put an arm around the man and helped him inside. As she did, he moved with a sudden, pronounced limp that hadn't been there before.

"Probably told her he'd been mugged," Overbey said, minimizing that recording and bringing up the other. "Now watch. This is twenty-nine minutes later."

Again, we saw the same street scene as before, from the same camera. After a moment, the man stepped outside and closed the door behind him. He turned left off the stoop, then started back up the block, moving easily with no discernible limp at all.

As he came near the camera again, we saw his face for the first time. He even looked up, right into the lens for a split second, as he passed under it and out of sight.

"Right there," I said.

"Yeah." Overbey stopped, rewound, and froze the image.

The man seemed to be looking right at us. Valente leaned in to see closer, and then cursed under his breath.

"Look familiar?" he said.

It did. The face was similar, but not exactly the same, as the old man we'd seen on the security tape at the parking garage the night Darcy Vickers was murdered.

He looked about the same age, maybe seventy, but unlike the last time, this guy had a mustache and glasses. Two white shocks of curly hair showed under the ball cap as well. The last guy had been mostly bald.

"Those are prosthetics," I said, at the same moment I realized it.

Valente nodded. "Some kind of mask, right? Jesus. That could explain a lot."

"I don't think he cares if we know it, either," I added. "He obviously had a bead on that camera, the way he looked right into it. Maybe he even wanted us to see him."

That could cut both ways, I thought. It might have meant he was confident for a reason, and we were never going to see past that disguise enough to pin him down.

Or, maybe he was starting to feel cocky— maybe a little *too* cocky for his own good—and we'd just turned a corner on this thing.

I looked up at Overbey. "Can you piece together his movements?" I said. "Try and figure out where he went from here? Or where he came from?"

"I'll do what I can," Overbey said. "Our service area only goes as far as Q Street. But you could pull from the city as well."

"On it," Valente said, tapping a number into his phone.

"Hey, Detective Cross?"

Someone else was there now. I turned around to see a uniformed cop trying to get my attention.

"What is it?" I said.

"You've got a visitor, detective."

"A *what*?" That didn't make sense. This was a closed crime scene.

The cop shrugged. "He said you called and

asked him to come right down. He's waiting over there."

I looked up the street the way the cop pointed. There, in his usual hoodie and cargos, was Ron Guidice.

"What the hell's that douche bag doing here?" Valente said. "You want me to get rid of him for you?"

"No," I said. "I'll take care of it. In fact, it's going to be my pleasure."

Somehow, Guidice had found his way into my crime scene. I was going to be sure to help him find his way out.

I'VE GOT NO QUALMS TAKING A REPORTER BY THE COLLAR AND WALKING THEM back, if they're compromising a scene. I've never actually had to arrest one before. But there's a first time for everything.

"Hey! Guidice!" I said, heading right for him. "You've got to go."

He stepped off the brick sidewalk to stand between a couple of parked cars as I came closer.

"Detective Cross, are you high?" he said, loud enough to be overheard.

"Very funny," I said. I had no doubt this little head game was for my benefit. Guidice was too smart *not* to know he was trespassing on the scene at this point. But I was also determined not to get sucked into his bullshit.

"You've got five seconds to get back on the other side of those barriers." I pointed to the top of the block, where a crowd had gathered. Some of them were even carrying protest signs—KEEP GEORGETOWN SAFE, WHAT THE HELL, MPD? I'm sure Guidice was loving those.

His eyes narrowed, and his pupils danced back and forth, taking me in.

"You are high, aren't you?" he said. "I didn't want to write about this until I was sure, but—"

"Ronald Guidice, you're under arrest for trespassing on a designated crime scene," I told him. I already had the bracelets out. "Turn around and put your hands behind your back."

He was still between the cars, and I had to step in there to try to get him moving. But then, as I did, I felt a sharp, stabbing pain in my leg.

When I looked down, it was just in time to see Guidice pulling his hand back. He was holding something, but I couldn't see what it was.

My next response was automatic. I hit him, hard. My fist sent a shower of blood out of his nose and down over his mouth. I probably should have stopped there, but the adrenaline had me, and Guidice was still standing. I countered the right punch with a left hook.

This time, he went down.

He landed on his back, looking stunned. My knee was on his chest now, holding him in place. My thigh was throbbing with the pain. He'd gotten me right in the muscle.

"What the hell was that?" I yelled at him. "What'd you stick me with?"

I'd barely started reaching for his pockets before two uniformed cops were pulling me off of him. A third cop knelt down next to Guidice and pulled him in the opposite direction, up onto the sidewalk.

Valente was there, too, and I saw Huizenga rushing over from her car.

"Alex? What's going on here?" she said.

"He's under arrest!" I pointed at Guidice. "Check his pockets! Book him!"

Guidice had gone slack, watching me as they held us apart. "Sergeant, your detective here is obviously on drugs. He just attacked me for no reason."

He wiped the blood off his mouth, keeping his hand up high for the cameras at the end of the block.

"Alex Cross did this to me!"

"Come here!" I yelled at him, but Huizenga put herself in the way and walked me back. Valente had me by the arm, too.

"Pull it together, Alex!" Huizenga said. "Now tell me there's a good goddamn reason for this."

"He just stuck me!" I said.

"What are you talking about?"

"I don't know...." I said. "I don't know what that...was."

It was hard to concentrate, and my thoughts were starting to swim. I felt a tingling all over my body. A warm sensation crawled up through my limbs and into my head.

"I think I'm..."

I meant to say, *I think I'm going to pass out,* but I never got that far.

It wasn't just a stab or an ordinary needle stick, I realized. It was something else. The last thought I can remember before I lost consciousness was that I'd just been poisoned.

Had Guidice killed me? Was I dying?

CHAPTER
57

I WOKE UP IN THE AMBULANCE. HUIZENGA WAS THERE. WE WERE MOVING.

None of it made sense at first, but quickly I remembered what had happened.

"Lie back," Huizenga said, pushing me onto the gurney when I tried to sit up.

Two paramedics were perched on either side. One of them had a blood-pressure cuff on my arm. The other was radioing my vitals, presumably to whatever hospital we were headed toward. Georgetown, maybe.

"He stuck me...."

"Just relax."

"He..."

I felt like Jell-O all over, except for a twitch in my hands. My head was still swimming. What the hell was this? I knew cognitively that something was terribly wrong, but somehow I couldn't quite *feel* that way. It was like a euphoric state more than anything, with the fear and dread somewhere way in the background. I felt like I was watching the movie of my own emergency more than I was actually in it.

My eyes rolled. A paramedic lifted one of my lids to have a look.

"He's nodding out," the guy said.

That was the last I heard.

CHAPTER
58

THE NEXT TIME I WOKE UP, I WAS IN THE HOSPITAL. A FLUORESCENT BOX fixture was shining down on me. Instead of walls there was a blue curtain pulled around whatever examination room or cubicle they'd stuck me in.

Huizenga was still there. Bree now, too, I realized.

"Hey there," she said, squeezing my hand. "How do you feel?"

I was still groggy, and floating on the last of some kind of cloud. I smiled, in spite of everything else. It was all a little blurry.

"How long have you been here?" I asked her.

"A couple of hours. It's six o'clock."

"What happened?"

"They found opiates in your bloodstream," Huizenga said to me. "Mostly OCs."

"Mostly?"

"A little morphine."

"Ah." I let my head fall back on the pillow. "I knew I recognized something."

I'd been through my share of scrapes before—been given my share of morphine, too. The last time was when I'd been shot, tracking a case up to Vermont several years earlier.

Now, everything started coming back in pieces.

I remembered the crime scene in Georgetown. The security company. Guidice—

I sat up all at once and threw off the thin blanket they had over me.

"Where's Guidice?" I said. "Is he in custody?"

"Whoa," Bree said. "Slow down, Alex. Take it easy."

"Where is he?" I repeated.

"I think they still have him over at the department," Huizenga told me. "But no. He's not arrested."

"What are you talking about? I was in the middle of putting the cuffs on him when he stuck me."

Marti took a deep breath and looked at Bree before she answered. They both knew something I didn't.

"There was nothing on him, Alex," she said. "Just ID, cash, and his camera."

"Well, he must have ditched the needle," I said. "I'm telling you—"

She cut me off. "Everything we found was on you. Including this." Huizenga held up a brown pharmacy bottle. "These were in your pocket when we got here. And his prints aren't on the bottle, either."

"*What?*"

"Guidice is claiming you were on drugs—which you were, one way or the other. Also, that you attacked him for no reason. If he stuck you, Alex, nobody saw it."

"Oh my God."

I lay back again. The full twisted reality of it all started to sink in. Huizenga wasn't done, either.

"He's also filing assault charges against you.

A restraining order, too. He says you've been out to get him ever since he started writing about you."

I looked up into Huizenga's eyes. "I'm being set up here, Marti. Jesus—do you even believe me? You know the history on this guy, right?"

She stood back from the bed, hating every second of this, I could tell.

"I don't want to say too much, Alex. Not until we know more. But I am going to need your gun, badge, and ID." She took another deep breath. "And I'm going to have to take you in when we're done here."

"Like hell you are!" Bree stepped in now. "You heard the man. He was attacked. Are you seriously questioning his word on this? He's one of the best cops in DC."

"*I'm* not questioning anything," Huizenga told Bree. "But the department's circling the wagons. We've got a whole city screaming for police accountability these days, and the fact of the matter is that—for whatever reason—Alex assaulted this guy."

"I don't believe this," Bree said. "You people have lost your minds!"

For the first time, Huizenga raised her voice.

"Bree, you're here as a professional courtesy, and I *am* your superior officer. You got that? Now dial it the hell back down, or I'm going to ask you to leave."

"Ask all you like," Bree said. "He's coming home with me."

"I can also have you removed, if necessary," Huizenga countered.

I couldn't believe everything I was hearing.

Everything that Guidice seemed to be getting away with here.

"Marti, what do you mean—take me in?" I said.

It could have gone one of two ways. Either they needed to talk to me back at the office, or she was actually putting me under arrest.

Huizenga ducked her chin and answered without answering.

"I'll give you two a few minutes alone," she said.

In other words, I wasn't coming home that night.

CHAPTER
59

I WASN'T PRIVY TO THE CONVERSATIONS HAPPENING BACK AT HEADQUARTERS, but by the time I got released from the hospital, word had been handed down. There would be no special treatment in this case. The department couldn't afford it. Not in the current environment. It was a game of political football, and right now, I was the ball.

Huizenga took me straight to headquarters. She bypassed the press gathered outside on Indiana and pulled into the parking garage without either of us talking about it. From the garage it's a straight shot down on the freight elevator to Central Cell Block in the basement.

The looks on the booking officers' faces when we got there were somewhere between dumbstruck and fascinated. I don't think they knew what I was doing there, but they certainly knew who I was. I'd brought hundreds of arrestees through that facility over the years.

Now the tables were turned in the worst possible way. I was printed and photographed. My pockets were emptied and their contents were catalogued in a plastic bag. I was given a thin sandwich and a blanket and was walked down the row to the cell where I'd be spending the night.

Central Cell Block is seventy years old. The cells are just about exactly what you might imagine—steel bar doors that clang shut, concrete floors, steel cots with no mattresses, and a steel toilet in the corner. More than once I've locked someone up and thought about how glad I was that I didn't have to spend the night down there.

Huizenga pulled enough rank to get me my own cell, and she offered to bring me some dinner from outside. But I couldn't even look at her by the time she was on the other side of those bars.

"We'll get this straightened out in the morning, Alex," she told me. "That's a promise."

I think she was desperate to leave me with some shred of optimism. The truth was, she couldn't possibly know how long this was going to take. When I didn't answer her, she said good night and left.

I sat down on my cot with my head in my hands. This whole thing was verging on the surreal—or at least, the nightmarish. I truly couldn't believe I'd landed here, much less for something I didn't do.

I wondered what Bree was telling the kids. I wondered how Ava was doing. What Jannie and Ali were making of all this. I even wondered what was up with the double homicide on Cambridge Place, and if Valente had made any progress.

We'd arrived at the cell block after lights out, so there was nothing to do until morning but sit there alone with my thoughts. God knows, I wasn't going to get any sleep.

In fact, every time I closed my eyes that night, I saw Ron Guidice's face. I kept thinking about that bloody palm of his. The way he'd held it up for the cameras. That was going to play beautifully for him, wasn't it? Especially alongside the stories about my arrest, which were no doubt all over the news by now.

If I could have wished that man dead, I just might have done it.

CHAPTER
60

IN THE MORNING I WAS ROUSED BY THE FIVE THIRTY CHANGEOVER, AS THEY brought in the overnight arrests from the districts and moved some others out for transport to the arraignment courts next door. Why they do that at five thirty, I've never been sure, but it wasn't like I was sleeping, anyway.

A few hours later they pulled me out of my own cell, for a 9 a.m. interview with Internal Affairs. IAD has a main office in the old homicide division at Penn Branch, but this meeting was in one of the interview rooms right there at the Daly Building—three floors down from my own desk in the Major Case Squad room. It was bizarre to be escorted around the building this way.

When the duty officer brought me into the room, I didn't recognize either of the investigators waiting for me. Neither of them moved to shake my hand. They just gestured to the empty chair on my side of the table.

It was a plain, small box of a room. A closed-circuit camera was mounted in the corner above the door, and on this particular morning, an AV cart had been wheeled in, with a DVD player and an old boxy television sitting on top.

The two suits introduced themselves as officers

Wieder and Kamiskey from the Public Corruption and Police Misconduct Section. Even that was enough to set my teeth on edge, as if I weren't already pissed off enough. Police misconduct? Unbelievable.

Still, this was a chance to tell my side of the story. Once I'd signed and initialed my Miranda rights card, I was ready to get straight to it.

"So, Detective Cross," Wieder started in. "I understand that you're alleging you were deliberately drugged during the incident in question yesterday. Is that right?"

"That's right," I said. I pointed to my hip. "I was stuck with some kind of hypodermic needle. The ER report can confirm the puncture mark."

"Sure, but not who made it," Wieder interrupted right away. "And was this alleged needle stick before or after you struck Mr. Guidice?"

"Directly before," I said. "That was the reason I retaliated against him. The *only* reason."

"Twice."

"Excuse me?"

"You struck him twice. The first time, you broke his nose. Then you knocked him down."

My heart was thudding. I didn't like this guy's tone, or the way the interview already seemed to be going.

"Let's take a look, shall we?" Wieder said.

Kamiskey used a remote to start a video playback on the TV. It looked like a clip from Channel Five news. What it showed was Guidice and me, standing between the two parked cars on Cambridge Place.

There was no audio, but the two of us were obviously in the middle of a heated conversation.

And then—seemingly out of the blue—my fists were up, and I was knocking Guidice to the ground, out of sight.

"That's one camera," I said. "There were at least a dozen others on-site."

"All showing the same thing," Wieder told me. He took a beat, long enough to give me a condescending look. "I'm not saying that your allegation about the needle stick is provably false, detective. And we do know about the case history between you and Mr. Guidice—"

"Technically, there is no case history," I said. "It was his fiancée. And it wasn't my bullet that killed her."

But Wieder wasn't about to let me take charge of the conversation.

"What I'm saying," he went on, raising his voice, "is that our job right now is to focus on the possibility of police misconduct in yesterday's incident. So far, we have no corroborating evidence to support your version of the events. But here's what we *do* have."

He opened his file. Inside there was an incident report clipped to the top of several other sheets. I didn't recognize the handwriting, or the signature at the bottom.

"We have a short but marked history of unflattering articles about you, by Mr. Guidice. We have a documented altercation, up at Lock Seven the other day, where by all appearances you behaved aggressively toward Mr. Guidice and threw a piece of his recording equipment. We have this, of course," he said, pointing at the frozen image on the TV. "And finally, we have a positive tox screen for opiates in your system, with a chemical match to the pills found in your pocket yesterday."

Wieder paused again and raised his eyebrows at me. He reminded me of every sanctimonious prick I've ever met—the ones who don't even try to hide how much they enjoy their own power.

"So let me ask you," he said. "You're an experienced detective. What conclusion would you draw if you were sitting on my side of the table?"

"If I were you?" I said. "I'd be asking myself *why* Ron Guidice is writing those articles in the first place. And I might be thinking—isn't this exactly what someone like him would like to see happen?"

The two investigators looked at each other.

"With all due respect, detective, that sounds like conspiracy theory to me," Wieder said, closing his file.

The gesture wasn't lost on me. These two weren't even interested in my story. They'd already interviewed their witnesses, they'd built their narrative, and this meeting was just—what? A formality? A necessary step toward the indictment they so obviously wanted?

In which case, there was no reason for me to be here. I pushed my chair back, stood, and pounded on the interview room door.

"Excuse me—" Wieder said.

"You want to build a case against me, you can do it on your own goddamn time," I said. "I'm ready to go back to my cell."

It was time to lawyer up.

CHAPTER
61

AS SOON AS I WAS LED OUT OF THE INTERVIEW ROOM, I FOUND CHIEF PERKINS waiting there in the hall. Not exactly the last person I might have expected—but not the first, either.

"Chief?"

"Come on," he told me and signaled to the duty officer that he'd take over from here.

Instead of heading back to the cell block, we walked around the corner, through a locked door, and out to the main elevator bank.

"Where are we going?" I said.

"You've been released," he told me. "The press has gotten their pound of flesh."

"What?" I wasn't following. "Did Bree post bail?"

The chief's features were set hard while he avoided my eyes. This wasn't easy for him.

"I'm just doing what I can, Alex."

I wasn't sure what to say to that. Perkins could have kept me from getting thrown into the cell block in the first place. Now, it seemed, he was pulling strings to save me from any more time down there.

"Thanks," I told him. "I guess." He didn't question my response, or say anything else until we were alone on the elevator. It was a strange vibe I was getting.

"Huizenga is expecting you back at the office. We've got you on noncontact status for the time being," he told me.

"Noncontact?" I said.

Whatever relief I'd been feeling had just been cut in half. Noncontact means that you come into work every day, sit at a desk, and answer the phones, or do the filing, or any of a hundred other things nobody else wants to do.

It also meant I was removed from all investigative duties at a time when the squad could least afford it.

"I don't suppose I can appeal to your better judgment," I said. "We've never been busier."

"Believe me, I wish you could," he said, shaking his head. "You're not out of the woods yet. You've still got these charges against you. If the US Attorney's Office decides to hand down an indictment, then it's out of my hands."

"As far as I can tell, Internal Affairs is gunning for it," I said.

"If the mayor had his way, you'd be sitting home without a paycheck. And not because he doesn't like you," Perkins said. "Dammit, Alex, I don't believe that druggie horseshit for a second—but I wish to hell you hadn't hit that guy."

"He deserved it," I said. "And then some."

"No doubt," the chief answered, just as the elevator doors opened onto the third-floor hall. "But that's justice. This is politics."

I think it might have been the most cynical thing I've ever heard from Perkins.

Which isn't to say that it wasn't also true.

CHAPTER
62

WHEN I WALKED INTO THE MAJOR CASE SQUAD OFFICE, I WASN'T EXPECTING much—a meeting with Sergeant Huizenga and a year's worth of backlogged filing to do. What I found instead was more like a surprise party.

"Here he is!" Valente shouted as I came through the door. Suddenly, everyone was on their feet, either prairie dogging out of their cubicles or coming my way. All of them were applauding and cheering, and slapping me on the back. And all of them were wearing the same yellow T-shirts pulled over their shirts.

The T-shirts all said FREE ALEX CROSS. It felt like the first laugh I'd had in days.

"Got any new tattoos?" Valente asked, with an arm over my shoulder. Jarret Krause handed me a cup of coffee.

"Good to see you, Alex. Welcome back."

"I wasn't even gone," I said.

"Close enough," Valente told me.

The truth is, I was deeply touched by the whole thing. Lying in that cell all night, I had no way of knowing who stood behind me on this, and who didn't. Now it seemed like a no-brainer. The Major Case crew is one of the best squads I've ever had the pleasure of working with. They gave me exactly the response I would have hoped for and the same support I would have given any of them.

Then I saw Sergeant Huizenga. She was standing in the door of her office, watching me as I came in. She wasn't smiling, and she wasn't wearing one of the T-shirts, either. But I did notice that she looked like hell. She was also wearing the same blazer and pants as the day before. It didn't look like Marti had gone home at all.

When I came into her office, the first thing she did was extend her hand across the desk.

"No hard feelings?" she asked.

I shook, gladly. "No hard feelings," I said. If anything, I respected her for locking me up herself and not passing it off to someone else.

"Have a seat," she told me. "We've got to do some technicalities here."

She gave me two release forms to sign and then returned my personal effects, with the exception of my Glock. Then she ran down the particulars of Guidice's restraining order. I wasn't to come within five hundred feet of him for as long as the temporary restraining order was in effect. If that went through, and it became permanent, I'd be informed accordingly.

It was one of the strangest twists of right and wrong I'd seen in a while. All things considered, wasn't it me who needed protection from Guidice?

"Have you seen the news?" Marti asked. "I think he gave a dozen 'exclusive' interviews last night. Plus, that goddamn blog of his."

"I'm sorry about all this," I said. "You're going to be down an investigator for a while."

"I don't think I'll be any worse off than you," she said. "I can tell, just looking at your face."

It was true. Maybe I was "free," but I was still in a holding pattern. Cop purgatory.

"Now, why don't you take the rest of the day off and go see your family?" Huizenga said.

"You sure?" I said. In fact, that's exactly what I needed.

"I'm sure," Marti told me, finally cracking a smile. "I think the filing can probably wait until tomorrow."

CHAPTER
63

IT'S LESS THAN A TWO-MILE WALK FROM HEADQUARTERS TO OUR HOUSE, BUT Bree insisted on picking me up that morning. My car was still in Georgetown, and I'd have to go get it later. For now I just wanted to go home, shower, and give my family whatever they needed for the rest of the day. The kids would be in school until three fifteen, so there was plenty of time to regroup with Nana and Bree.

So I thought.

When I got into Bree's white Explorer in front of the Daly Building, I expected her to be glad to see me but also still pissed about my arrest. What I got instead was tears.

She put her arms around me and we kissed. "Are you okay?" she said. I could see then how red her eyes were, and how long she'd been crying.

"I'm fine," I said. "Are *you* okay?"

She clearly wasn't. "I was going to try and get you home first, but—you have to know, Alex. They're removing Ava from the house. Today."

"What? Who's taking her?" I said.

"Child and Family Services. Stephanie called first thing this morning. Given that Ava's been using lately, and now these drug charges against you—"

I went straight from disbelief to anger. "This is bullshit," I said. "I've barely even been charged, much less convicted."

But it was just the anger talking. I knew better, and so did Bree.

"They don't have a choice. They have to err on the side of caution," she said. "And they're not waiting, either. Stephanie's coming at five o'clock to get her."

In other words, the whole guilty until proven innocent thing was now reverberating into my personal life. My *family* life. And Ron Guidice was to blame for all of it.

"Where's she going?" I said.

"For now? Into a group home, up in Northeast. They're moving her in tonight."

It just got worse and worse. DC's group homes are a random mix of kids who have nowhere else to go—orphans, thugs, bangers, all of it. Other than actually living on the street, a group home was the last place I'd want Ava to land.

Bree told me we had an eleven o'clock appointment with our family attorney, Juliet Freeman. That was good. We'd already consulted with Juliet on some preliminary adoption issues for Ava, and Bree had gotten her up to speed on the current situation. Now I just wanted to get home so we could turn around and start doing something about this.

The morning traffic was still aggravatingly thick. It took way too long to crawl up Constitution Avenue, past the white dome of the Capitol and into Southeast. By the time we were passing Seward Square, where we'd first found Ava, Bree and I had both fallen into a depressed silence.

Nana wasn't in any better shape, either. When I came into the house, she was tearing around the kitchen as fast as a ninety-year-old woman can do. She likes to keep busy when she's upset, and it looked to me like she'd been cooking all morning. I could smell fresh bread baking in the oven.

When she saw me, she stopped, and her arms dropped to her sides. I went over and hugged her tight.

"We were just getting somewhere with her," Nana said. "Just starting to crack that little shell of hers. And now—"

"Now, we're going to get Alex some breakfast," Bree said. "We're going to meet Juliet at eleven. And we're going to fight this."

She's a cop, all right. She knows how to shake off the stress and take charge of a situation when she has to. That included the eggs she'd already started whisking in a bowl.

"What are you doing?" I said. "Don't worry about that."

"You need a decent meal, after the night you just had," Bree said. "What did they give you this morning, a doughnut? And I'm guessing you didn't eat that, either."

"She's right." Nana patted my hand. "Go get cleaned up, and come back down here ready to eat."

"Yeah." Bree's whisk was going about a hundred angry miles a minute by now. "And ready to fight," she said.

CHAPTER
64

"COME IN, COME IN. PLEASE."

Juliet Freeman isn't the kind of person you might tag as an attorney if you saw her walking down the street. She's almost as short as Nana, is fairly big around the middle, and she doesn't exactly dress to impress when she's not in court.

Likewise, the inside of her Pennsylvania Avenue law office feels more like it's part of somebody's home. I liked that she kept a laundry basket of toys in the corner for her clients' kids, and that the books on her shelves covered everything from constitutional history to *Green Eggs and Ham*.

Juliet doesn't just know family law—she understands *family*, and what it takes to keep one together. As far as I'm concerned, she's impressive in all the right ways.

I got right to it, even as we were sitting down.

"I have three questions," I told her. "How do we get Ava back? What do we do in the meantime? And how does all of this play with the other charges I have hanging over my head?"

Juliet poured tea from an old ornate samovar on her sideboard as she answered. "In a way, that's really just one big question," she said. "But a complicated one. I assume you want me to be blunt."

"Of course," Nana Mama said, accepting a cup. "I'm an old lady, Juliet. I don't have time for a lot of false hopes."

"Okay, then. The fact that Ava's been using drugs, combined with these charges against Alex, makes this an uphill battle. And even without that, you still don't have any superior rights to her, or any foster child."

"No, but we have a relationship with her," Nana Mama said. "That has to be worth something, for a girl who has nobody else in the world. Ava's part of our family now."

Juliet nodded, but only to acknowledge what Nana said, not to agree with her.

"Legally speaking, she's not. If they end up placing her with another family, and it sticks, then that's it. She won't be coming back to you."

That news settled heavily over all of us. Bree squeezed my hand in the silence. "What do you suggest?" I asked.

"You need to make it clear to your social worker that whatever drugs Ava has been using, she hasn't been getting them from you," Juliet said.

"I've been over that with her already," Bree said.

"She needs to hear it from Ava. If you can make that conversation happen, it's a good first step."

I wasn't so sure. "Couldn't that be taken as some kind of tacit admission about my own drug use?" I said.

"One thing at a time," Juliet told me. "First and foremost, address Ava's situation, and then your own charges. When's your court date?"

"A week from today."

She went to her desk and scribbled a note. "See what you can do. In the meantime, I understand you've got a restraining order against you?"

"Yes, but I was set up," I told her. "I can't prove anything—not yet. I'll countersue, if I have to. Whatever it takes."

Juliet leaned forward and caught my eye over the top of her red-framed glasses. "Alex, listen to me. If you've ever had a reason to stay above board, this is it. Whatever you do, don't start bending the rules, or God forbid, breaking the law to expose this guy." She knew me, maybe a little too well. It was good advice. Still, somewhere in the back of my mind, I was resolved to keeping my options open.

That fact that Ron Guidice had injected me with the same class of drugs Ava had been taking was no coincidence. That much I knew. I had no idea how he'd found out about her—maybe by bribing someone for lab results, or chatting up the cop who had dropped her off at our house that day. In any case, it wasn't the first time he'd dug up confidential information. Maybe Guidice was more of a reporter than I'd given him credit for.

A reporter, and a vindictive son of a bitch.

Now I just had to prove it. One way or another.

CHAPTER
65

WHEN THE KIDS GOT HOME FROM SCHOOL, WE SAT THEM ALL DOWN FOR THE hardest talk I've ever had as a parent. We had to explain to Ava that she needed to pack her things, and we had to explain to all of them why.

I didn't go into details about the hot water I was in. I just told them that there had been some legal complications, and that we had to get those worked out before Ava could come back to live with us again.

Stephanie held off for as long as she could, but they had to check Ava into the group home by six. When she showed up at five, Ava's suitcase was next to the door, and our house was quiet as a morgue. We'd all settled into the living room, waiting for the inevitable.

Even Stephanie was upset. She had tears in her eyes when I answered the door. We'd already spoken about the drug charge, and asked her to please interview Ava about it the first chance she got. Stephanie had promised she would. Meanwhile, there was a forty-eight-hour waiting period before we could visit Ava in her new place. That meant we wouldn't know anything else for at least two days.

"Ava, honey, you ready to go?" Stephanie asked, trying to stay upbeat.

Ava just shrugged and shuffled over to the door. I could already see the hardness coming back into her eyes. It was like she'd been expecting this all along. The only constant in this girl's life up to now had been impermanence itself. Why would she expect this situation to be any different?

"Hold your horses there," Nana said. She unclasped the silver locket from around her neck as she followed Ava to the door. Inside, I knew the locket had a tiny picture of the whole family on one side, and a goofy little baby picture of me on the other.

"Here." Nana put the chain around Ava's neck. "This is a loan, so don't you dare trade it or sell it. I'm going to want it back the minute you're settled here again."

Ava raised and lowered one shoulder, staring at the ground. "Thanks for being nice to me," she said, without any discernible emotion. "I'm sorry I wasn't always so good."

At that, Nana's expression went dark. She reached up and took Ava by the shoulders with her own small, bony hands.

"Girl, you've got nothing to be sorry for," she said, her voice starting to shake. "You are *loved* in this home, Miss Ava Williams. Do you hear me? Nothing you do is ever going to change that. Nothing!"

She wrapped Ava up in a big hug, and we all gathered around. I could feel Ava there in the middle of us, as stiff as a board. It was like she was trying to feel as little as possible. The girl who had cried in my arms a week ago was now packed up and put away, just like the rest of her things. To me, that felt like a tragedy.

"I'm sorry, everyone, but we really do have to get moving," Stephanie said. "It's getting late."

"Bye, Ava," Jannie said. "We're going to miss you so much!"

"Bye, Ava!" Ali said, crying in my arms, as we followed her down the front stairs.

By the time we got to the curb, where another woman from Child and Family Services was double-parked, Ava wasn't even looking at us anymore. She climbed into the backseat and took her suitcase from Bree.

"We love you, Ava," Bree said. "And we'll see you in two days."

Ava stared straight ahead, up Fifth Street, with dry eyes. "Bye," was all she said.

A moment later, they were gone.

CHAPTER
66

RON GUIDICE WATCHED HIS REARVIEW MIRROR AS THE LADY FROM SOCIAL services walked Ava down the front steps. He hadn't been able to overhear much from inside the Cross home. His listening mike on the first floor was in the kitchen. But still, this little scene spoke for itself.

There was a time when he might have felt sorry for the Crosses on a day like this. Now, it felt more like a checkmark. If he needed any reminder about why, every glance in the mirror showed him the bandages across his broken nose. He had a black eye, too, and his jaw was as stiff as concrete.

An undeniable line in the sand had been crossed. Alex was on the run now, and he knew Guidice was coming for him. But Guidice still had the upper hand. Anytime he felt compromised, all he had to do was pull the trigger—literally, and figuratively. That's what the Kahr 9mm was doing under the seat. From here on out, he'd keep it with him at all times.

Meanwhile, his thumbs jumped around the touchpad on his phone, finishing up a quick piece for *The Real Deal*. As Ava climbed into the tan minivan in front of Alex's house, he jotted down his last few thoughts for the day.

Then, as the car took off from the curb, and before Guidice pulled out to follow, he hit Send.

UNFORTUNATE, AND INEVITABLE
Posted by RG at 5:28 p.m.

It seems that Detective Cross of the MPD has gone off the rails. Anyone who has been following this story might call the events of the last twenty-four hours unsurprising. I call it an unfortunate inevitability.

Before anything else, let me reiterate that I am making this information available as a matter of public record. I have no intention to sell, package, or profit from my own story beyond what you see in this space.

In a nutshell: Detective Cross beat the s**t out of me yesterday. This was not the first unprovoked confrontation I've had with the detective, but it was certainly the most violent. (Click *here* for an overview of Cross's most recent lapses in judgment.)

From the moment I encountered him, outside the Georgetown Ripper's most recent crime scene, I suspected that Detective Cross was altered in some way—either drunk, high, or both. When I asked him about it, he quickly grew angry and belligerent.

As I pressed the question, it sparked a reaction that surprised even me. After six years of reporting on police practices both in and out of the US, I've never experienced anything like this. I received one punch to the face, where I sustained a broken nose; one punch to the jaw; and one kick to the stomach while I was on the ground.

Click *here* for pictures (warning—graphic content, not suitable for children). I will be using these images as evidence in my civil suit against Detective Cross, against whom I have already filed a restraining order.

The story doesn't end there, either. Immediately following this incident, the detective was seen passing out, and was then taken away in an ambulance. (I know this because MPD attended to his medical needs before mine.) Given that I never hit him, or even touched him, I feel more certain than ever that he was, in fact, under the influence of some illicit substance.

The city seems to agree with me, too. Just this evening, the foster child in Detective Cross's care was removed from his home. Hopefully, that child will now be living in a safer and healthier environment.

Lastly, for the record, I fully admit to using this platform for making an example of Detective Cross over the past several weeks. After what happened yesterday, I wonder if anyone could blame me. If even one corrupt police officer is taken off the streets as a result of my investigations, then this work (and yes, my recently sustained injuries) will have been worth it.

Comments? Thoughts? Share them *here*.

Part Three

DROP DEAD, GORGEOUS

CHAPTER
67

ELIJAH CREEM STOOD ON A DARK STRETCH OF PALM BEACH, ADMIRING HIS OWN house from a distance.

"You know, I'm actually going to miss this place?" he said to Bergman over the phone.

"Don't worry about it. It's just a house," Bergman told him.

"Yeah, but it's a *nice* goddamn house, and I paid for it. Not her."

Even at night, and all closed up, the place fairly glowed from the pearlescent white finish on the sleek modern exterior. Miranda had insisted it be reclad that way when they bought it, to the tune of three hundred thousand dollars. It was a ridiculous bit of real estate vanity, but she'd been right in the end.

The bitch had good taste. There was no denying that.

She'd also made it clear through her mouthpiece of a lawyer that she was coming after the Palm Beach place in the divorce. Absent a thriving private practice, and the cash flow that went with it, Miranda was taking her revenge in real estate. Creem wouldn't have expected anything less.

"Ah, well," he said. "I guess I'll have to make it up to myself somehow."

"You're wearing one of those crazy masks again, aren't you?" Bergman asked. "I can hear it in your voice."

They'd been talking for a full five minutes before Josh even noticed the slight aspiration that followed Creem's consonants, as they tripped over his latex lips. That was a good sign. These masks were an outstanding bit of business.

Even if someone did take notice of him down here, what would they see? An elderly white gentleman in a Members Only jacket. Not exactly a stellar lead, in a place like southern Florida.

This would be the last time Creem was using the old man prototype. Now that the DC police had gotten wise to the whole mask thing, they were running with it in the media—which was fine. All he had to do was change the template. Just be someone else the next time. Simple as that.

In the meantime, he realized, Josh was still talking.

"...not sure I like you running off like this," he said. His own voice was low and slow, and fairly soaked in Scotch. "This little field trip of yours wasn't part of the plan."

"What plan?" Creem answered. "You said it yourself. This can be whatever we want it to be. Hell, I haven't felt this free since—"

"Fort Lauderdale. Yeah, I know. That's the whole point. I thought we were in this together," Josh said.

Creem took a deep breath. He loved Bergman, but the man could be a bit needy.

"We are, Josh. All the way to the end, I promise. Just don't start getting all vaginal on me. The last thing I need right now is another wife."

"Tha's funny," he half slurred. "Oh, and PS, I've already figured out how you can make this up to me. When are you coming back?"

"Soon," Creem said. "We'll talk then. But right now, I've got to get busy."

"Can I listen? Please? Pretty please?"

Creem smiled down at the sand in the dark. He would have been surprised if Josh *hadn't* asked.

"Of course," he said. "Just keep your mouth shut until I'm done."

CREEM WATCHED THE BEACH AS A SHADOWED COUPLE WORKED THEIR WAY along the shore, arm in arm. Once they'd passed off into the dark, he crossed the sand and cut through the high grass to the back of his own property.

"What exactly are you doing, anyway?" Josh whispered over the Bluetooth.

"Something a little different this time," Creem told him. "Wait and see."

Bergman chuckled out his excitement, as a few more ice cubes dropped into his glass, a thousand miles away.

Inside the gate, Creem skirted around the pool enclosure to the house's side entrance. The stone chess set on the patio was exactly as he'd left it, nearly eight months ago. He'd played Roger Wettig from next door. Beaten him, too, if memory served. The set had gone untouched in the meantime. Chess was a little above Miranda and the girls' mental pay grade.

At the utility room door, he stopped and tried the knob. It was secure, of course, but the alarm system on this entrance had been fritzed out since two Christmases ago. He twisted the suppressor onto a small Beretta handgun from the inside pocket of his jacket, and shot the door handle right off. There was a fast, loud ping of metal. Nothing that would carry past the property line, anyway.

A moment later, he was in.

It was more than a little strange, sneaking into his own house like this. He left the lights off as he padded into the echoey back hall and up toward the kitchen. As he passed through the butler's pantry, Creem stopped to take a white kitchen garbage bag out of a drawer, and stuffed it in his pocket.

He continued on, making a quick circuit around the first floor, just to look around. The whole place was making him ridiculously senti-mental. There had, in fact, been some decent times in this house. A few Christmases and such, back before everyone started hating each other.

And it wasn't the sex that had bothered Miranda. Not even close. She had her dalliances, and he had his.

No, it was the scandal in DC, and everything that had gone with it. There would be no more seven-figure income, no more white-cloth reputa-tion, no more perfect imperfect life. It gave her all the excuse she needed to pull the trigger on some-thing they both should have done a long time ago.

Except now, Miranda was pissed. And she was getting greedy, too.

Creem climbed the sculptural bamboo and steel staircase to the second floor. He took his time, opening doors along the hall. First was Chloe's suite, then Justine's. Neither of them had left much behind, but he did find a pair of diamond studs in Chloe's dresser, and the opal ring he and

Miranda had brought Justine from Santorini a few years back.

He'd loved his little blond beauties, once. But it was painfully clear what kind of women their mother was turning them into. Neither one had called in over a month, not even to say hello. There had been exactly one text, when Chloe wanted an increase on the limit of her Amex card.

Yes, indeed—just a couple of chips off the old bitch block. It was too late to save them now.

Creem kept moving. He passed the upstairs gym and a guest room, then up another half level to the master suite.

Inside Miranda's dressing room, he opened every drawer, spilling her panties and knickknacks onto the carpet. He took what little of value was there, and a few old prescriptions from the medicine cabinet. It wasn't much—not that it mattered. Tonight was all about appearances.

Finally, he turned and headed back outside.

"Josh?" he said, halfway up the hall. "You still conscious?"

"Still here," Bergman answered. "Getting a little bored, though. What's going on?"

"Just hang on," Creem told him. "It's about to get much more interesting."

CHAPTER
69

FROM THE UTILITY ROOM DOOR, CREEM TRAVELED LATERALLY. HE SKIRTED THE side yard and pushed right through the ten-foot arborvitae between his own property and Roger Wettig's next door.

It was a little like passing through the looking glass. The house on this side of the hedge was all lit up, with a soft golden light showing through the expanses of glass on both levels.

And in fact, Roger and Annette Wettig themselves were like some kind of skewed mirror version of the Creems. Roger was twenty years older than Elijah, and Annette was at least ten years younger than Miranda—the prototypical Palm Beach trophy wife, all set to be rich and single as soon as Roger had that inevitable second heart attack of his.

As he came onto the Ipe-planked deck around Roger's pool, Creem went into his bit. He dragged his right leg behind him and held a hand up to the back of his head, limping the last twenty yards to one of the Wettigs' back doors.

Inside, he could see Roger watching a Marlins game on an enormous television. His back was to the door, with his hands laced over the monk's cap of bald scalp on his head.

When Creem banged on the glass, Roger nearly fell out of his chair.

"Hello?" Creem called through.

Roger stared back, squinting, but not coming any closer. "Who the hell are you?" he shouted.

Creem gestured toward the beach. "I was just attacked," he said. "Could you please help me?"

From the way Roger was looking at him so intently, it was clear he had no idea who Creem was, inside the mask. Just some old stranger who'd had the nerve to be mugged on his spit of Palm Beach. He didn't even try to hide his annoyance as he came closer.

"Hang on, hang on," he said. He beeped out a code on the glowing keypad by the floor-to-ceiling sliders, and then pulled one open with a whoosh of air. The Marlins game inside was up at top volume.

"Reyes's been looking good in early season play...."

"Do you want me to call the police?" Roger said.

"No," Creem told him. "That won't be necessary."

"Whether we'll see last year's kind of batting remains to be seen...."

"Well...can I help you?" Roger said. "Are you hurt?"

"Hurt?" Creem said. "Just my feelings, I suppose. You know, you could have at least called."

Softly in the background, he could hear Josh laughing with a hand over the phone.

"What the hell are you talking about?" Roger demanded.

"A swing and a miss."

"It's me, Roger. Elijah Creem."

That was all the fun Creem allowed himself. He produced the handgun from behind his back and fired into Roger's left man boob before he could even try to turn away. So much for the heart attack. He dropped dead right there.

"Strike two! Maybe this isn't José's night, after all."

Creem kept moving. He stepped over Roger's heft and continued farther into the house. He'd been here for a few beers, a few dinner parties, and he knew the basic layout. The master bedroom was on the ground level, in its own wing off to the right.

As he left the great room behind, he could hear another TV up ahead, with whatever Annette was watching on her own back there.

"Roger?" she called out, just as Creem opened the bedroom door and fired his third shot of the night.

It caught her in the shoulder as she started to scramble off the bed. The next bullet hit her in the face, and she went down for good. She died in her husband's Dallas Cowboys jersey, with little white pieces of cotton between her toes and a fresh coat of red on the nails.

A little knife work would have been more to Creem's liking—probably Josh's, too—but not tonight. There was no sense drawing any parallels for the police down here.

He emptied Annette's drawers quickly, and bagged the two velvet boxes that fell out as he did. He dumped her purse, took the wallet, and then took Roger's wallet as well, from the tall dresser in the closet.

That was enough. It didn't really matter what he might have missed, and it was best to keep moving.

But then halfway out the door, Creem's curiosity got the best of him. He turned around and went back to where Annette was laid out, all angles and wide eyes on the bed. With one gloved hand, he lifted up the hem of her nightshirt to have a look.

Sure enough, her breasts had a noticeable asymmetry, with the shadow of a scar still showing on either side. Roger had cheaped out on the one thing it made the least sense in the world to skimp on, and it showed. What a fool.

Two minutes later, Creem was back on the beach, walking north toward the lot where he'd parked his rental.

"That's it, Josh," he said. "It's done. I'm calling it a night."

"I still don't get it," Josh said. "What just happened?"

"Well, for one thing, I might have just single-handedly brought down the property values on this little stretch of Gold Coast. But more important? I made sure that Miranda and the girls are never going to want to use this place again."

Not bad for a night's work. Inside his mask, Dr. Creem smiled.

CHAPTER
70

THE NEXT DAY AT WORK STARTED WITH SOME DECENT NEWS. I GOT MY GUN and badge back from Sergeant Huizenga. The chief himself had to sign off on the Glock, so that felt like a vote of confidence in the right direction.

Too bad it didn't change my work status. I was still stuck in the office, and basically spent the whole day doing three things—answering the phones, logging cold case reports in the file room, and taking the temperature of everyone I'd been working with up until now.

Technically I was off the Elizabeth Reilly case, off the Georgetown Ripper, and off the River Killer. But you don't just work a multiple homicide one day and then stop caring about it the next. I wanted to know what was going on.

I also still had Ava on my mind, and Ron Guidice as well. In fact, my first detour that morning was over to Jarret Krause's desk.

"Alex. How's it hanging?" he said, sitting back as I came into his cube. I noticed he'd shut down whatever window he'd been working on, too.

"I'm fine," I told him. "Just wondered if you have anything new on Ron Guidice."

Krause leaned farther back, with his hands on

top of his head, like he was trying to get them as far off the keyboard as possible.

"Jeez, I'm not sure what to say," he told me.

"Meaning what?" I asked, just to keep the pressure on. I knew what he meant.

"Huizenga was pretty specific. You're noncontact, right? And frankly, aren't you supposed to be laying off of Guidice?"

I wasn't going to answer that one. The truth was, I understood where Krause was coming from. He was a newbie, and probably more ambitious than he was bold. That can change over time, but right now he was working his way up by staying inside the lines. It wasn't up to me to change that for him. So I moved on.

The person who was the most open to me that morning was Errico Valente. The last we'd really talked was at the double homicide on Cambridge Place, right before my big blowout with Guidice. I still had access to the investigative files online, but Errico let me look through his notes as well.

What I learned was that the knife work on the mother and daughter victims was strikingly similar. The incisions were close enough to each other in placement and scope to indicate some level of expertise. Most of the seemingly random flesh tears were secondary, almost as if the cutter had deliberately gone back and added some messiness to the whole thing. At a minimum, our killer was getting better with practice.

Errico had also been researching mask fabricators. Based on the security camera footage, he'd narrowed it down to three possible companies, in North Carolina, Texas, and California. It seemed doubtful that the Barbie Killer, or Georgetown

Ripper, or whoever he was, would do anything so obvious as to have these things shipped to a traceable address. But either way, MPD was now talking about the masks publicly, including at the press briefings.

It was a good move. If nothing else, it might put the killer on the defensive, and maybe even push him to make some kind of mistake. Anything you can do to upset a serial killer's pattern can be a potent tool, especially when you have nothing else to work with.

By the end of the day, I knew a lot more than I had when I walked in that morning. But I was still frustrated. I wanted to help. Instead, all I could do was pace around the outside of it all, just waiting to get back in.

And so far, there was no sign of that changing anytime soon.

CHAPTER
71

ANOTHER ADVANTAGE TO WORKING THE SO-CALLED RUBBER GUN SQUAD WAS the hours. I went in at eight and signed out at five. There's only so much office work you can do.

For the first time in a while, I beat Bree home, and even better, sat down to dinner with the family. If there's one thing I could change about my life, it might just be all those dinners I miss.

After the ice cream was eaten and the dishes were washed, I was helping Jannie with some algebra, when Sampson came up onto the back porch.

"Knock knock," he said, coming in. We were all feeling pretty down about Ava, but Sampson's family. He's welcome anytime.

"How are you holding up, Nana?" he said, giving her a hug in her chair.

"I'm just fine," she said, but I think she'd been on the same page of Madeleine Albright's new book for the last half hour. "You want some ice cream, dear?"

"Actually, I was hoping to grab Alex and Bree for a minute," he said, thumbing over his shoulder. "Maybe outside?" He leaned down to kiss Jannie on the cheek as we headed out to the picnic table in the yard.

"What's up?" I asked, once John had closed the back door behind him.

Sampson settled his bear-size frame across from us and clasped his hands on the table. It took him a second to figure out what he wanted to say, or at least, how he wanted to start.

"Let me give you a hypothetical," he said. "Suppose there's some guy pressing charges against someone else—charges he knows are false. And say this guy's gone to some lengths to set that person up, and make life difficult. Maybe he even breaks the law to get it done, but no one can prove it."

"Okay," I said. We were obviously talking about Guidice—but also *not* talking about Guidice. I knew enough to keep my mouth shut and follow John's lead for the moment. "Go on."

"I'm thinking that sort of guy might have a few skeletons in his closet," Sampson said. "The kind that don't show up on a regular background check."

I noticed Bree was sitting very still, not saying a word.

"What kind of skeletons?" I said.

Sampson leaned back and shrugged. "Drug habit? Bad debt? I don't know, maybe he's sleeping with his best friend's wife. But just for the sake of argument, let's say someone else finds out about it. Someone like me, for instance. That kind of information might be used to make a person reconsider these charges he's pressing. And maybe *that* makes life a little easier for the other guy. Him, and his family."

"Jesus, John," I said. If I weren't so on the rack about all this, the pretense might have almost seemed funny. "I couldn't ask you to do something like that—"

"If we were even talking about it," John said. "Which we're not. But just for the record, Alex, you *have* asked me to do that kind of thing before. More than once."

"Yeah, when I'm in on it," I said. "This is different."

Finally, Bree spoke up. Her voice was low, and I got the impression she'd been expecting this.

"My two cents?" she said. "I don't think John would have come over here if he didn't want to."

"That's true," Sampson told me.

I believed him, but it was also true that Sampson would do anything for us. The same way I'd do anything for him. That's not always a good thing. This was John's career we were talking about.

"I don't know, Sampson," I said.

"But I do," Bree told me. "There's a lot at stake here, Alex, and you're right in the middle of it. Let me call this one. Please."

When I looked into her eyes, I saw something else. There was something she wasn't saying—and I finally got the whole picture. Unless I was very much mistaken, this wasn't just John's idea. Bree had asked him to come over tonight.

I still felt conflicted about it all, but she was right. There was a lot at stake here, either way. I was the one with the restraining order, and they were doing whatever they could to protect me—but also Ava.

Under other circumstances, I might have also still been caught up on the loss Guidice himself had incurred, back in 2007. But he'd trumped that issue the minute he'd started messing with my family.

So instead of saying anything else, I just stood up from the table and started back inside.

"I'm going to finish helping Jannie with her homework," I said. "You two come on in when you're done talking."

CHAPTER
72

BY THE END OF THE NEXT DAY, WE WERE FINALLY PERMITTED TO GO VISIT Ava. Sampson's wife, Billie, was nice enough to come over and watch the kids, while Nana, Bree, and I drove up to Quarles Street in Northeast.

The home where Ava had been placed was on the fringes of one of the city's worst neighborhoods. It was a converted single-family house, called Howard House now. They had twelve girls living there, along with a house manager, a pair of overnight staff, and a couple of part-time counselors.

I don't expect miracles from the city, and I've got plenty of respect for the job these people are up against. Still, I had to keep my feelings in check as we walked up the cracked sidewalk and rang the bell.

Inside, the place reminded me of a few of my college apartments. The furniture was old and mismatched, with a threadbare wall-to-wall carpet that looked like it had been new sometime in the seventies.

Several young women were hanging out in front of the TV in the living room, watching *Judge Judy* on a wall-mounted TV. I could hear cooking sounds from farther back, and half of a phone conversation, at full volume, from somewhere upstairs.

"Yes, I did. *Nuh-uh!* Don't start, Lamar. Don't even start with that shit!"

The truth was, Ava could be just as street as the next girl. I had no doubt she could stand up for herself, and even hold her own in a fight, if it came to that. But it made me sadder than I could say to know she was living here now. Just looking at Nana and Bree, I could tell they felt the same way.

Eventually, a middle-aged woman in braids came out from the back, drying her hands on a dish towel. The T-shirt over her enormous bosom had a portrait of James Baldwin, one of Nana's favorites. I chose to take that as a good sign—our first one of the day.

"Can I help you?" she said.

"We're here to see Ava Williams," I told her.

The woman threw the towel over her shoulder. "And you are?"

"We're her family," Nana said. There was a little edge of stress in her voice.

"Her foster family," Bree added quietly.

"Stephanie Gethmann from Child and Family Services said we could see her today after five," I told her.

The woman nodded and took a deep breath. I imagine she took a lot of deep breaths, in her job.

"Ava's had some issues today," she finally said. "Now's not a good time. Maybe you could come back tomorrow."

"Is she here?" Bree eyeballed the open staircase, where the loud phone talker was on her way down.

"*Damn,* Lamar, what you want from me?" she

said into her cell, but then stopped between us and the woman we were talking to. "Can I go to the store?"

The woman held up five fingers, as in, you've got five minutes to be back. The girl continued out the door and down the steps, cursing Lamar the whole way.

"Sorry," the woman said. She stepped out of the foyer and into the empty dining room, which I guess was the closest thing to privacy around here. "Anyway—no. Ava's not here right now."

"What kind of issues are we talking about?" Bree said. "Is she hurt?"

"She'll be fine," the woman said.

"Is she high?" Bree asked.

At that the woman paused, and looked me in the eye instead of Bree. "I really can't talk about it," she said.

"She's high," Bree said. "Unbelievable. Two days here and she's using again."

I tried to step in before Bree's or Nana's temper got us into trouble.

"We can help, if you'll let us," I said. "How about if we wait for her?"

"I'm sorry," she said. "Visiting hours are over at seven, and she won't be back until later. You should really call first."

There didn't seem to be anything more we could do. For a minute we all just stood there, not wanting to leave. It was incredibly disappointing.

"Well, you give her this," Nana said between clenched teeth. She handed over the tin she'd brought, filled with her homemade brownies and Ava's favorite butterscotch candies. "I want every

single one of those to get to Ava. Do you understand?"

"Don't worry, ma'am. I'll make sure she gets
them."

"Hey, lady, what's that?" someone called out
from the living room. "Something good?"

"Shee-it, nobody be bringing me nothing. Who
those people here to see, anyway?"

Nana looked over her shoulder. "You watch
your mouth, young lady," she said. Then she
reached over and took the tin out of the manager's
hands. "I changed my mind. We'll bring these tomorrow," she said.

The manager was doing her best, she really
was. I don't know anyone in the child welfare
system who isn't overworked, underpaid, and un-
derappreciated.

Still, as we left the house, I'm pretty sure all
three of us were thinking the same thing. If Ava
was going to have any kind of chance, we had to
get her out of there.

CHAPTER
73

MY THIRD DAY OF DESK DUTY WENT PRETTY MUCH THE SAME AS THE FIRST two. I was starting to feel like some kid stuck with an in-school suspension.

Then, late in the afternoon, another call came in.

"Homicide," I answered, for the hundredth time that day.

"Yes, hello, this is Detective Penner from Palm Beach Police down here in Florida. I'm looking for Detective Cross."

"You've got him," I said. I've done a fair amount of collaborating with departments all around the country. It's not so unusual to get a call like this. My guess was that he wanted some kind of consult.

"First of all, can I just say I'm a fan of your book?" Detective Penner told me. "I'm hoping you're going to write something else one of these days."

"Sure, in my spare time," I deadpanned. "How can I help you?"

"We've got a double homicide investigation going on down here, from two nights ago. It's a husband and wife, with all indications of a simple robbery. The reason I'm calling is we just heard from the caretaker at the house next door to this one. Looks like it was hit, too, when no one was home."

"And you're calling me because…"

"I'm having a hard time locating the owner of that second house. As it turns out, this guy is someone you arrested a while back. A doctor by the name of Elijah Creem. Ring any bells?"

It sure did. There was no forgetting that name, just for the name's sake. But beyond that, the night of Creem's little underage sex party, and the bust we ran, was pretty hard to forget.

He'd also made a few headlines in the meantime. They'd been calling him Dr. Creep in the rags. I was pretty sure he and his friend, Bergman, had a trial coming up, where Sampson was going to be testifying.

"I was wondering if you might be able to send someone over to see if Dr. Creem is home, or even in town," Penner said. "He hasn't been answering any calls."

"Is he a suspect?" I said. The guy was such scum, I was prepared to believe anything about him.

"Depends on where he was two nights ago," Penner said. "At a minimum, I need to notify him of the robbery and ask a few questions."

Technically, it was a breach of my noncontact status to start interacting with the public. But everyone else was flat out, and truth be told, some part of me wanted to see how far this guy had fallen since the night I put the cuffs on him. If it turned into anything, I'd pass it on to Sampson. He worked out of Second District, where Creem lived, anyway.

I waited until five, then clocked out and headed over to Creem's house.

CHAPTER
74

DR. CREEM LIVED IN AN IMPRESSIVE TUDOR ON A LITTLE CUL-DE-SAC IN Wesley Heights. The whole property butted up against Glover-Archbold Park, with plenty of privacy all around. From what little I knew of Creem's situation, I assumed his next address was going to be something a bit more downscale, with guards and a roommate.

Then again, money like his has been known to buy justice—and freedom—every once in a while. I hadn't been planning on following the trial, but now that he was back on my radar, maybe I would.

There was no answer at the front door when I rang, but the garage was open, with a midnight-blue Escalade parked inside. I let myself around through the side gate, toward the wooded back half of the property.

That's where I found him. He was standing with a cigar clenched in his teeth, bent over a putter on a big kidney-shaped green that had been worked into the patio at the back of the house. A small yellow flag stuck up from each of the three cups sunk into the fake turf.

"Dr. Creem?"

He didn't seem to recognize me at first. I'm

pretty sure all he saw was some black guy in a suit, standing there on his property.

"Don't you believe in ringing the bell?" he said.

"I did," I told him, and showed my badge. "I'm Detective Cross from MPD. We've actually met before."

A flash of recognition showed on his face then. I wondered if he remembered trying to bribe me, too.

Either way, he played it off. He took a ball from the pocket of his sweats, dropped it on the green, and put both hands back on the putter. The guy just oozed arrogance. I tried not to take too much pleasure from the fact that I was here with bad news.

"What exactly can I do for you?" he said.

"We had a call from Palm Beach," I said. "The police department's been trying to reach you."

"Yeah? What did I do now?" he said and executed a smooth, twenty-foot putt that just missed its mark.

"Apparently there was a robbery at your house the other night. Your place and the one next door. Unfortunately your neighbors were both killed by the intruder."

"You don't say." Creem dropped another ball onto the ground. "Are we talking about the Wettigs or the Andersons?"

"I'm sorry, but I don't know."

"Jesus, I hope it's the Wettigs," he said. "No disrespect, but that guy's an ass, and he plays his TV way too loud."

No disrespect? It was a little late for that. I knew I couldn't stand this guy for a reason.

I interviewed Creem a little bit and got his

story. He'd been home the night of the Florida murders and said I could check it out with his friend, Josh Bergman, if necessary. I told him I'd pass it all on to the Palm Beach Police Department.

"Now, if that's all, I need to keep moving, detective. I've got a social engagement." He stopped and looked me in the eye, with a familiar grin. "Believe it or not, there are still some people in this town who will associate with me."

In a strange way, it made me think of Ava, the way Creem deflected any and all sense of real emotion—about himself, or anyone else for that matter. In his own way, the man was shut up tight against the world. Just like Ava.

The difference being that I wished Ava well.

CHAPTER
75

CREEM HAD BEEN EXPECTING SOME KIND OF NOTIFICATION FROM PALM BEACH PD. He just hadn't expected it to come from someone like Detective Cross. It was more disarming than actually alarming. A nasty little coincidence that he chose not to share that evening.

Supposedly, this was make-it-up-to-Josh night, for the imagined little infraction of running off to Florida without him. Whatever big surprise Josh had planned—and Creem was fairly sure he knew what it was—there was no sense in muddying the waters with paranoia. At least not beforehand.

Still, some cover was in order. He waited until they were halfway through dinner, and then brought it up as casually as he could.

"By the way, if anyone asks, you and I were at my place on Friday night," he said. "We grilled a couple of steaks, just like the ones we're having right now, and watched a movie. Let's say *Taxi Driver*. You left just before twelve."

Josh grinned. He liked this part of the game. It also helped that he was in such a good mood tonight—maybe even a little too hyped. Creem poured him another draught of cabernet, and dug back into his own excellent Montana *wagyu*. There was no better place for beef in

Georgetown than Bourbon Steak, at the Four
Seasons. Josh had picked the place, but he knew
Elijah loved it.

"So, what's the big surprise, anyway?" Creem
asked. "Where are we headed from here?"

Josh set down his fork and leaned in. "Elijah,
I need you to stay open-minded about this, okay?
It's nothing we haven't done before. It's just been
a while. Like...twenty-five years."

Creem looked him in the eye, holding back for
the moment, as the understanding settled silently
between them.

"I don't ask for much," Josh said. That was
debatable, but whatever. He was putting on the
puppy dog's eyes now. Obviously, he'd already
settled on what he needed Creem's answer to be.

"Please don't say no. They're meeting us upstairs. I gave them a wad of cash, and they booked
the room themselves. All very high-end." Josh
leaned a little closer and lowered his voice again.
"I even had them pick up a rubber mattress cover
for the session. They probably think I'm totally
kinky, but that's okay. The point is—it's all taken
care of, Elijah. Every last detail."

Creem let him hang for another few seconds,
but then shrugged nonchalantly. "What am I going to say?" he asked.

Josh fairly beamed, and sat back with his glass
in his hand. "You won't be sorry," he said.

"Of course, I do have to ask—"

"Actually, you don't. This is me, remember?
She's absolutely perfect," Josh told him. "So is he,
if you care."

Creem nodded, and sniffed his wine. The bouquet in the glass was almost enough to get drunk

on. He'd go slow. He wanted to stay sharp, no pun intended.

"What time?" he said.

"Ten o'clock."

It was nine thirty now. "We'll have to skip dessert," he said.

Bergman signaled to the waiter from across the room. He playfully twirled the wine in his glass with his finger, then licked it clean and downed the rest before he threw a white napkin over the half-finished meal in front of him.

"Hardly," he said.

CHAPTER
76

UPSTAIRS IN THE SUITE, JOSH INTRODUCED ELIJAH TO THE ATTRACTIVE YOUNG couple waiting for them.

"This is Richie. And this," he said, with a barely contained laugh, "is Miranda."

Creem looked twice at the girl. "Is that your real name?" he asked, but she only stared awkwardly over at Josh. "Never mind," he said. She was more of a Chloe than a Miranda, but he appreciated the sick little gesture, anyway. Josh was trying to make this special for him, and in any case, she was tall, lithe, blond, and yes, perfect.

It looked like Richie and "Miranda" had started in without them. A bottle of tequila was open on the bedside table, and even though there were no loose tabs in sight, the ready-to-ball looks on their faces told Creem they were all X'd up and good to go.

He poured himself a small shot of the tequila and settled into a comfortable chair by the bed. A stolen knife from the steakhouse downstairs was in the breast pocket of his blazer. To his own surprise, he was starting to feel quite into this. Maybe Josh knew him even better than he realized.

"So, Miranda," Creem said. "Tell me what turns you on."

With a little prodding, the prelubricated couple-for-hire got right into the swing of things. They sat perched on the edge of the king-size bed while Creem and Bergman directed them, and watched.

Soon, the boy was running his hand up the girl's skirt. The girl, in turn, put a well-manicured hand over the boy's crotch.

"Not too fast," Josh told her. "Just unsnap his pants, and then leave them like that for a while."

There was no need for cross talk. They'd been here before. Josh told the girl what to do to the boy, and Creem told the boy what to do to the girl.

"Put your finger in her. That's it. Very nice."

After a while, Creem started to wish they'd brought a camera. The little beauty didn't seem to have a single hair below her neck. He recorded it with his eyes instead, watching from the side while Bergman sat on the upholstered bench at the foot of the bed.

Over the course of several minutes, the two were undressed, and then eventually going at it, flagrante delicto. The girl reached up, pressing her hands against the headboard with her back arched and her eyes closed, while the boy did his thing.

When Creem had seen enough, he gave Josh a nod, to let him know he was ready.

Josh held up a finger. He wanted to see the boy finish. But he did take a pistol out of the briefcase he'd carried in, and laid it flat on his own bulging lap. The two little bunny rabbits on the mattress didn't even notice.

It wasn't such a bad way to go, actually.

Slowly, Josh got onto his feet. The thousand-volt look in his eyes was unmistakable. It was his killing face. Creem had only seen it once before— twenty-five years ago, in Fort Lauderdale. That was the last time they'd killed together.

"That's it, kids," Josh told them. "Exactly like that. Don't stop now. Please, whatever you do, don't stop."

The boy probably couldn't have if he wanted to. He thrust a few more times and then ground furiously into the girl, as she squealed underneath him. He squeezed his eyes shut, and threw his head back.

That's when Josh went for it.

With a muffled pop, he fired one bullet straight into the crown of the boy's head. It sent him collapsing back onto the girl, like a naked rag doll, already dead. She didn't even seem to notice what had happened at first.

By the time she did, Creem's knife was out and it was far too late for her to do anything about it.

CHAPTER
77

decided to call it a night. They sat parked in the deserted lot next to Fletcher's Cove, looking out toward the river.

Both Richie and "Miranda" were on their way downstream by now. The bottle of tequila sat mostly empty on the car seat. Josh had even smoked a cigar with Elijah, though he'd clearly just pretended to enjoy it. Still posing, after all these years.

"There's something you should know," Creem told him. "I didn't want to say anything before, and it's not as bad as it sounds, but a detective came to see me today."

Josh kept his cool, which surprised Creem a little. "A detective?"

"Cross. One of the ones who arrested us that night. He came to tell me my place in Palm Beach had been burgled. The neighbors are dead, too. Imagine that."

"Why him?" Josh said.

"I have no idea, but it was all about the robbery. I'm not too concerned."

"Whatever you say, Elijah."

Creem was relieved to hear Josh speaking like

this. Of course, he was also half-drunk, and still riding the high of the evening. He lolled back against the headrest and closed his eyes as the silence stretched on in the car.

"What would you do if the police *were* onto us?" Creem said finally. "If you knew they were coming after you?"

Bergman shrugged. "Whatever I had to."

"Would you run?"

"If I could, sure. I hear Vietnam is nice. Cute boys, good food. Or Argentina."

"And what if you couldn't get away? What then?" Creem asked. "There's still the trial to consider."

"Believe me, I've considered it," Bergman said. "And in the words of my alcoholic mother"—he stopped and put on a shaky, Katharine Hepburn voice—"always leave the party before the party's over, darling."

He raised his head then and looked across at Creem with a sudden seriousness.

"I meant it about not going to jail, Elijah. I'm sorry, but I don't need to turn fifty that badly. Nobody does."

Bergman's ready answers seemed to explain a few things. Maybe that was the upside of Josh's paranoid streak—always considering the exit plan, one way or another.

"You said something the other day," Creem reminded him. "Something about how we'll finish this together, when the time comes. Is that what you were talking about?"

Bergman picked up the bottle between them and took a swig. "You ever see *Thelma and Louise*?" he asked.

"No."

"Well, never mind," he said. "But to answer your question—yes. That's what I was talking about. I love you, Elijah. You can make fun all you like, but I do. Without you...without all of this...I really don't have anything worth sticking around for. Not anymore."

There were tears in his eyes now. The conversation had shifted in a way that Creem hadn't anticipated. He even allowed himself to be hugged, which was not something he usually went in for.

"I feel the same way, Josh," he said. "About all of it. I wouldn't trade the last several weeks for anything."

"Me either, Louise," he said.

"I don't know what that means," Creem said.

"Never mind."

CHAPTER
78

AT THE END OF THE NEXT DAY, WE FINALLY GOT TO SEE AVA. I HAD ALL KINDS of questions for her, but I knew we couldn't push too hard on this first visit. She'd been through a lot since we'd last seen her.

It was quiet at Howard House when we got there, and Ava herself answered the door. Whether or not she was happy to see us, we got a cool breeze of tolerance when we went to hug her— arms at her sides, and no smile at all. I found myself scanning the exposed skin on her arms, and even behind her ears, for puncture marks. It made me sad to even consider that Ava might be injecting, but I've seen junkies younger than her.

After that, we settled on the front porch in some old lawn chairs, with Cokes and the tin of Nana's day-old brownies. Nana did a lot of the talking at first, and told Ava about the KIPP school she'd already scoped out for her.

Bree and I gave her a homemade "We Miss You" card from Jannie and Ali. That got the first and only smile of the day. It was all kind of stilted and awkward, but better than being kept at a distance. I was glad just to see her.

Still, after fifteen minutes of nodding and one-word answers from Ava, I decided to address the elephant in the room. We knew from Stephanie that she'd been enrolled in a mandatory drug counseling program, but not a lot more than that.

"Ava, there's something we need to ask you about," I said.

She went perfectly still then, and rested the toes of her sneakers against the concrete. It reminded me of a sprinter in the blocks, ready to bolt.

"We know a little about what's been going on the past few days, and I want you to know how concerned we are about you," I said. "Not about what you did. About *you*."

Nana looked at me like I was going too fast, but Bree picked it up from there.

"Sweetheart, listen to me. It's really important that you tell us where you've been getting these drugs. Which corner, or dealer, or friend—"

"I don't gotta answer that," Ava said. "You two are police."

Even after months of living in our home, she saw us as a threat. That distrust of authority was in her DNA.

"We're not here to bust anybody," I said. "The problem is, you never know what you're getting out there. Kids accidentally overdose every single day, especially on the kind of stuff you've been taking."

"I ain't taking any drugs!" she said suddenly.

I knew her well enough to recognize the knee-jerk lying she did when she felt cornered. It wasn't about being believable. It was about saying whatever she had to in the moment.

Before we could say anything else, the front door opened and another girl came outside. It was the loud phone talker from the other day. She was about Ava's age, but going on thirty, with low-slung jeans and a tight denim jacket.

"W'sup, Ava?" she said. "These your people?"

"I'm Alex," I said. "This is Bree, and Nana. We're Ava's foster family."

The girl's eye landed on the brownies, and Nana held up the tin.

"Thank you, ma'am," she said, taking two, with a little grin. "Ava tell you what she been up to lately?"

"Shut up, Nessa!" Ava blurted out. "You mind your own business."

"Whatever," the girl said. I assumed she was talking about the drug counseling, but either way, she didn't seem to take Ava too seriously. In fact, she held up her phone to snap a group shot of us, like nothing had happened. "Say cheese, y'all."

"Cheese," we said—except for Ava, of course. I gave the girl my number and she texted the picture right over before taking another brownie and disappearing back inside.

"She doesn't seem so bad," Nana said. "Is she a friend?"

"My roommate," Ava said. "She's a'ight."

We offered to take both girls out to dinner, if she wanted, but Ava said they were making tacos that night, and she wanted to stick around. We all nodded and acted like we understood, but we also left frustrated when the visit was over.

I didn't see Ava as ungrateful, or bratty. I saw her as broken, and unable to process everything she was feeling. It's the kind of void kids try to fill up with drugs all the time. Once you add in a history of neglect, like Ava had, and the pressure of living in the foster system, meaningful change can start to be nearly impossible.

It's all about baby steps, at best. And that's on the good days.

Today was not one of them.

CHAPTER
79

MEANWHILE, THE HITS JUST KEPT ON COMING.

Back at work the next morning, I went to log into the case files, and the system spit back an unwelcome message.

Login ID not recognized.

I tried a few more times but kept getting back the same message. Clearly, my access to the system had been revoked sometime in the last twelve hours. My noncontact status at work was now complete.

I shouldn't have been surprised. All it took was a routine case review for anyone up the food chain from me to see my virtual fingerprints all over the River Killer, Georgetown Ripper, and Elizabeth Reilly files. Based on the rules of my suspension, I wasn't supposed to be poking around the system to begin with.

But that didn't stop me from going in to complain to Sergeant Huizenga.

"Don't start, Alex," she said, as soon as I showed up in her door. She knew why I was there. "I'm not in the mood."

"This isn't about me," I told her. "We've got three potentially active serials on the books right now. When was the last time we were stretched this thin?"

"Not the point," she said. "All Commander D'Auria saw when he caught this was something I should have already taken care of. Chewed my ass out about it, too, at ten o'clock last night, thank you very much."

"I'm not talking about getting back in the field," I told her. "I'm talking about reading files, so I can be up to speed when I'm reinstated."

"What don't you understand about noncontact status?" she shouted at me. "You think I *want* you on the sidelines? Jesus! Why are we even having this conversation?"

It was day eighteen of the crisis, and progress wasn't nearly what it needed to be. The longer these investigations went on, the more Huizenga was going to have management breathing down her neck, micromanaging her life and demanding results. That's usually when the yelling starts.

And it was about to get worse.

Just then, Detective Jacobs pushed past me into Huizenga's office. Whatever she had, it was big. I could tell just from the way she was moving.

"Bad news, sergeant," she said.

"Hang on." Huizenga put up a hand and turned her lasers back on me. "That's it, Alex. We're done here."

I hadn't been left out of a Major Case Squad conversation since I could remember. The whole thing had me steaming mad, but there wasn't much choice.

I didn't go far, though. Instead of heading back to my desk, I stopped right outside Huizenga's door and listened in. It's not a move I'm especially proud of, but like I said, it wasn't about me. It was about the victims, and their families, and maybe most of all, the potential victims still to come. All those people deserved every resource we had to offer, and at the risk of tooting my own horn, they weren't getting it.

"What is it, Jessica?" Huizenga asked.

"We just got word from CIC about two floaters in the Potomac. They washed up on Roosevelt Island about an hour ago. One young white male, shot in the head and stabbed all over the groin. One young white female—"

"Don't tell me. Blond. Three carefully placed stab wounds. Bad haircut."

"Unfortunately, yeah," Jacobs said.

"And you're saying they were found at the exact same time?"

"That's the freaky little kicker to the whole thing. The two vics were handcuffed together in the water. Whatever that means."

I took a deep breath. It meant that our two Georgetown killers were back in business together. More than ever, from the sound of it.

I heard Huizenga's chair push back, and some jangling keys. "Does Valente already know?" she asked.

"Not yet."

"Call him. I'll notify the chief. And tell whoever's on the scene not to touch a damn thing."

When Jacobs came out, she glared at me but kept moving. Ten minutes later, all off-duty Major Case Squad personnel had been called in, and the office was empty. Except for me, of course. I was left back to answer the phones and twiddle my thumbs, like some kind of lackey in a cage. Again.

I really wasn't sure how much more of this I could stand.

CHAPTER
80

AS SOON AS I HAD THE OFFICE TO MYSELF, I PUT IN A CALL TO BREE.

I knew she was working a gang shooting over at the Garfield Terrace projects in Northwest. She'd left the house early that morning when the call came in. Hopefully, she'd be wrapping up soon and could go take a look at the scene on Roosevelt Island—or at least, get a little closer to it than my radioactive ass was ever going to get.

"I've still got about an hour to go here," she told me. "But I can drive by after that, if it helps."

"Anything helps," I said. I was determined to track this case, one way or another. "See if you can find Errico Valente. He'll keep you in the loop, if anyone will."

Working the same homicide—much less several of them—was something Bree and I had set out to avoid when we got married. It only made family life that much harder, in terms of being around for the kids and keeping things running smoothly at home. But somewhere along the way, between the Ava situation, and Ron Guidice, and now my own troubles at work, the rules of the game had shifted.

And for better or worse, we make a pretty good team. I like working with her.

After that, I spent the next few hours alone on the desk, taking calls and mulling over everything I knew about these cases.

Whatever our killers were getting out of their double homicides, it was clearly working for them. Two handcuffed victims in the river was a step up from a body dump in Rock Creek Park. It was staged. They were getting into it now.

And *staged* seemed like the right word. It was as if they were putting on some kind of show with all of this. For us? For each other? For the world?

Who knew? It was all just questions in a vacuum, while I hung there on the desk, answering call after call.

Finally, around midafternoon, I heard back from Bree.

"I just got here," she said. "And I'm already back at the perimeter. D'Auria tagged me out before I could even get a look at the bodies."

"Did you tell him you've got a prior connection to the case?"

"He wasn't having it," she said. "They've got this place tied down tight."

"What about Valente?" I asked.

"He's down by the water. I'm going to hang out a little and see if he comes up for air, but I've got to be at the ME's office before five, and then..." Bree's voice trailed off. "Oh, for crap's sake," she said then. "You've got to be kidding me."

"What is it?" I asked. I hated getting all of this secondhand.

"It's Ron Guidice. He's over on the line with the other reporters. Son of a bitch just took my picture," she said.

My face started burning, just thinking about it.

Of course he was there. He was everywhere these days.

"Don't give him the satisfaction of a response," I said. "That's exactly what he wants."

"I'd like to wrap that camera strap around his throat."

"Believe me, I know how you feel," I said. "But don't do it, Bree. Ignore him."

I heard her take a deep breath. I did the same.

"Yeah, okay," she said. "I'll let him live. But listen, I've got to go. I'll call you if I get anything off of Valente. Love you."

"You too," I said, and then she was gone.

Usually, I can read Bree pretty well. Not this time. After we hung up, I sat there wondering if she'd told me what I needed to hear, or if she really was going to give Guidice some distance. She hated the guy just as much as I did.

For all I knew, she'd already punched his lights out before I'd even taken my next call.

CHAPTER
81

Eyes on Guidice. Go now if u can.

They'd been waiting for this opportunity. Instead of continuing down Mass Ave. to the police training he was supposed to hit that day, he took a hard right on K Street and headed off to Virginia instead.

Accurint records showed Ron Guidice's name on a house rental in Reston for the last three years. The place belonged to a developer out of Atlanta, with a management company based in DC, but none of those people had anything interesting to say about their tenant. Guidice had decent credit, paid his rent on time, and looked normal on paper.

The house itself was surprisingly suburban, for lack of a better word. It was a simple little Cape, painted an ugly light blue, in the middle of a tightly packed neighborhood, Sampson saw as he drove in. It wasn't nearly the hole in the ground you might expect a bottom-feeder like Guidice to crawl out of.

At the front door, he rang the bell just in case.

When no one answered, Sampson stepped off the low porch and did a quick half lap around to the back. There was no car in the driveway, no garage, either. Just a nonexistent scrub of fenced-in backyard.

If there was any concern at all, it was the lack of deadbolts on Guidice's doors. There weren't even shades or curtains on the windows. Going by first impressions, it didn't seem like the guy had anything to hide. But there was one way to find out.

Sampson slipped the license out of his wallet and easily carded his way past the cheap lock on the back door.

From there, it didn't take long to case out the first floor. Empty seemed to be the operative word. There wasn't much of anything in the fridge, and just a single recliner next to a folding TV table in the living room. A stack of newspapers by the front door went back about three weeks—*Post, New York Times,* and *Al-Sabah,* for whatever that was worth.

He continued upstairs and found a simple lay-out of three small bedrooms. One was completely empty. One had a futon on the floor, with a few piles of folded clothes against the wall.

The third bedroom seemed to be Guidice's makeshift office. There was a card table piled with Pendaflex files, and a cheap Lexmark printer on the floor. The files didn't seem to have much rhyme or reason. There were clippings about everything from police brutality to financial planning, car engine repair, and even the White House vegetable garden.

The whole place was kind of depressing, actually. It was pretty easy to imagine Guidice living out his pathetic nights here, working up his conspiracy theories, and writing his shitty little blog.

Still, Sampson had been hoping for something he could run with. He took another twenty minutes or so, checking the closets, the floorboards, and the air vents, just in case. But there was nothing.

Back outside, he was halfway to his car when he spotted one of the neighbors. He was an older man in golf pastels, wheeling his garbage out to the curb. It seemed worth a shot, anyway. Sampson stopped to take an empty interoffice envelope off his backseat, and headed over.

"Excuse me," he said. "I'm looking for Ron Guidice. Can you tell me if this is where he lives?"

The old man regarded the little blue Cape house and shook his head.

"Sorry. I know he's a tall fellow with a beard, but I don't know his name."

"That sounds like him," Sampson said. He held up the envelope. "He's got to sign for this. Any idea when he tends to be home?"

"Hard to say." The man stopped to lean on his mini-dumpster. He had lonely bachelor written all over him—the kind who liked to talk. "Ever since the old lady and that little girl moved out, he just kind of comes and goes. Mostly goes."

Sampson nodded, keeping a poker face. Old lady? Little girl? Why hadn't there been any mention of that in the background checks? And why didn't they live here anymore?

"So, I guess that's his family, huh?" he asked.

The man shrugged. "I think she was the grandma. Big fat lady, anyway. The little girl was cute as a bug, though. Same age as my granddaughter, just about. Five, maybe six, I'd say."

Sampson's mind was turning it all over while the neighbor talked. It explained a thing or two—like why Guidice might choose a place like this.

"I don't suppose you know where I could find them," he said, but now the man stepped back.

"Son, I don't even know who they are. How am I going to know where they got to?"

"Fair enough," Sampson said. "I'll just try back."

"If I see him, I'll tell him you're looking for him. What's your name?" the man called out as Sampson headed to his car.

"Joe Smith," he said. "But don't worry about it. I'm pretty good at finding someone when I want to."

CHAPTER
82

ABOUT HALFWAY THROUGH THE AFTERNOON, I GOT A SECOND CALL FROM Detective Penner down in Palm Beach.

I'd already passed Elijah Creem's information on to Penner, and for all I knew Creem's alibi for the night of the Florida murders had checked out. So what was this?

"What can I do for you?" I said.

"Actually, I might have something for you," he said. "We've been seeing some of the coverage on your Georgetown serial cases up there. Sounds like some pretty crazy stuff."

"To say the least," I told him.

"So, these masks your perp is using. What can you tell me about them?" he asked.

Penner had no way of knowing about my restricted work status, and I wasn't in any hurry to clue him in. I wanted to see what he had to say. For that, I was going to have to share a little information.

"They seem to be fabricated from latex," I said. "Definitely high-grade, and convincing enough to pass on the street. If you look closely, you can pick up on a little bit of stiffness in the footage we've got, but not much."

"Yeah, that's what I thought," he said. "We've

got a little security footage of our own down here. We picked up a guy getting into a dark sedan, a quarter mile north of our double homicide, and about half an hour after the estimated time of death for our two victims. There was just something about him—"

Penner hadn't gotten all the way through what he had to say, but I saw it coming.

"Older white guy? Maybe six feet, and a hundred and eighty, two hundred pounds?"

"So you know what I'm talking about," he said.

"I know that much," I told him.

"I was hoping we could do an image swap, and see if we aren't talking about the same guy," Penner said.

"And by same guy, you mean Elijah Creem."

"At a minimum, it's highly suspicious," he said. "He's got homes in Georgetown and Palm Beach, which just happens to be where these masks are popping up."

I was already on my feet, with the blood pumping in my ears. Considering the kind of sociopathic tendencies Creem had shown me both times we met, it all felt entirely plausible. Creem was also a surgeon, which meant a high degree of knife skill, whether that was with a scalpel, or with our killer's signature serrated blade.

In homicide, circumstantial evidence can be an easy trap. I've been around long enough to avoid getting carried away by how things *seem* to be sometimes. But even so, by the time I hung up with Penner, this didn't just feel like a theory to me.

It felt a whole hell of a lot like the solution.

IT DIDN'T TAKE LONG TO CONFIRM WHAT DETECTIVE PENNER HAD SUSPECTED. Other than a few cosmetic details, the old man mask in the Florida surveillance image was a clear match to the ones we'd seen in Georgetown. It was time to move on Dr. Creem.

The first thing I did was call Errico Valente down at his crime scene on Roosevelt Island to brief him. Then I printed everything I had in hard copy and left it in a plain envelope on Valente's desk. I'd already gotten enough heat for one day. I didn't need an e-trail leading back to me on any of this, and I knew Errico could handle it. Also, that he'd be discreet. If he got the credit, that was the least of my worries.

After that, all I could do was finish out my day, head home, and wait to hear what they'd made of it all.

Of course, that didn't stop me, Bree, and Sampson from putting our heads together that night, up in my office at home. There was still plenty to talk about.

It was starting to feel like we had our own PI firm running out of my attic. It was a little ridiculous, with all the secrecy—but also exciting. After three days on the desk, I felt like I was actually getting something done.

I caught Bree and John up on everything I'd learned that day, and we swapped a few theories. My best guess was that Elijah Creem would be in for questioning by morning, if not actually in custody. This also put a bright light on his friend, Josh Bergman, who was starting to look pretty good as our River Killer. Valente would be speaking with him, too, no doubt.

After that, we moved on to the Elizabeth Reilly case, and her phantom boyfriend—the man we knew of only as Russell. Bree had continued checking NCIC records, flagging any arrests for someone with that first or last name. So far, none of the hits she'd gotten had shown even a remote possibility of being related.

It was the same deal with Rebecca Reilly, Elizabeth's kidnapped daughter. I'd been checking in with Ned Mahoney at the FBI, but there was no movement on that front, either. The hard truth was that our best shot at finding this baby would be if "Russell" came out of the shadows to go after another pregnant girl. I hated to even think about it.

All of which left the subject of Ron Guidice on the table.

"What about our other friend?" I said. "The one we don't talk about."

Bree and Sampson looked at each other. Whatever they had going on Guidice, they'd been keeping it to themselves.

"Not much to tell," John said.

"Not much?" I said. "Or nothing at all?" I was too curious to leave it alone. Or maybe just sick of being out of the loop.

Sampson shrugged and killed the last of his beer. "Supposedly, there was an older woman and a little girl living with him until recently. The neighbor thinks they were Guidice's mother and daughter, but he couldn't say for sure. Either way, they're gone now. That place of his out in Reston is like a ghost house."

"I thought we weren't talking about this," Bree said.

"We're not," Sampson said, and laid himself across my old leather couch.

I gave John a thumbs-up by way of thanks. I wished I could be in on this, but as long as Guidice's restraining order was in place, I wasn't going to touch it. If that meant Guidice got to win a few battles along the way, so be it.

I was still determined to win the war.

CHAPTER
84

RON GUIDICE SLID HIS HEADPHONES OFF.

Son of a bitch! He almost wanted to turn the whole operation ninety degrees and go after John Sampson instead. No way that pathetic excuse for a cop was going to get any closer to his family than he already had. That was for damn sure.

Either way, the signs were unmistakable. It was time to make a big move. The only question was—what first?

When the phone in his pocket buzzed, Guidice gritted his teeth. He didn't have to look at the ID. His mother was the only person who had this number, and it was the fourth time she'd tried him in the last hour. It was getting ridiculous.

"*What*, Mom?" he finally answered. "I'm working."

"Daddy?"

Instead of Lydia, it was Emma Lee at the other end. Immediately, he regretted his tone.

"Hey, sweetheart," he said softly. "What are you doing up so late?"

"When are you coming home?" his daughter asked. Her little Virginia accent coaxed at him, pulling his heart right through the phone. He felt guilty as hell, but that couldn't be helped right now.

"Just a few more days," he said. "Not much longer."

"The baby's been crying a lot. I think she misses you."

"That's what babies do, sweet pea. Don't worry about it. Now, put Grandma on the phone, okay?"

"I love you, Daddy."

"I love you, too. More than the moon."

After a short pause, Lydia came on the line. "Ronald?" she said.

Guidice could feel his gut turn a one eighty at the sound of her voice. "What the hell is she doing up?" he said. "You're supposed to be looking after her."

"Don't you curse at me," his mother said. "Your daughter misses her daddy. Can you blame her? You move us all the way out here and then don't come around for days. And we're out of milk, by the way. I can't keep walking back to that store on these ankles."

Guidice gave himself a ten count. There was nothing to do but suck it up. He needed Lydia now more than ever.

"Mom, we've talked all about this," he said slowly. "As long as I've got this lawsuit going, I don't think it's safe for me to be around you and the girls too much. It's no secret the police are out to get me."

"But you're the victim! You're the one who got his nose broken."

"That's exactly what I'm talking about. The last thing you want is cops like that coming around, asking questions. Then it's just a matter of time before you've got reporters out there, trying to snap pictures of you and the girls. Right through the windows, even."

"Stop it," she said. "Now you're scaring me."

"I'm not trying to, Mom. I'm just explaining."

In fact, he *was* trying, a little. If there was one thing Lydia Guidice hated, it was seeing pictures of herself. The fat ones reminded her she was fat, and the skinny ones reminded her that she wasn't skinny anymore. Somewhere there was a box of family snapshots—including half a dozen of Guidice's old man, standing there with his arm around nobody anymore—where she'd torn herself right out.

It was too bad the old man had dropped dead instead of her. He might have actually appreciated what Guidice was trying to accomplish here.

"Don't trust anyone, Mom," he said. "You know your rights, don't you?"

"Yes, Ronald. You've told me a thousand times."

"If someone comes around asking questions, you tell them you're not required to identify yourself, and that you want to speak to your lawyer first."

"Oh, for pity's sake. I know, I know."

It was one of the best ways to get Lydia off the phone. She hated talking about this stuff.

"I'll try to get out there when I can," he told her. "I just need you and the girls to hang on a little longer without me, okay?"

"Do we have a choice?" she asked, edging back into that childish tone of hers—the one that made Guidice think maybe the old man had been the lucky one after all.

"No, Mom," he said before he hung up again, "I guess you don't."

CHAPTER
85

THE NEXT MORNING, VALENTE BRIEFED THE ENTIRE INVESTIGATIVE TEAM ABOUT Elijah Creem. At least, that's what I inferred. I wasn't permitted into the briefings, or the Joint Operations Center, where they took place.

But as soon as everyone started filtering back into the office, I could feel the buzz. Valente waved at me from across the room before he took off again, followed out the door by Huizenga and Jacobs. I didn't expect him to catch me up in front of everyone, but it was clear that this case was now moving forward.

Before I could start sorting anything out, I got an unexpected call. It was Chief Perkins's office telling me I was wanted upstairs. Perkins's assistant, Tracy, didn't offer any details. She just said to come right away.

I knew this summons could cut either way—good or bad news. Up to now, Perkins had been looking out for me as much as not. He'd let me spend the night in jail, but he'd also pulled me off the cell block early. He'd kept me on the sidelines all this time, but he also made sure I got my gun and badge back, which he didn't have to do.

So what now?

"Go on in," Tracy said, waving me past reception when I got there. "He's waiting for you."

Perkins's door was open and he was sitting behind his huge maple desk—Old Ironsides, we call it—signing a stack of paperwork when I came in.

"Have a seat if you like," he said.

I stayed on my feet while he signed a few more forms. When he finally looked up, he took a separate page out of his inbox and held it out for me.

"What's this?" I said.

"A letter of declination from the US Attorney's Office," he told me. "It looks like today's your lucky day. They're citing insufficient evidence for prosecution."

I felt like a weight had just been lifted off me. A letter of declination meant they were declining to advance my case to an indictment.

"I'm a little surprised, to be honest," I said. "Internal Affairs has been riding me pretty hard since this whole thing started."

"Let's just say you owe me one. Or two or three," Perkins said without a smile.

Whatever he'd done, it had tilted the scales in my favor—which I appreciated, but quite frankly it shouldn't have been that hard to do, since I was innocent on all counts.

"And you're still going to be taking piss tests for the next couple months," he added.

"I can live with that," I said.

There was also the possibility of administrative charges, and Guidice would undoubtedly move forward with his own civil suit. But none of that was going to stop me from finally getting back to work. I was four days out of the loop by now, and that's like dog years in homicide. I had some catching up to do.

"Anything else?" I said.

"Yes. Not everyone's going to be happy about this. We're going to take some heat," Perkins said. "I need you to keep your mouth shut about the whole thing. Don't defend yourself to the press, don't talk about Ron Guidice, nothing. Just keep your head down and go back to work."

"That's all I ever wanted, Lou," I said.

"Good," he said. "Because I think they're expecting you downstairs. We've got Elijah Creem in for questioning right now."

CHAPTER
86

BY THE TIME I GOT DOWN TO THE INTERVIEW SUITE ON FOUR, THEY ALREADY HAD Dr. Creem alone in a room with Detective Valente.

I found Huizenga, D'Auria, and Jacobs sitting at the end of the suite's L-shaped hallway, gathered around a laptop and watching and listening in. Chief Perkins must have said something to Huizenga at the morning briefing, because she just nodded and made room for me at the table.

"Good to have you back," she said.

"Shh," D'Auria said, and tapped the screen in front of us.

I could feel the tension in the group. I wasn't sure how long Creem had been in there, but something told me it wasn't going well.

Creem was seated on an aluminum chair bolted to the interview room floor. His body language was open, with his hands at his sides and his legs wide. If anything, it looked studied to me. Arrogant, even, as if he were enjoying this—or at least, wanted us to think so.

Valente had pulled in a folding chair of his own and sat with his back against the door. The wedge-shaped table in the corner was empty, and the only pop of color in the room was the red panic button on the wall.

"Dr. Creem, do you recognize this signature?" Valente asked. He'd just taken a sheet out of an accordion file on the floor and turned it around to show Creem.

"That would be one of my intake forms," he said.

"Yes. For Darcy Vickers," Valente said.

"I can see that."

Valente took the form back and stowed it. He wanted Creem looking at him, not the page.

"Her most recent procedure with you was a neck lift," he said. "Eleven months before she was murdered."

"A platysmaplasty, yes," Creem said. "It's unfortunate. I did some of my best work on her."

I didn't know what his exact goal was here, but he'd played the same game with me while he took putts in his backyard. The last thing Elijah Creem wanted us to think was that he cared about anything but himself. He was going out of his way to make the point.

Valente sat back and crossed his arms. I could tell his patience was running thin.

"It's a lot of coincidences, don't you think?" he said. "Your former patient. Your neighbors in Palm Beach—"

"Now, you see there?" Creem said, suddenly more animated. "Why would you need to ask that question, unless you were short on information? I'm no detective, detective, but even I know that you don't prosecute on coincidences."

To my mind that sounded a lot like *Yes, I'm guilty, but you can't prove it*. One of the most important aspects of any interview is what isn't said. And Creem seemed to be *not* saying a lot.

He *liked* us knowing what he'd done, didn't he? Just as long as he stayed on the right side of that very thin line he was treading. It was a game of thrills for him—the killing itself, but this part, too.

"Okay," Valente said. He got up and folded his chair against the wall. "Let me ask you a different question. Did you kill Darcy Vickers?"

"Let's say I wish I'd gotten to her first," Creem said. "That's not illegal, is it?"

"Did you kill Roger and Annette Wettig in Florida?" Valente asked.

Creem seemed to consider it. "Same answer."

"So, you did kill them," Valente pressed. "That's what I'm hearing."

All at once, Creem jumped onto his feet. The two of them were suddenly inches apart. I jumped up, too, but D'Auria held out a hand for me to wait.

"What do you think you're doing?" Valente said.

"You see this?" Creem held his hands up between them. "No cuffs. Not like the first time you people came after me. That means I haven't been arrested, and *that* means I don't have to be here."

"Sit down!" Valente barked at him.

"No, I don't think I will," Creem said. "I'm ready to speak to my attorney. So you can either give me your phone, or you can let me out of this ridiculous little closet of yours. Either way, this conversation is over."

The fact of the matter was, Creem knew the score. We were onto him, but every piece of evidence we had was circumstantial. All we could do now was keep peeling the layers away until we found a little more blood on the doctor's hands.

In the meantime, he was about to walk out of here, and there was nothing we could do to stop him.

CHAPTER
87

BY SIX O'CLOCK THAT NIGHT, ELIJAH CREEM WAS HOME AGAIN, AND GETTING ready to go out for the evening. When the doorbell rang, he was tying a godforsaken bow tie around his neck for the first time in months.

From the bedroom window, he saw Josh standing outside, looking as strung out as some kind of junkie. It was tempting to ignore the bell, but probably ill advised.

When he went down to answer, Bergman walked right past him and made his usual beeline for the bar. The pits of his wrinkled linen blazer were stained right through with sweat.

"Josh?" Creem said, following him inside.

Bergman's hands trembled as he dropped a couple of ice cubes into a glass, and a few on the custom Oriental carpet, too. He didn't seem to notice.

"They came to my house, Elijah! Asking all kinds of questions."

"Who did?"

"The police! Who do you think?"

"What did you tell them?" Creem asked.

"Nothing! I told them I wanted to speak to my goddamn attorney."

Bergman threw the first shot down his throat

and poured another. He was probably on a
Klonopin or two as well. Not that it seemed to be
helping.

"First of all, just calm down," Creem said.

"Calm down?" Bergman turned on him, wild-
eyed. "I'm lucky to be here at all. If I'd known
they were coming...well, it all happened too fast,
and my gun was in the safe—"

"Whoa, whoa, whoa," Creem said. He walked
over and put both hands on Bergman's quivering
shoulders. "Believe me, I know how you feel. I
was with the police all morning."

"What? Why didn't you warn me?"

"It was the same," Creem said. "I didn't see
it coming, and frankly, I've been afraid to call. I
know they're watching me now."

Bergman searched his face, before he turned
away to take another swig.

"Can you get us out of the country?" he asked.

"No," Creem admitted. "Not anymore. It's too
late for that."

His best friend laughed then, a little maniacally,
and completely without humor. "Well that's it
then," he said. "Game over. I guess we knew it
was coming."

When Josh pulled the small black and silver
pistol from the back of his waistband, Creem's
eyes went wide. The gun shook in Bergman's
hand, but he pulled it out of reach when Creem
tried to take it.

"Don't you dare try to talk me out of this!"
Bergman said. "Not now!"

"I'm not," Creem said. "I even have my own
gun upstairs. And I'm not afraid, Josh."

"So? What are you waiting for?" Bergman

looked toward the foyer, where the main staircase wound up to the second floor. He was crying, too. Tears ran down from the corners of his eyes and over the cheekbones he'd always been so proud of.

"I need one more night," Creem told him. "And...I need a favor."

That was worth another few fingers of Scotch, apparently. Josh was back at the bar now, and he set the pistol down to pick up a crystal decanter.

"You are unbelievable," he said. "A favor? What kind of favor?"

"What kind do you think?" Creem told him. "You can do it however you like. Shoot her, cut her up, I don't care. I just want it done. After that, we can call it quits."

"Why can't you do it yourself?"

Creem pointed at the tall front window over-looking the lawn. "Did you see the car parked outside? They're all over me, Josh. If they were on you, too, you'd know it. Please—one last favor. That's all I'm asking."

Bergman got to the bottom of his glass one more time before he finally answered.

"Okay, fine," he said. "But you have to do something for me, too."

"What's that?" Creem asked.

Looking him right in the eye, Bergman said, "I want you to kiss me, Elijah."

Creem laughed before he realized how serious Josh was. Of course he was. It was like the longest-running inside joke they had—the kind that grows around a kernel of truth. Josh had wanted him since college.

And clearly, this was going to be his last chance to do anything about it.

"I'm not going to kiss you, Josh," Creem said.

"Fine, then."

In one fast gesture, Josh dropped his glass to the carpet and raised the pistol to his own wide-open mouth.

"No!"

Creem lunged and knocked his hand away. Josh stumbled, weeping, and came to rest against the back of a slipcovered dining room chair. One of his front teeth was chipped and his lip was bleeding, but he didn't seem to notice.

"You can't stop me, Elijah," he said.

"You're unbelievable, you know that?" Creem said. "Jesus Christ!"

There was obviously only one way around this. He took Bergman by the shoulders again and stood him up. Then he pulled him in close. He even let it last a long time. It was a little disgusting, a little strange, and it smelled strongly of booze.

When they pulled apart, Bergman's eyes were red and puffy, but he'd stopped crying, anyway. His mouth was smeared with his own blood.

"I know you didn't feel anything," he said. "But that's okay. I also know you love me."

"I do, Josh. But for God's sake, enough with the histrionics. Let's finish this with a little bit of dignity. Like men."

Bergman grinned, looking more tired than anything now. Spent.

"Whatever you say, Elijah. Just tell me what to do."

CHAPTER
88

NOW THAT WE HAD A PRIMARY SUSPECT, ELIJAH CREEM QUICKLY BECAME THE subject of MPD surveillance. Commander D'Auria was making the assignments at this point, and mine was to cover a shift at Creem's house that night, whether he was home or not.

When I showed up to relieve the first shift at eight o'clock, word from command was that Creem had gone out in a tux around seven thirty. Hired car service had dropped him off at a private home on the 3000 block of Q Street, one of Georgetown's highest-dollar neighborhoods. Intel on the event said that it was a juvenile diabetes fundraising dinner.

That made sense. I didn't really see "Dr. Creep" being welcomed into society circles anymore, unless he was buying his way in.

My partner for the night was a thick-necked detective from the Second District warrant squad, Jerry Doyle. According to Sampson, the guy's nickname was The Mouth, and it didn't take long to find out why. He was complaining within the first five minutes.

"What are we even doing?" he said. "Creem's out for the night while we sit here getting kidney stones and he makes nice with the richies, eating caviar or whatever. Yeah, sure, that makes a lot of sense."

"Well—" I said, but that was as far as I got.

"Not to mention, if they're going to do this, they should be doing it right," Doyle went on. "Management's pulling all kinds of extra staff and overtime, and if you ask me, we still don't have this guy covered good enough. I mean, if I were him and I wanted to give us the slip, I'm pretty sure I could do it."

"No argument there," I said. "I don't know if I've ever seen the investigative units stretched so thin before."

"Speaking of which, I thought you were out of commission," Doyle went on. "I mean, no judgment. I'm just a little surprised to see you here, I guess."

I wasn't so keen on discussing my situation with The Mouth, so I mostly listened instead. For hours. Doyle didn't seem to notice the difference.

Finally, around midnight, we got a radio call that Creem was on his way. He'd left the party with an unknown female and seemed to be heading home.

"You've got to be shittin' me," Doyle said. "I mean, he knows we're all over him, right? And he's going to bring a broad back here?"

I nodded. "I think it's all part of the show."

Creem didn't do anything without a reason. He was trying to rub his own freedom in our faces, wasn't he? Never mind that the pornography charges alone were enough to send him to jail. He was clearly milking this for all it was worth in the meantime.

Ten minutes later, a black town car pulled up the block and idled to a stop in Creem's driveway. A uniformed driver got out, but Creem was a step ahead of him. He ducked around and helped his date out of the car himself. A faux gas lamp from the front porch threw just enough light to show me that she was tall, blond, and as far as I could tell, exactly Dr. Creem's type.

That was as much as I could sit still for.

"What are you doing?" Doyle asked when I reached for my door handle.

"Whatever I can," I said, and got out of the car. I headed straight across the lawn to cut the couple off as they came up Creem's brick front walk.

"Excuse me," I called out.

The woman started and clutched Creem's arm.

"It's all right," he said to her. "This is one of the police officers I was telling you about. Sheila Bishop, I'd like you to meet Detective Cross. He's here to make sure I don't cut you up into little pieces."

The woman actually rolled her eyes and kept her arm locked onto his. A pair of high-heeled sandals was dangling off one finger, and she had on a long, shimmery dress that pooled around her bare feet.

"I'm sorry to startle you, Ms. Bishop," I said, "but I'm not at all comfortable with you going inside. I'd like to call you a cab, if that's all right."

"And I'd like you to mind your own damn business," she snapped back at me.

Creem only smiled, as if he were leaving this up to the two of us.

"You should know the reason we're here," I told her. "Dr. Creem is the primary suspect in a series of murders in Georgetown. You've probably heard about them. I'd strongly suggest—"

But Ms. Bishop cut me off.

"Just inside, there's an antique mahogany coat-rack," she said, pointing at the front door.

"Excuse me?"

"Upstairs, to the left, is the master bedroom. That's where Elijah and Miranda keep their Rookwood pottery collection. There's also a fantastic Lucien Freud hanging over the bed. Should I go on?"

I'd thought Ms. Bishop was embarrassed by my presence, but I was wrong. As far as I could tell now, Dr. Creem's mistress was just pissed off and anxious to get inside.

He'd laid the bait, and I'd taken it, just like he wanted. Unbelievable.

"Don't worry, detective," Creem said ingratiatingly. "It's an understandable mistake. For what it's worth, I don't imagine Sheila could be any safer, with you and your partner out here. Am I right?"

He didn't wait for an answer, and keyed the door to let Ms. Bishop in ahead of him. As she led the way, Creem turned back to me and spoke low from the porch.

"If it makes you feel any better, I'll leave the curtains open," he said with a smile.

Then he went inside, closed the door, and turned off the lights behind him.

CHAPTER
89

THE NEXT SEVERAL HOURS WERE THEIR OWN KIND OF TORTURE. I FELT MORE than a little burned by Creem, and I hated the way he was playing this.

To make things worse, Doyle kept his own personal monologue going pretty much the entire time. He knew a thing or two about surveillance and had some valid opinions about how these investigations ought to be structured, but most of that was bookended with one long, pointless story after another.

Around 3 a.m., a yellow cab pulled up in front of the house. A minute later, the porch light came on and Creem walked Ms. Bishop outside. She was carrying a shopping bag now and wearing street clothes that, for all I knew, came straight out of Mrs. Creem's closet.

Neither of them even glanced our way, until Creem had put her into the cab and sent her off. Then he turned, gave us a friendly wave, and went back inside.

"What a tool," Doyle said. "I don't get it. What is it about hot women and rich assholes? Actually, never mind. I just answered my own question. But still—"

Bottom line, I don't like to talk when I'm losing the game. I couldn't stand the idea of five more hours of this.

"Doyle, don't take this the wrong way," I said, "but is there any chance we could finish out this shift with a little less conversation?"

It got him all huffy and cold-shouldered, but if that was the price of silence, I was ready to pay it. With any luck, this would be our first and last detail together.

After that it stayed pretty quiet, both in and outside the car. Creem kept the lights on and puttered around the house, doing whatever he was doing in there. At five, he took the paper off his front porch and went back in—upstairs, I think. I didn't see him after that.

Then, just after sunrise, my cell rang.

It's not so unusual for me to get calls at all hours. I expected to see a departmental number on the ID or maybe Bree. But it wasn't either of those. It was Stephanie Gethmann, Ava's social worker. Right away I knew something had to be wrong.

"Stephanie?" I answered.

"I'm sorry to call so early," she said. "I actually wanted to call last night, but...well, it's complicated, of course."

"Something's happened to Ava," I said. It wasn't a question. My heart was thumping, and I was already running through the possibilities in my head. Overdose? Runaway? Accident?

"She's missing, Alex."

"Missing? What does that mean?"

"She didn't come home from school yesterday, and nobody knows where she is. I hope this isn't inappropriate, but I know you and Bree are police officers. I was thinking maybe—"

I only wished Stephanie had called sooner.

"Of course we will," I said. "We'll get right on it. Tell me everything you know."

Part Four

ALL FALL DOWN

BREE AND I SPENT THE MORNING IN OUR CARS, KEEPING IN TOUCH BY PHONE and hitting up every resource we could think of to track Ava down.

I started with the Youth Investigations Bureau contacts I knew in the first, third, and sixth police districts. Those covered Ava's group home, her school, our house, and Seward Square, where she used to hang out. The department has a centralized database of missing kids, but there's no substitute for face time with people who are working the streets every day. For that, you have to go district by district.

As it turned out, the picture Nessa had taken of us at the group home was even more valuable than I'd thought. It wasn't much of a shot, but it was something to show people. I texted it to everyone I could think of.

Bree started at Howard House and interviewed several of the girls there, as well as Sunita, the braided house manager we'd met the other day. From the sound of it, nobody had seen Ava since breakfast the previous morning. She'd been quiet, but that was nothing new. And it didn't look like anything was missing from her room, either. That meant she hadn't intentionally run away.

After that, Bree headed over to Seward Square, walking the neighborhood and looking for any of Ava's old friends. She told me over the phone that she'd found two of them—Patrice and K-Fly. Supposedly, neither of them had seen Ava in weeks, but you have to take anything street kids tell you with a grain of salt. Bree gave them each a card and promised a hundred bucks for anyone who might help find her. Whatever it took.

I hit up all the area hospitals, and then finally headed over to MPD's main Narcotics Unit on Third Street in Northeast. I was starting to grasp at straws, but I thought if anyone knew of specific dealers who pushed Oxy, or fake Oxy, on the streets Ava had frequented, it might be a way in.

The longer this went on, the worse I felt about it. Especially if drugs were involved, which I all but assumed was the case.

Opiates are probably the least-controlled substances out there these days. The high-grade pharmaceutical stuff is highly desirable on the street, and sellers take advantage of that fact all the time. They pass garbage off as true Oxy, and there's no way to control the dosage, much less the contents of street drugs like that. It wasn't just empty talk when we'd told Ava that kids OD all the time. This country has an opiate epidemic, and it's largely being driven by people under twenty-five.

By midafternoon, we'd come up completely empty-handed. It was getting hard not to play out some worst-case scenarios in my head, and it drove me crazy to think that Ava was around here *somewhere,* while we ran out of ideas about where to look.

I knew I had to stay positive, for Nana's sake and the kids' sake, if not my own. But the truth was, I had a terrible feeling about this.

CHAPTER
91

"ALEX, WHERE THE HELL ARE YOU?"

It was Sergeant Huizenga on the phone. I was driving from the Sixth District station house back to my own place in Southeast when I took the call.

"I'm sorry, sergeant. Something's come up at home."

"Yeah, well, we need you. Now."

"What is it?" I asked.

"Sheila Bishop, Dr. Creem's date from last night. She's been found dead in her apartment."

It might have hit me harder, but I was practically numb by now. Still, this was one more smack in the face on top of everything else.

"Is Creem in custody?" I asked.

"No," Huizenga said tightly. "That's part of the cluster hump we've got going on. The son of a bitch is missing."

That got me. I actually braked right there on D Street and pulled over. "Missing? How is that even possible? We've been on him since yesterday."

"Slipped out right through the back of his property, it looks like," she said. "Into the woods and God knows where from there."

The first thing I thought of was Jerry Doyle. He'd gone on and on about how Creem's surveillance detail was insufficient—and he'd been right.

I remembered how the place was bordered by Glover-Archbold Park. It's a piece of land that runs from Cathedral Heights all the way down to the Potomac. We'd covered the front of Creem's house, but there had been no way to completely cover the entire track of open ground at the back. It made for a perfect hole in our net. That much was clear—now.

"We've got a BOLO out on him, but meanwhile, I want you over at Sheila Bishop's apartment."

She gave me an address on Logan Circle. There was no question of yes or no. If I wanted to keep showing up for work, I needed to be there.

Still, once I hung up with Huizenga, I continued on home. Screw protocol. I needed to check in with my family, too.

Bree actually encouraged me to go, when I saw her. She and Nana were parked by the home phone, waiting for any word from Stephanie, while Bree worked her cell to be in touch with the districts, the hospital, and Howard House. The kids were with Aunt Tia, and could spend the night there if necessary.

"Go," she said. "You're just a phone call away if anything comes up. I've got Sampson and Billie driving the neighborhood right now, keeping an eye out. You can spell them later."

"You okay?" I asked.

"No," Bree said. "But so what? Just go."

I looked at Nana, who had her hands clasped

under her chin. I wasn't sure if she was praying or just thinking, but she didn't look good, either.

I gave them both a kiss good-bye, and kept on moving, out the back door.

CHAPTER
92

SHEILA BISHOP'S APARTMENT WAS HALF OF A TURRETED BRICK AND STONE town house on the north side of Logan Circle. Other than a handful of people watching their dogs run around John Logan's statue, and the usual daytime traffic, it was quiet when I got there. No reporters, anyway. That was a relative blessing.

Most of the investigative team was on-site, along with the Mobile Crime Unit from Forensics. They had techs in blue windbreakers on the front door, up and down the stairs, and all over the master bedroom, where Ms. Bishop's body had been discovered by a housekeeper a few hours earlier.

That's also where I found Valente. He was kneeling by the body, and looking from Ms. Bishop to each of the doors and windows when I came in.

She'd been shot once in the chest, and by all appearances had collapsed in front of the open double doors of her walk-in closet. I couldn't say for sure, but it looked like Ms. Bishop was wearing the same clothes she'd had on when she left Dr. Creem's house.

A Barneys shopping bag was on the bed, with

her evening gown and shoes inside. And according to Valente, the tub in the adjoining bathroom was just under half full.

"Looks to me like she came in, left the bag on the bed, and started drawing a bath," he said. "Then she comes back out here to get undressed, and bam. He's waiting for her in the closet. No signs of forced entry, either. Creem could have easily had a key to this place."

Most of what Valente had worked out made sense to me—except for the part about Creem himself.

"I watched him put her in a cab at three in the morning," I said. "He didn't go anywhere after that. At least not before five. There's no way he could have beaten her over here."

"I guess the question then is time of death," Valente said.

"That's one question," I said.

"Detectives?"

Errico and I both turned around to see Manny Lapore, one of the forensic techs, standing in the door to the bathroom. He was holding up a clear acrylic lifter with the dark impression of a handprint on it. Even at a glance, the print was too big to have come from Ms. Bishop.

"I got this off the bathroom tile over the tub," Lapore said. "There's a couple of matching partials on the hot and cold taps, too. Could be something."

My first thought was that the killer had gone in to turn off the tub, to avoid an attention-drawing flood in the bathroom. My second thought was that it seemed like a pretty sloppy mistake—unless he just didn't care. Or wasn't thinking straight.

We followed Lapore downstairs to see what, if anything, this print turned up. With the mobile automated fingerprint ID scanners we're now using, a process that used to take hours—not to mention a trip to the lab—can happen anywhere, and in a matter of minutes. I didn't even have time to check in with Bree before Lapore had found a match and was printing off the results.

"Here's your guy," he said, handing me the report. "Does the name Joshua Bergman mean anything to you?"

CHAPTER
93

I CAUGHT UP WITH BREE ON THE PHONE WHILE VALENTE AND I DROVE FROM Logan Circle over to M Street, where Josh Bergman lived. There was no new word about Ava. It was all eerily quiet on that front.

Meanwhile, I had to focus on this if I could.

It can take an hour or more to pull SWAT together, but that was time we didn't have. Instead we dispatched a quick in-house team for the operation. Within thirty minutes, we had five tactically trained officers with one sergeant all ready to go in a parking lot on Water Street, a block from Bergman's building.

Bergman had a high-dollar loft on the top floor of a converted flour mill, from Georgetown's nineteenth-century industrial days. Word from our spotter, stationed on the roof behind his, was that Bergman seemed to be home alone.

After a fast briefing with Commander D'Auria, we piled into two plain white panel vans and pulled around the block. The drivers stopped in front, the van doors slid open, and we made a beeline for the entrance.

Besides the half dozen tactical personnel, the entry team included me, Valente, and two more D-1 detectives from Major Case Squad, winding our way up the three flights of stairs to the top. We had officers stationed around the block, EMTs on standby, and D'Auria with a small crew in a mobile command center back down on Water Street.

The breach team was armed with AR-15 rifles and SIG P226 sidearms. Tasers and pepper spray were standard issue as well.

I had my Glock out, for the first time since I'd been reinstated. All of us wore Kevlar, too. We had more than enough manpower to take Bergman in, but he was very possibly armed and dangerous. Maybe also a little desperate. He might try to get off a few shots of his own.

When we got to the third-floor landing, the sergeant at the head of the line wagged two fingers at a pair of officers, who came forward with the forty-five pound battering ram they'd carried up. Everyone was wired with headsets, but the protocol was for radio silence once we'd entered the building.

Inside I could hear Bergman talking. It sounded like half of a phone conversation.

"Where the hell are you? You said you'd be here an hour ago," he said. He also sounded agitated, and seemed to be moving around. When he spoke again, his voice faded off toward the back of the apartment. "I don't care," he said. "Just...no, you listen to me. Just get here! Now!"

That was it. I could feel the collective pulse of the group start to go up, as the sergeant gave a visual countdown on his fingers—three, two, one. The two cops at the front pulled back with the ram and swung it at Bergman's steel front door.

It sent a resounding boom up and down the stair-well. Any cover we had now was blown.

"Units C and D, standby," the sergeant radioed. "He may try to make a run for it."

It took two more fast swings before the door finally tore away from the frame and blew open. My vision tunneled straight ahead as the sergeant corkscrewed his arm, ushering the team inside, double time.

"Go, go, go, go, go!"

CHAPTER
94

VALENTE AND I DIDN'T WAIT FOR CLEARANCE. WE FOLLOWED RIGHT IN BEHIND the breach team. Normally, investigative staff is meant to hold their position until we get an all clear, but neither of us were feeling that patient right now.

The apartment door opened into a wide-open loft space that looked pristine to the point of sterility. Bergman didn't seem to have any *stuff* at all. There was a set of white modular furniture on a huge gray rug, like an island in the middle of the room, with a single tall rubber tree that reached up to the exposed I-beams in the ceiling. A stainless-steel kitchen off to the side looked like it had never been used.

There was no sign of Bergman anywhere in the front. The team quickly moved through, leapfrogging each other across the loft, and then down a long hallway toward the back of the building.

"MPD! Joshua Bergman?" I shouted. "Stay right where you are! Don't move!"

At the very end of the hall there was an open door, with light streaming in through several iron-framed floor-to-ceiling windows. As soon as the first officer got there, I heard Bergman start to yell.

"Get away from me! Stay back!"

"Sir, put down the gun!" one of the officers shouted. "Keep your hands where we can see them and get down on the floor!"

"Go to hell!"

When I came into the room, Bergman was sitting up, cross-legged on a king-size platform bed. He had his back against the painted concrete block wall, with a white iPhone in one hand and a small Smith & Wesson revolver in the other. It could have easily been the same .32 he'd used to kill all those boys, as well as Sheila Bishop.

"Bergman, put the gun down!" I told him. "You don't want to do this."

"Oh yeah? I don't?" He was clearly agitated, but also relatively focused. He looked me right in the eye when he said it.

"Just try to calm down," I told him. "Let's go one thing at a time."

I lowered my own gun and took a step toward him, but only until he pressed the Smith & Wesson up to his chin.

"You think I'm kidding around here?" he said.

"Josh—don't," I said. "Please."

"Too late," he said. He held the phone up to his ear and spoke a single word to whoever was there. "Good-bye," he said.

Then he pulled the trigger on that Smith & Wesson and blew himself away.

Whatever horrible things Bergman might have done to other people, it was god-awful to see him go out like that. This was an act of pure, irrational desperation. Maybe even insanity.

Not to mention a truly stomach-churning mess.

Everyone started moving at once. There was no question of survival, but Bergman's death had to be confirmed. The sergeant went straight to the body and felt for a pulse on the wrist, while Valente called it in.

"One round fired, subject is down. Self-inflicted GSW," he said. When the sergeant shook his head, Valente added, "No signs of life."

Bergman's gun had dropped onto the blood-stained comforter, and his phone was on the floor. That's what I focused on. I was pretty sure I knew who he'd been talking to, but I needed to confirm it if I could.

I went straight to the phone, picked it up, and hit redial. On the first ring, it sent me right into voice mail.

"Hello," I heard in a familiar voice. "You've reached Dr. Elijah Creem. I can't take your call right now, but please leave a message. Thank you, and have a pleasant day."

THIS WASN'T THE END OF ANYTHING. WE WERE RIGHT IN THE MIDDLE OF IT ALL.

Up until now, with only circumstantial evidence against Creem, it was all we could do to put a surveillance detail on him. Legally speaking, it's one thing to watch someone at home, from the street. It's another to go inside. The courts are jumpy about that kind of thing.

So it was ironic to get the push we needed, not from Creem but from Bergman, our presumed River Killer. The fact that he'd called Creem's cell and home numbers multiple times in the hours before he killed himself was enough to put us over the top. Within an hour of Bergman's death, we had a warrant number for secreted evidence in Creem's house and a one-sheet for Creem himself, circulating up and down the Eastern Seaboard. The special note on this one was that Creem might have been traveling in disguise. The one-sheet included his DMV photo alongside the clearest image we had of the old man mask he'd been using, but we weren't cutting off any possibilities. He could have easily switched up his look by now— and probably had.

My guess was that Creem had been planning this exit all along. It would explain the way he'd flaunted himself to the police so brazenly. Not to mention Sheila Bishop's and Josh Bergman's deaths. Was that all just one big, high-stakes smokescreen for him?

If so, it had worked. We'd already lost between five and nine hours on Creem, depending on what time he'd slipped away from us.

To search the house in Wesley Heights, Valente and I brought a team of three other detectives, plus four from mobile crime. It's a slow, methodical process—aggravatingly so when your perp is already on the move. We spread out over the home's three floors when we got there, to cover as much area as we could.

I started on the lower level, where Creem had an office, an examination room, and a waiting area with its own separate entrance. There was also a TV room and a garage down there—plenty of places to look.

As it turned out, there were a few things Creem hadn't even tried to hide. Within the first few minutes, I found a makeup kit in his top desk drawer. There were tinting pigments, a dozen different small brushes, a bottle of spirit gum, and several items I didn't recognize. Maybe he'd even worked on his latest mask right there at the desk, while I'd been sitting outside on the curb, watching his house the night before.

The other thing I did while I searched was to keep dialing Creem's number. I didn't really expect him to pick up, but I figured it was worth trying. He was the type who might like to take a parting shot at the cops, given the opportunity.

For the first hour, I got the same response, over and over—straight to voice mail. He'd probably shut the phone down to keep it from pinging off of cell towers and leaving a trail behind him.

But that doesn't mean I was wrong about Creem. He must have tracked my incoming calls somehow, because the next time my phone rang, it was him, calling me back.

On his terms, of course.

CHAPTER
96

I DIDN'T RECOGNIZE THE NUMBER ON THE ID AS I PICKED UP.

"Detective Cross," I answered.

"It's me," Creem said. "The man of the hour."

I banged my knee on his desk as I jumped up. Valente was just coming into the room, and I snapped my fingers to grab his attention.

"Dr. Creem," I said pointedly. "I'm a little surprised to hear from you."

Right away, Valente took out his own phone and started making a call, presumably to try to run a trace.

"I wanted to ask about Josh," Creem told me.

"What about him?" I asked.

"Is he dead?"

Valente motioned at me to take my time and go slow with him.

"I'm not going to discuss that with you over the phone," I said. "Tell me where you are. I'll meet you anywhere you like. No other cops."

Creem paused, maybe even just to smile to himself. He was enjoying this, no doubt.

"Don't bother with this phone, by the way," he said. "I bought it an hour ago and I'm throwing it away after this call."

He was probably using a convenience store burner, or something like it. From a cop's perspective, those are the worst. They can be impossible to track down.

I figured the best way to keep Creem talking would be to feed that oversize ego of his. It was the only language he seemed to speak.

"You know, there's a massive manhunt going on right now," I said. "You've given us quite the slip."

"Any luck so far?" he asked.

"If there were—"

"Of course. We wouldn't be having this conversation," Creem said.

I also knew better than to condescend to him. One thing about Creem—he wasn't stupid. If I lost him now, something told me that would be it.

"I'd love to know how you pulled this off," I said. "It's been a fascinating case. You, Bergman, all of it. I assume you were in it together from the start."

This time Creem sighed, almost nostalgically. "All the way back to college, in fact. We got a bit of a taste for it then, just like old Jack Sprat and his wife."

"Excuse me?"

"He liked the boys, I liked the girls. And between the two of us, we licked the platter clean."

His calm, collected pride in the whole thing gave me the creeps. Wherever he was headed, I didn't think for a second he'd be able to stop himself from killing again.

"So what now?" I said. "You disappear, never to be heard from?"

"That's the idea," he said.

"Are you leaving the country?" I asked, but Creem demurred.

"I called because I wanted to know about Josh," he told me. "If you don't have anything to say about that, I'm hanging up."

When I looked at Valente, he just shook his head and raked his fingers through his hair. It wasn't going well.

"What do you want to know?" I asked.

"Is he dead or not?"

"Yes," I told him. It would all be in the news soon enough anyway.

"Where did he do it?" Creem asked.

"In his loft, on M Street," I said, stalling.

"No. I mean, it sounded to me like he shot himself. Was it in the mouth?"

"Under the chin," I said.

"Lord. Must have been a terrible mess."

"It was," I said. "Is that hard for you? He was your friend, after all."

Creem paused again. I listened hard for any kind of telltale background noise, but there was nothing.

"Are you a doctor, Alex?" he asked then.

"I am. A psychologist," I said.

"Ah. One for the books, then."

"Now, I told you about Josh. Give me something in return," I said. "Are there other victims we should know about? Tell me how many you've killed over the years."

"I'm sorry," Creem said, "but we're out of time for today. Isn't that what you shrinks always say?"

"Hang on. One more question."

"It was fun while it lasted, detective, but I think

we both know I'm already well beyond your reach. I wouldn't go to too much trouble if I were you."

"Creem, wait!" I said, but it was too late. He'd already hung up.

When I set down my phone, I could see on Valente's face that he hadn't gotten anywhere. Also that he was good and pissed by now. We'd just had a decent shot at Creem, and once again he'd slipped through our fingers.

Maybe for the last time.

CHAPTER
97

I TRIED CALLING CREEM'S NEW NUMBER BACK, BUT ALL I GOT WAS A GENERIC machine-generated voice mail. He'd probably destroyed the phone as soon as he hung up on me.

Right away, I turned my attention back to his home office. Maybe it would give us some clue about where he'd planned on running.

By all appearances, Creem was fastidiously tidy. Possibly even a little OCD. Everything about his house was well ordered, right down to the matching letterboxes, pencil cup, and stapler sitting at perfect right angles on the desk. It was easy to see as the outward manifestation of a man who needed to control every aspect of his universe—from the mundane physical details to the repetitive, hyper-precise way he'd cut up each of his victims.

Bergman's murders had been self-similar as well, but there was a difference. With every kill, Bergman had been less controlled. Each one of those young hustlers had been stabbed and mutilated a little more than the one before. In retrospect, Bergman was the ticking time bomb, waiting to go off. Creem was more like the Swiss clock.

From his desk, I worked my way around the

office, opening drawers, checking files, and even lifting up furniture to look underneath. It wasn't until I got to the black lacquered media console by the door that I found anything at all out of place.

There, at the back of the cabinet behind a boxed set of date-ordered AMA journals, I found three matching pewter photo frames. It looked like they'd been thrown back there, rather than placed in any kind of deliberate way.

When I pulled them out, I saw the glass was mostly gone, with several shards sitting on the floor of the cabinet itself. Each photo was of the Creem family. There was a group shot in front of a massive Christmas tree; one picture of Miranda Creem, standing on a beach somewhere; and a hinged double frame, with side-by-side school photos of Creem's two daughters.

All three women—Miranda, Chloe, and Justine Creem—were attractive, tall, and blond, I saw. If anything, the two girls were an even closer match to Creem's slate of victims than their mother was.

And then there was the undeniable kicker. Each photo had been pierced with some kind of sharp object, like someone had driven a pair of scissors right through them. Three times each. Everything in threes.

That's who he was trying to kill, wasn't it? Creem had been methodically—and symbolically—erasing the three women who had left him after his scandal. If he'd gone straight for them, it would have been too suspicious. So he did the next best thing. He went after a theoretically endless supply of surrogates, maybe as a way of keeping himself from actually having to kill his own family.

Or maybe he was just building up to it.

I ran upstairs to find Valente. He was in the second-floor master bedroom, going through Mrs. Creem's desk when I got to him.

"What's up?" he said.

"Where's Creem's family right now?" I said.

"Rhode Island. They've been staying at her parents' house in Newport, last I heard. Why?"

I held up one of the mutilated photos to show him.

"Because I don't think he's done yet," I said.

CHAPTER
98

"BUS 53 LEAVING FOR NEW YORK, BRIDGEPORT, PROVIDENCE, AND BOSTON *will be boarding in ten minutes. Ticketed passengers should proceed to the loading area at this time.*"

Elijah Creem stood at the bathroom mirror in a downtown Philadelphia bus station, looking at himself and making sure he was good to go for the next leg.

He touched the back of his neck, where the latex was invisibly spirit gummed to his skin. He patted the dark wig and adjusted the undergarment. It was a whole new appreciation, really, for what women went through. The makeup was no problem, but the body shaper alone was an all-day ordeal.

Still, it was incredibly effective. It wasn't himself he saw looking back from the streaked, dirty mirror. It was a vaguely unfortunate woman of a certain age, with liver-spotted skin and a small but pronounced wattle under her chin. Even the yellow smoker's teeth were individually rendered veneers. If Creem had ever had a masterpiece, this was it.

So far, nobody had even batted an eyelash in

his direction. Not the old fatty who sold him his bus ticket at Union Station, and not the numbnut kid who sat next to him all the way from DC. The whole getup had allowed him to sail right out of Washington unnoticed, even if it was on a god-damn Greyhound bus. This wouldn't be the last indignity of his little tour, but hopefully it would all be worth it in the end.

Rhode Island. Florida. South America. That was the idea. He'd already arranged passage on a Trinidadian cargo ship out of Miami. After that, it was just a skip to the mainland. Once he made his way to Buenos Aires, he could start to feel out the surgery community to see who might be safe to approach about some major work.

It wouldn't be too much trouble lying low in the meantime. He had eleven million in gold, held in a numbered account at Banco Macro. Plenty to live on, if he was careful. And with US extradition priorities being what they were, he'd be more than safe. It was all about the drug wars now. No-body paid attention to someone like him once you reached a certain distance.

Meanwhile, as long as he was stateside, Elijah Creem knew full well how to stay invisible—even standing in the middle of a public ladies' room.

When the bathroom door opened, Creem let his hand fall away from his face. He took a plum-colored lipstick out of the purse he carried—one of Miranda's cast-offs—and busied himself with it at the mirror.

He kept his eyes forward, watching the young woman's reflection as she passed behind him and let herself into one of the toilet stalls. She was blond, and pretty, in a trashy sort of way. The kind of girl you might see riding alone on a Greyhound bus.

Was she perfect? Not by any stretch, but it sent a slight itch through Creem's palm, all the same. As he put the lipstick back in the purse, he let his fingers graze over the handle of a number eighteen scalpel, tucked into one of the side pockets.

As the girl's yellow panties slipped down to gather around her sandals near the floor, he turned slowly to face the row of stalls. He checked the entrance again.

It was tempting. So tempting. It had been too long since he'd been able to use a real instrument.

Still, the bus station was crowded. He had a transfer to make. And there would be plenty of opportunity to use the scalpel, soon enough.

"*Hey!*" The girl's voice cut right through his thoughts. "Someone's in here!"

Creem looked down to realize he'd already put a hand on the stall door. His size twelve canvas espadrilles were no doubt showing under the partition wall.

"Oh!" he said. "Sorry!"

His affected voice was something less than ladylike, but it passed well enough. He could see the girl now, just a sliver of her through the crack, hunched over and reaching to hold the stall door closed between them.

"You can relax, sweetheart," he added. "You're safe."

She didn't offer any response, and really, why would she? There was no way for her to know that, on this particular day, she was the luckiest little piece of trash in Philadelphia.

As Creem reached the bathroom door, he turned back one more time.

"You know, you might think about those bags under your eyes before they get away from you," he said.

"*What?*" the girl called back.

But Creem was already gone.

CHAPTER
99

SEVERAL HOURS LATER, DR. CREEM STEPPED OUT OF A TAXI IN FRONT OF THE house in Newport. The driver took his suitcase from the trunk, called him ma'am, and wished him a good night before he took off.

So far, so good.

The place was dark, but he'd brought one of Miranda's keys from home. He let himself in through the porte cochere entrance and up to the grand hall that ran down the center of the old place. It was one of those eight-bedroom, twelve-bathroom deals they called a "cottage" around here. Typical WASP understatement.

It was ridiculous, really. Miranda had been rich as Croesus long before the two of them had ever met. Her parents—in Provence for the season—had some kind of bottomless fortune, tied to half a million acres of sugarcane in Hawaii and Australia. Miranda's stock options alone were worth a hundred million. She may not have married Creem for his money, but she sure as hell was divorcing him for it. The last six months had turned her into a vindictive, greedy little bitch. Her, and her two little clones. There was no preserving those relationships anymore, and no sense trying.

Just the opposite, in fact.

Creem skipped the nostalgia tour this time and went straight to the so-called blue room on the third floor. It was the one Miranda favored. He'd stayed in it several times himself. Chloe was even conceived in the room's nineteenth-century sleigh bed. That's where he stopped to change.

He peeled off the mask, the dress, and the god-forsaken undergear, folding them carefully onto the bed. A duplicate pair of masks were rolled in Bubble Wrap inside his suitcase, for the two-day bus trip to Miami.

In the meantime, he took out a few of his own things and quickly re-dressed. He also took out three pairs of steel handcuffs, a roll of black packing tape, and a small, sealed bottle of chloral hydrate.

From the game table in the corner, Creem took one of the straight-back chairs and moved it to the space under the window by the bed. It was all planned out. Miranda would be the last to go, but she'd get the show of her life before she did.

The only thing he kept on him was the scalpel. He slid it carefully into his back pocket as he crossed to the window again and looked outside.

From here he could see where the white crushed-gravel driveway curved around the back of the house to a parking courtyard. There was no sign of Miranda or the girls yet, but there had been a Newport paper in the front hall, open to the movie section. Chances were, they wouldn't be long.

As he stood there at the window, surveying the back of the house, something suddenly caught Creem's eye. A flicker, or a reflection of movement in the glass.

He turned around fast to see the tall shape of a man, silhouetted in the bedroom door against the light from the hall.

"Elijah Creem?" the man said. "You need to come with me. You're under arrest."

Creem still couldn't make out the face, but he recognized the deep tone of the man's voice right away.

It was his new best friend, Alex Cross.

CHAPTER
100

MY GUESS IS THAT CREEM THOUGHT FLYING WOULD BE TOO RISKY. IT HAD taken him the better part of the day to reach the house in Newport over land.

Not me. With the favor of a Bell helicopter from the Bureau—and specifically from Ned Mahoney, who was now on the list of people I owed, big-time—Valente and I had gotten to Rhode Island in two and a half hours. We'd also contacted an investigative unit with the Newport County sheriff's office. The house where Miranda Creem and her daughters were staying had been vacated long before Dr. Creem ever got there.

Given my previous contact with Creem, my psych background, and the disaster of Josh Bergman's suicide, it was agreed I'd approach Creem first. I had a two-way radio clipped to my belt, with a backup mike on my cuff. A full team of local police and detectives were all now in position, just outside. Help was a word away, if I needed it.

When I flicked on the bedroom light, it looked to me as if Creem had some kind of lacerations around his face. Then I realized I was looking at the remnants of latex and glue from whatever mask had gotten him this far.

"I'll be honest," Creem said. "I'm surprised to see you."

I motioned with the Glock in my hand. "Get down on your knees and lace your fingers behind your head," I said.

Creem didn't move. I could see him regrouping, and taking in the room around us. He was looking for a way out, even now.

"I have every right to be here," he said, settling back into his usual superiority. "I let myself in with a key. You're the one who's trespassing. I'm here to see my wife."

"I'll bet you are," I said. "Were you going to kill your daughters, too, Creem?"

He grinned at that, in a way I'd seen before. It was pure Elijah Creem, treading that fine line between confident and sociopathic.

"This is a bit of déjà vu, isn't it?" he said. "That night we met in Georgetown, I offered you twenty thousand, or maybe it was thirty, for a little head start out the bedroom window."

"I remember it didn't get you anywhere," I said.

"No. It didn't, did it?" he said. He nodded several times, as if he were finally coming to the logical conclusion here.

But instead, Creem made a break for it. He put his hands on the back of a tall wooden chair and swung it all at once, right through the bedroom's picture window. It brought down a shower of glass, even as he was climbing onto the sill to jump out.

I was right behind, nearly too late to grab him—but not quite. My hand closed around the back of his shirt just as he dropped. It pulled and ripped, but then he snapped back. His body bounced hard off the side of the house. For a brief moment, I lost my footing and nearly went out the window with him. If there had been any broken glass on the sill right there, it would have gone right into my gut.

"Give me your hand!" I shouted, even as he struggled, dangling at the end of my reach. A stream of cops was coming around the house now, and I could hear several others coming into the room behind me.

"Get off me!" Creem said. When he tried to slip out of his shirt, I leaned over and got a grip on his arm, to drag him back in.

That's when he pulled the scalpel I didn't even realize he had. He brought it up all at once and drove the tip right into the back of my hand.

A nauseating bolt of pain ran up my arm. I yelled out and let go before I could stop myself. It was a reflex as much as anything. Drops of blood from my hand followed him down to the ground, three stories below.

Creem pinwheeled his arms as he fell. The motion of it twisted his body around in the air, and there was no time to get himself upright. His legs would have broken anyway, but instead, he landed flat on his back, hitting the patio beneath us with a sickening thud.

Several officers, including Valente, closed in around him with weapons drawn.

"Don't move!" one of them shouted. "Stay right where you are!"

It was a nonissue. At first I thought Creem was dead. Then I heard a slight moan. He turned his

head a few inches to the side, and moaned again,
but that was it.

Dr. Creem's career was over.

Finally.

CHAPTER
101

ONCE I GOT MY HAND WRAPPED BY THE EMTS ON THE SCENE, I LEFT VALENTE in Rhode Island and flew back to DC in the middle of the night.

I didn't hear anything en route, but Errico called me just as I was disembarking in Quantico. It turned out that Elijah Creem had snapped his spine in the fall, breaking two vertebrae. He'd also given a full confession before they even got him to Newport Hospital. The way Valente put it, Creem had been broken in more ways than one by that fall. Not only was he headed to jail for the rest of his life, but he was going to be spending that time in a wheelchair. I can't say I was too sorry.

I'd see Creem again at his trial, but for now I had other things on my mind.

Actually, just one. Ava.

I went straight to the office without going home. The best way to get back to my family was to get my report done in the quiet of the night, before the office started filling up.

The amount of administrative paperwork on something like this is staggering. The primary burden would fall to Valente, and also to Jacobs for the River Killer case. Each file would have to go through no fewer than seven levels of review at the department before it got its final sign-off. I've seen the process take upwards of six months. It's a big part of what keeps me from trying to go any higher at MPD than I already am. At a certain level, you wind up spending all your time on paperwork and politics instead of in the field, where the real police work gets done.

By seven that morning, I'd written up a full account of the last twenty-four hours, and handed it off to Sergeant Huizenga when she came in for the day. She'd already been in touch with Valente, and her mood was as good as I'd seen it in weeks.

Just as well, since I had to give her my paperwork and ask for a few days off in the same breath.

"I know I just got back on," I said, "but Ava's been missing for three days now—"

Huizenga was blessedly cool about it. She waved me out of her office with the file I'd just handed her.

"Go, before I change my mind," she said. "Find your girl, and get back here as soon as you can. And leave your phone on!"

There would be a dozen or more calls that day, with half a million questions about Creem and Bergman, but this at least gave me the space I needed to get my priorities back in order.

First stop—home.

CHAPTER
102

I LEFT HEADQUARTERS AND SWUNG THROUGH THE HOUSE LONG ENOUGH TO see the kids before school. Exhausted wasn't really the word. At a certain point, it pushes past that and back into adrenaline. I'd figure out the whole sleep thing when I could.

"Who are you again?" Jannie asked, grinning over her eggs at me as I came down from a quick shower.

"I'm the Invisible Man," I said. "You can call me Ralph E."

"Hi, Ralphie!" Ali said. "Nice to meet you."

"Not funny," Nana said. "You're going to burn yourself out, right down to the nub. And if you hadn't noticed, we've still got a family emergency on our hands."

"That's what I'm doing home, Nana," I said. I gave her a sideways hug at the stove and stole a piece of her amazingly flat bacon off the paper towel where it was draining. "I'll drop the kids at school, and then I'm heading out to look for her again. All day if I have to."

There was no talk of Elijah Creem or Josh Bergman. Bree already knew, and nobody else in the family needed to be worrying themselves about all that. We made sure to leave the TV off that morning, too.

"I want you to make an appointment with Dr. Finaly," Nana told me, once the kids were in the hall, putting on their jackets. "You need to tend your own garden as well, mister."

"Funny you should say that," I told her. "I had the same thought."

Adele Finaly is the shrink I see from time to time—sometimes more than others. She's always there when I need a smart, objective opinion about my life, my work, my family—and most of all, about the habit those three things have of crashing into each other. First chance I got, I was going to put my figurative feet up on Adele's couch. Just not today.

As soon as I dropped Ali and Jannie off for school, I circled back around to touch base with each of the street cops and Vice Unit detectives I'd been working with since Ava disappeared.

Mostly it was an exercise in frustration. There was no new word anywhere. Things were starting to look worse, and I knew it. I told everyone the same thing. If they so much as spotted someone who looked like Ava, they were to put the grab on her and call me immediately. I'd come and take it from there.

The toughest calls were the ones I'd started making on the Prostitution Unit and their out-reach teams. Like it or not, there was one very nasty and unavoidable possibility in all of this. With a drug habit, no money, and Ava's family history, she might very well have started turning tricks by now—for cash, or for the drugs them-selves, if she was desperate enough.

It ground me down every time I thought about it. The girl was fourteen years old! Was that unheard of? Not at all. Nobody knows better than me that life on the streets of DC can get pretty damn bleak.

But this was Ava. *Our* Ava. And nothing I did seemed to get me any closer to finding her.

I was starting to wonder if anything would.

CHAPTER
103

IT WAS A FULL TWO DAYS MORE BEFORE WE FINALLY GOT WORD ON AVA.

I was home for a few hours that Wednesday, just grabbing some time with the family before I headed back out. I'd been alternating day and night, trawling the long list of streets where I thought Ava might turn up.

When the doorbell rang, I got up from the couch with the kids and went to answer. Every ring of the bell those days brought a combined sense of hope and dread—maybe this would be the one that gave us some kind of answer.

And in fact, it was.

When I opened the front door, Sampson was standing there on the stoop. It didn't take long to read him. Between the fact that he hadn't come in the back, as usual, and the tears in his eyes, I knew right away why he was there.

It felt like a crater opened up in my chest. My jaw went tight, and some part of me started trying to come up with a different conclusion. Maybe I was misreading Sampson, I thought—even though I knew it wasn't the case.

He didn't have to say a word. I stepped outside and pulled the door closed behind me.

"Jesus, John," I said, choking up.

He pulled me in tight, with his hand on the back of my head.

"I'm so sorry, Alex. I'm so goddamn sorry."

I've been here before. I've lost loved ones, and I've had to give other people the worst news they could possibly get. Nothing—but nothing—ever makes that easier.

Ava was gone. I knew it for sure now. But even so, it didn't feel real.

I stood back from John on the stoop. "Where?" I said.

"An abandoned apartment building on the waterfront, across the river. Junkies flop there all the time. It was a...Jesus, Alex, it was a terrible scene. They took samples, but..."

The tears were streaming down my face, even as the anger started flooding in. Sampson was having a hard time getting through this himself.

"Just tell me everything," I said. "What else do you know?"

John took a long, slow breath. "The body was burned. Beyond recognition. I don't know why. Maybe she'd scored a hit and someone wanted it. Maybe someone killed her on accident and tried to cover up."

"But it was her?" I said. "For sure?"

"It was a young woman. African American. Ava's height and build. And Alex? They found this on the body."

He opened an envelope and poured the blackened pieces of Nana's locket into my hand. The two hinged halves had come apart from the chain, and the photos were either burned up, or missing. But it was most definitely the necklace that Nana Mama had given Ava on the day she'd moved out.

I could just make out the engraved R. C. on the back—for Regina Cross.

Suddenly, the front door opened and Nana was there with Bree.

"What is going on out here?" Nana said. She stopped short the second I turned to look at her. It was the same way I'd seen the truth on John's face.

As her eyes traveled down to the pieces of the locket in my hand, I reached over and pulled her close.

"No," she said, stiffening up at first, but then buckling at the knees just as fast. "No, no, no. Not our Miss Ava. Oh, Lord. Please, no!"

"She's gone, Nana," I said. "I'm so sorry."

Bree was crying now, too, and I could see the kids standing behind her, moon-eyed and watching. It was like waves of heartbreak, just seeing their faces and knowing what I had to tell them.

My mind went somewhere else, in a way. Without a word, we all moved back inside as a family. Sampson didn't even come in. There was no good-bye. He left us to grieve, and to try to explain to Jannie and Ali how something like this could possibly happen.

How it could possibly be true.

CHAPTER
104

I DON'T BELIEVE IN A VENGEFUL GOD, BUT I WILL SAY THAT I FELT CONFUSED as much as anything in those first few hours. How could something like this happen? And why? Most of all—*why?*

Had I done something to bring all of this down on my head? On my family's heads?

And Ava's?

It's not the kind of question I ask too frequently—or lightly. But I had to confront the fact that whatever choices I'd made had brought me to this point, in some small or large way. I'd never know now if I could have done something else to stop it.

Jannie and Ali took the news very differently from each other. After we all sat and talked, and cried together, Jannie withdrew. She said she wanted to be alone and think it all over in her room, which we let her do.

Ali stuck close. I think he was just old enough to understand what had happened, but too young to have ever felt anything like this before. I read to him in bed for a long time that night, and held his hand after I turned out the light, like he asked me to.

"All the way to asleep," he said. "Okay, Dad?"

"You got it, bud," I said, and I stayed right there while he slowly drifted off.

I wasn't sure which of my kids my heart was breaking for more. All of them, I suppose. Ava, too.

When we spoke to Damon on the phone, he asked to come home the next morning, on the first bus. I told him he didn't have to if he didn't want to, but I was glad when he insisted. It felt like the right thing, having all of us together now.

Nana went to bed early, but Bree and I sat up late in the attic, talking for hours. Part of me would like to say that I wasn't already thinking about the investigation on this, but I was. Bree, too. We'd been so engaged in looking for Ava, it felt like we already had a blueprint for where to start asking questions.

"Whoever sold to her, or whoever did this...we're going to find them," Bree said. "And they're going to pay, Alex. You can be sure about that."

Bree was the strongest one of all of us that night. In a way, she'd become this linchpin in our family that we didn't even know had been missing until she was there. I love her more every time I think about it.

"Thank you," I told her. "Thank you for being my wife. And for coming into my life exactly when I needed you most. I don't know if I could have—"

"Of course you could," Bree said. "You already did, for years. But I'm glad I'm here now, too. I love you, Alex. And I love this family. That's never going to change."

When we finally went to bed, we made love,

and even cried some more in each other's arms before we finally drifted off ourselves, holding each other close.

All the way to asleep, just like Ali.

CHAPTER
105

BREE AND I TOOK SHIFTS THE NEXT DAY. I STAYED HOME WITH NANA AND THE kids through the morning while she went out and spoke with as many people at Ava's school as she could.

When she got back, we all had lunch together, though nobody was too hungry. Then I went out for the afternoon. Technically I was on bereavement, and off duty. I left my gun at home but took my badge.

One of my first stops was Howard House. I'd been in touch with Sunita, the manager, and she'd agreed to call a full house meeting, first thing after school that day. By the time I got there, all eleven girls were already waiting with the staff in the living room.

They knew Ava had died, and I could see there had been some tears, but it was all reined in by the time I was standing in front of them. It actually reminded me of Ava, the way they seemed so intent on showing as little emotion as possible.

"I know you've already answered some of these questions," I told the group. "But I want you all to think hard. Has anyone remembered anything else about the day Ava disappeared? Anything you hadn't thought about before, or since then?"

What I got back was a room full of silence. Part of it had to do with the fact that we'd been over this before, but that wasn't all. There's an unwritten rule out there on the streets, where a lot of these girls came from. The line between helping and snitching is gray, at best. The safest bet is to just keep your mouth shut, especially if anyone else is listening. It can come off as apathy, but I knew it was more complicated than that.

I asked a few more open-ended questions, but didn't really get anywhere until I moved on to individual interviews. Sunita let me use her office for privacy, and she brought the girls in, one by one.

Ava's roommate, Nessa, was the fifth girl I saw. I could tell she'd been crying again, although she tried to hide it.

I could also tell she was sitting on something the second she walked in the door.

We sat on the same side of Sunita's desk, in two folding chairs. Nessa kept her feet pushed out in the space between us and looked at her phone more than at me, while she flipped it around and around in her hand.

"You seem nervous," I said.

She didn't look up when she started talking. "Just so you know, I wasn't trying to hide nothin' before, okay?" she said. "I even kind of asked you about it, when you was here the first time."

I tried pulling up whatever memory I had of the day we'd met, outside on the porch. She'd taken our picture—I remembered that much.

"Asked me about what?" I said.

"Well, not asked you, exactly," Nessa said.

"Come on, Nessa. Spit it out. What are we talking about here?"

"Ava's boyfriend, okay? She always sayin' how he wasn't nothing to her, but if you ask me, I think she was just embarrassed. This boy was *old*."

"Who is he?" I said. "How did she know him?"

Nessa gave a shrug and pushed her lips out. "She just said his name was Russell. That's where she gettin' her junk."

That name, Russell, hit me like an electric shock all at once. Could this be *the* Russell? The same phantom boyfriend we were looking for in the Elizabeth Reilly case? Rebecca Reilly's kidnapper?

Or was this just some horrible coincidence?

I tried to stay cool as I pushed on, but it wasn't easy. My mind was racing.

"Nessa, what can you tell me about him?" I asked. "Do you know what he looked like? Or maybe what kind of car he drove?"

"It was a jeep," she said right away. "He was white, too, but Ava didn't care. I think she liked that jeep—and whatever else he was givin' her, if you know what I mean. No disrespect."

I felt sick to my stomach. I still couldn't know if this was the same man, but the similarities were there—to Elizabeth Reilly, and to Amanda Simms as well. All these girls were disconnected from their families in some way.

Young. Vulnerable. Alone.

The idea of this monster plying Ava with drugs, promises, sex—whatever it had been—made me want to excuse myself and puke my guts out in the bathroom.

"You said he was white," I went on. "What else?"

She sat up a little straighter then and started

thumbing at her phone. "I got a picture, yo," she said. I think she was just relieved that I wasn't giving her a hard time for holding back this long.

She swiped past several dozen images before she came to the one she was looking for, and then held it up to show me.

"Here," she said. "I used to see her over on Eastern, talkin' to him in that jeep, see? Ava didn't even know I took it, but once I showed it to her, she stopped talkin' shit about not havin' no boyfriend."

The picture had been snapped from maybe half a block away. Ava had her back to the camera, but I easily recognized her long, thin frame, and the suede boots she'd worn almost constantly since Bree bought them for her.

That wasn't all. I also recognized the gray-green jeep in the photo, and the tall, bearded man behind the wheel.

It was Ron Guidice.

I DON'T KNOW IF I CAN EXPLAIN WHAT HAPPENED TO ME NEXT. OR IF I EVEN fully understand it myself.

When I left Howard House, it was as if there were no words for anything I was feeling. There was nothing inside me at all but pure, white-hot anger. That, and the image from Nessa's phone, burning into my brain, as clear as anything else.

I barely remember driving home. When I came in, Bree was there, with Sampson and Billie at the kitchen table. I must have looked like hell, because they all stopped what they were doing and stared at me.

"Alex?" Bree said. "What is it?"

I stood at the head of the table, holding myself up with both hands on the back of a kitchen chair.

"Where are the kids?" I said.

"On a walk with Nana. Billie wanted some cornstarch from the store. Why? What's going on?"

"It was Guidice," I said. Already, I was walking out of the room. I headed up the hall toward the stairs at the front.

"Wait—what?" Bree said, catching up behind me. "*What* was Guidice?"

I took the stairs two at a time, even as I tried

to explain to Bree what Nessa had shown me. The words practically stuck in my throat. It was hard focusing on anything except what I'd come here to do.

"Did you call it in?" Bree asked as we came into the bedroom.

"No. I'm going out to find him myself."

I opened the closet door and started working the combination on the safe. No electric keypad here—it was twenty-three right, thirty-nine left, nine right.

I took out my Glock and a magazine, slapped it home, and stuck the gun in my jacket pocket. I didn't bother with a holster.

"Hold on," Bree said. She grabbed her own gun out of the safe before I closed the door. "If you're arresting him, I'm coming, too."

"I'm not arresting him," I said.

She grabbed my arm then and looked me deep in the eyes. If I'd been anywhere near myself, I might have seen enough right there to stop what I was doing and pick up the phone. Or even to send Sampson out instead of me. But I didn't.

The only thing I knew for sure in that moment was that nobody had ever deserved to die as much as Ron Guidice did.

Before Bree could stop me, I was already out of the bedroom, down the stairs, and heading for the back door. Maybe I'd find some sense, or a reason not to do this, by the time I tracked Guidice down. And maybe I wouldn't.

I truly didn't know.

CHAPTER
107

RON GUIDICE TORE HIS HEADPHONES OFF, PULLED THE BERETTA 9MM OUT FROM under the driver's seat, and got out of the jeep.

It was like a starter pistol had gone off. This was all fast-twitch muscle stuff coming back to him, the way his body had been trained to respond without the interference of the mind. The moment he'd heard Alex mention his name, Guidice knew. This operation was about to come to a sudden end.

Looking up Fifth Street from where he'd parked, he could see the front door of Alex's house. There was no sign of him yet, but it wouldn't be long now. His car was right there at the curb. He'd left it wide open when he went inside just moments earlier.

Guidice kept the Beretta pulled up inside the sleeve of his jacket, out of sight. There were several people on the street. A man clipping his hedges. A woman with two small kids riding their trikes up the sidewalk. There was no sense drawing any attention to himself yet. When this happened, it was going to be out in the open, and he needed a certain element of surprise.

It wasn't the time, place, or method Guidice might have chosen, but that was irrelevant now.

He'd gotten greedy. He'd let himself watch Alex suffer for one day too many, just long enough to connect the last few dots.

But maybe that was okay. In fact, maybe it was perfect, Guidice thought, as he stood watching the door. Alex was going to take a bullet to the brain, right there on the street where he'd tried so hard— and so much in vain—to keep his little family safe.

And when he did, Detective Alex Cross, paragon of the Metropolitan Police Department, was going to single-handedly prove his own incompetence to the world, in the most definitive possible terms.

So then fine, Guidice thought. Alex wanted to come looking for him? He wouldn't have to look very far.

CHAPTER
108

"DON'T DO THIS, ALEX!"

It was only when Bree followed me off the back porch that I remembered I'd come in through the front of the house. Usually I drove around and parked in our garage—but there was nothing usual about today.

When I turned around, she was right there.

"Just give me thirty seconds," she said. "I'm going to tell Sampson to call this in. And then I'm coming with you. At least do that for me."

I think she was grasping at straws. Maybe she thought she could talk me down in the car.

"Yeah, okay," I said. "I'll wait for you out front."

"Good." She looked at me one more time before she ran back into the house. "I'll be right there."

In fact, I had no intention of waiting for Bree. Whatever was going to happen with Guidice, it was going to be just him and me when it did. There was no sense getting her involved. Or anyone else, for that matter.

I walked up the narrow passage between our house and the neighbors', through the locked gate, and out onto Fifth Street, where I'd parked.

I didn't look back once. I just got into the car, started it up, and pulled away from the curb. In fact, if I hadn't taken a quick glance in the rearview mirror for oncoming traffic, I never would have seen Guidice at all. He was standing right in the middle of the street, and he raised his arm in my direction just as I spotted him. I didn't actually see the gun, but I recognized the posture right away.

Even as I swerved, and cut the car hard to the left, my back windshield exploded in a shower of glass gravel. When I looked again, Guidice was on the move. He was coming right for me, his gun still raised.

Heart thumping, I rolled onto the seat, threw open the passenger door, and fell out onto the street. My Glock was out now, and I looked over the edge of the door to see him closing the gap between us. I could tell he was trained. He didn't just pepper the car with bullets as he came. He was waiting for a clean shot.

So was I. There were people screaming up and down the block, and running for cover in any number of directions. At this distance, I couldn't afford the possibility of a stray bullet. If I missed him, I might hit someone else.

Guidice didn't have the same problem. As soon as he spotted me over the passenger door, he tried again, with a quick double tap this time. I ducked down and heard the shots hit the side of the car with two dull thuds.

I could still hear a few people running up the sidewalk behind me, too. The situation was only going to get worse if I didn't do something.

Working mostly on instinct, I stayed close to

the ground and made my way around the front of the car. Maybe—just maybe—I could catch Guidice off guard as he came within range, too close to miss.

When I got to the front, I tried another quick look. He was right there, less than ten yards away now, and moving at a run. This was it. One of us was going down.

I stood up fast, with a two-hand grip on the Glock, ready to fire—but I never got that far. At the moment I came eye to eye with Guidice, another shot sounded from farther off.

Guidice stumbled hard and fell, face-first onto the street with his arms splayed out in front of him. He didn't even try to catch himself.

"Alex!"

I looked over and saw Bree coming down the front steps of our house. Her own Glock 19 was up, still pointed in Guidice's direction where he lay.

"Are you all right?" she shouted.

"I'm fine," I said.

She'd gotten him in the neck, I saw. Probably hit the carotid artery, too, from the way his blood was pumping. A pool of it had started to spread on the pavement around him.

Sampson was outside now, too, close behind Bree. "EMTs are on the way," he said, and stopped short when he saw Guidice.

I tore my shirt off and pressed it to the wound at his neck, but there was no way to stop the bleeding. Not with a shirt. I think Guidice knew it, too. He struggled to roll over and looked me in the eye, where I was kneeling next to him.

"Congratulations," he slurred out. "Didn't think you had it in you—"

"Yeah, well think again," Bree said, her own voice shaking.

"Listen to me," I said. "Where's Rebecca Reilly? Did you take her, Guidice? Was it you? Are you Russell?"

I was still putting the pieces all together, but if I was right about this, I also knew I didn't have much time here. He was nearly gone already.

Guidice grabbed my arm then, and pulled himself a few inches off the pavement. He tried to swallow back whatever was clogging his throat, and his jaw went slack.

"Tell my girls...tell them—"

"Answer my question first!" I said. Even then I was fighting my own feelings. It was everything I could do to keep from stepping back and letting him bleed all the way out.

Before I could say anything else, Guidice convulsed. He spit up a large amount of blood all over himself, shuddered one more time, and then went still. When his head fell back on the street, his eyes were open—still on me. At least, it seemed that way.

I could hear a siren somewhere, coming closer.

"That's it," Sampson said. "He's gone."

"He can rot in hell," Bree said.

When I looked at her, she had an expression on her face I'd never seen before. She's the most caring person I know. In a way, it was as if everything I'd been feeling had shifted to her.

She was crying again, too. Thinking about poor Ava, no doubt. Whatever else Guidice may have done, he'd used her as nothing more than a pawn, just to get back at me.

The most we could say now was that no more

lives would be wasted in Ron Guidice's name. I suppose if this were any other case, it might feel good to know that.

But not this time. Rebecca Reilly was still out there somewhere. And Ava was dead. Nothing was going to make us feel better about how all of this had gone down. Certainly not right away. We'd have to get there on our own, and in our own time.

Still, somehow, I knew we would.

Epilogue

CIRCLE OF LIFE

CHAPTER
109

NOT LONG AFTER RON GUIDICE DIED, HIS FULL SITUATION CAME TO LIGHT. It was his mother who called the authorities, when her son's name became a national headline.

It took another five days after that and two independent DNA tests to confirm that the baby in Lydia Guidice's care was in fact Rebecca Reilly. Also, that her sister, Emma Lee Guidice, was the biological daughter of both Ron Guidice and Amanda Simms, the first pregnant girl in our pregnant girl cases.

It brought up all kinds of reverberating speculation about Ava, and what Guidice might have had planned for her before she died. But Ava's cremation was already behind us now. A small, intimate memorial service had been held. She had no dental records at all, and her remains had been identified to the extent that they could.

But that was it. None of us were prepared to confront the possibility that she'd been pregnant at the end. That question was just going to have to fade off into the great unknown, which was probably for the best.

But I'll always wonder, of course. I'll wonder about a lot of things from this case.

When Child and Family Services took custody

of Guidice's two daughters, Bree and I worked with the agency to make sure Mrs. Guidice could see the girls from time to time. She may not have been competent to raise them, but she also wasn't criminally negligent here. I felt sorry for her more than anything.

Stephanie agreed to shepherd their case, and she also promised not to give up until she found a home where both girls could live together. In the meantime, they were placed into emergency foster care at a small, well-run facility in Foggy Bottom.

Taking in Rebecca and Emma Lee ourselves wasn't something we could even contemplate, starting with the fact that we'd just lost Ava. But Bree and I did make several visits to the home in those early months.

"Look at you," I said, the first time Bree actually met Rebecca. She was cradling the baby in a rocking chair, going slowly back and forth like she'd done it a million times. "You're good at that."

Bree just shrugged and kept her eyes on Rebecca in the way that—yes, I'm going to say it—only a woman can look at a baby.

The subject of having our own kids wasn't really on the table anymore. We'd talked about it before we got married, and had already put it behind us. But life's a circle sometimes, isn't it? The thing you thought you left behind can come back around, until it's sitting right there in front of you, all over again.

I'm not saying Bree and I made any kind of new plans that day, or even that there were going to *be* any new plans. But if I had to guess, I'd say that we were probably feeling some of the same things as she sat there, rocking Rebecca back to sleep.

After a while, Bree looked up and caught me staring at her.

"What is it?" she said.

"Nothing," I said.

She smiled like she could read my mind. "Nothing, huh?"

Now it was my turn to shrug. "You just look really beautiful right now," I told her. "That's all."

"It's this little girl," she said. "She looks good on me."

And I couldn't argue with that.

CHAPTER
110

"ALEX, COME ON IN. HAVE A SEAT. IT'S GOOD TO SEE YOU."

I admire Adele Finaly quite a bit. I think she's one of the finest psychotherapists I've ever seen in action.

I guess that's why I put up with her No Shoes rule during sessions. I didn't even think about it anymore. I just left my trainers on the mat by the door of her plant-filled office, and went to sit in my usual spot on the couch.

"It's been a while," she said, settling into her own flowered armchair. "Was there anything specific that precipitated this call?"

She reminds me of Audrey Hepburn, or Lena Horne. Adele has a way of being incredibly smart and accessible at the same time.

"Just the oldest question in the book," I said. "My book, anyway."

"Ah." She smiled sympathetically. "That one."

I spent a good chunk of the session with her just explaining everything that had happened in the last month. She knew who Ava was, but not how badly it had all turned out.

I told her about Ron Guidice, too. Not just what he'd done, but what had happened to me on that last day—and also what *might* have happened if things had turned out differently. I don't know that I've ever been so consumed by my own hatred of someone before, and it scared me.

"I tell myself it was different this time," I said. "It was *personal*. Having Ava involved changed everything, and I got in over my head. That's not even accounting for the two other major cases I had going."

"Well, yes," Adele said. "It *was* different. You had this girl living in your home, and very possibly lining up to become a legal part of your family. She would have been your daughter."

I nodded, not really sure I could talk about that part without breaking up.

"But Alex," Adele said. She leaned over and put a hand on my wrist. "It's *always* different with you. There's always a reason why you end up pushing yourself—and why you land back in those very dark places."

It was true. In fact, I didn't even know what to say to that. So Adele went on. I can always count on her to show me both sides of any coin.

"You know what else is true?" she said. "There are evil people out there in the world. Someone has to do the work that you do, and we're all very lucky that you do it so well.

"But that doesn't mean you can't care too much sometimes, Alex. I think you do. And that's when I worry about you—about what this might be doing to ... well, to your soul."

"You worry about me?" I said, grinning. "Adele, I'm touched."

She knew I was trying to sidestep something and didn't take the bait. Instead, she kept pushing.

"Maybe we should stop asking why you are

this way, and start focusing on what, if anything, you want to do about it," she said.

I looked at her, a little sheepish. "I want to keep showing up here until I'm so sick of hearing myself talk that I finally make a change. A real one."

Adele sat back and looked at me like I'd just won the spelling bee.

"That's a pretty good answer. For a start."

"What about you?" I said. "If you were a betting woman, would you say I was going to be seeing you for the rest of my life? Coming in here, and asking the same damn questions, over and over?"

"My God, I hope not. You're twenty years younger than me."

Adele's always good for a well-timed laugh. She gets me, in that way.

"You know what I mean," I said. "When are we going to figure this one out, Adele?"

"If you keep coming in to see me?" she said. "Then . . . eventually."

"Eventually? That's your answer?"

"And I'm sticking to it," she said.

In fact, she was probably right. We *would* get there one of these days. We'd figure it out.

Unless, of course, we didn't. Nobody knows better than me that *eventually* is an idea, not a given. There's no guarantee I'm going to *eventually* make it to anything, including breakfast tomorrow. But by the same token, I have to allow for the possibility.

Otherwise, I've got nothing. And that's not me.

About the Author

JAMES PATTERSON has created more enduring fictional characters than any other novelist writing today. He is the author of the Alex Cross novels, the most popular detective series of the past twenty-five years, including *Kiss the Girls* and *Along Came a Spider*. Mr. Patterson also writes the bestselling Women's Murder Club novels, set in San Francisco, and the top-selling New York detective series of all time, featuring Detective Michael Bennett. James Patterson has had more *New York Times* bestsellers than any other writer, ever, according to *Guinness World Records*. Since his first novel won the Edgar Award in 1977, James Patterson's books have sold more than 280 million copies.

James Patterson has also written numerous #1 bestsellers for young readers, including the Maximum Ride, Witch & Wizard, and Middle School series. In total, these books have spent more than 220 weeks on national bestseller lists. In 2010, James Patterson was named Author of the Year at the Children's Choice Book Awards.

His lifelong passion for books and reading led James Patterson to create the innovative website ReadKiddoRead.com, giving adults an invaluable tool to find the books that get kids reading for life. He writes full-time and lives in Florida with his family.

Books by James Patterson

FEATURING ALEX CROSS

Cross My Heart
Alex Cross, Run
Merry Christmas, Alex Cross
Kill Alex Cross
Cross Fire
I, Alex Cross
Alex Cross's Trial (with
   Richard DiLallo)
Cross Country
Double Cross
Cross (also published as Alex
   Cross)
Mary, Mary

London Bridges
The Big Bad Wolf
Four Blind Mice
Violets Are Blue
Roses Are Red
Pop Goes the Weasel
Cat & Mouse
Jack & Jill
Kiss the Girls
Along Came a Spider

THE WOMEN'S MURDER CLUB

12th of Never (with Maxine Paetro)
11th Hour (with Maxine Paetro)
10th Anniversary (with Maxine Paetro)
The 9th Judgment (with Maxine Paetro)
The 8th Confession (with Maxine Paetro)
7th Heaven (with Maxine Paetro)
The 6th Target (with Maxine Paetro)
The 5th Horseman (with Maxine Paetro)
4th of July (with Maxine Paetro)
3rd Degree (with Andrew Gross)
2nd Chance (with Andrew Gross)
1st to Die

FEATURING MICHAEL BENNETT

Gone (with Michael Ledwidge)
I, Michael Bennett (with Michael Ledwidge)
Tick Tock (with Michael Ledwidge)
Worst Case (with Michael Ledwidge)
Run for Your Life (with Michael Ledwidge)
Step on a Crack (with Michael Ledwidge)

Daniel X: Demons and Druids (with Adam Sadler)
Med Head (with Hal Friedman)
FANG: A Maximum Ride Novel
Witch & Wizard (with Gabrielle Charbonnet)
Maximum Ride: The Manga 2 (with NaRae Lee)
Daniel X: Watch the Skies (with Ned Rust)
MAX: A Maximum Ride Novel
Maximum Ride: The Manga 1 (with NaRae Lee)
Daniel X: Alien Hunter (graphic novel; with Leopoldo Gout)
The Dangerous Days of Daniel X (with Michael Ledwidge)
The Final Warning: A Maximum Ride Novel
*Saving the World and Other Extreme Sports: A Maximum
    Ride Novel*
School's Out—Forever: A Maximum Ride Novel
Maximum Ride: The Angel Experiment
santaKid

STANDALONE BOOKS

Mistress (with David Ellis)
Second Honeymoon (with Howard Roughan)
NYPD Red (with Marshall Karp)
Zoo (with Michael Ledwidge)
Guilty Wives (with David Ellis)
The Christmas Wedding (with Richard DiLallo)
Kill Me If You Can (with Marshall Karp)
Now You See Her (with Michael Ledwidge)
Toys (with Neil McMahon)
Don't Blink (with Howard Roughan)
The Postcard Killers (with Liza Marklund)
The Murder of King Tut (with Martin Dugard)
Swimsuit (with Maxine Paetro)
Against Medical Advice (with Hal Friedman)
Sail (with Howard Roughan)
Sundays at Tiffany's (with Gabrielle Charbonnet)
You've Been Warned (with Howard Roughan)
The Quickie (with Michael Ledwidge)
Judge & Jury (with Andrew Gross)
Beach Road (with Peter de Jonge)
Lifeguard (with Andrew Gross)
Honeymoon (with Howard Roughan)
Sam's Letters to Jennifer
The Lake House
The Jester (with Andrew Gross)

For previews of upcoming books and more information about James Patterson, please visit JamesPatterson.com or find him on Facebook or at your app store.

JAMES PATTERSON PRESENTS A THRILLING NEW NOVEL IN HIS SIZZLING SERIES

Tasked to solve the most extreme crimes in the world's most extreme metropolis, NYPD Red must hunt the most elusive killer in the city's history...

Please turn this page for an exciting preview of
NYPD Red 2

Part One

THE HAZMAT KILLER

CHAPTER
1

THE TWO HOMELESS men were sitting on the cobblestone in front of the World War I memorial on Fifth Avenue and 67th Street. As soon as they saw me heading toward them, they stood up.

"Zach Jordan, NYPD Red," I said.

"We got a dead woman on the merry-go-round," one said.

"Carousel," the second one corrected.

His hair was matted, his unshaven face was streaked with dirt, and his ragtag clothes smelled of day-old piss. I got a strong whiff and jerked my head away.

"Am I that bad?" he said, backing off. "I don't even smell it anymore. I'm Detective Bell. This is my partner, Detective Casey. We've been working anti-crime out of the park. A gang of kids has been beating the shit out of homeless guys just for sport, and we're on decoy duty. Sorry about the stink, but we've got to smell as bad as we look."

"Mission accomplished," I said. "Give me a description of the victim."

"White, middle-aged, and based on the fact that she's dressed head to toe in one of those Tyvek jumpsuits, it looks like she's the next victim of the Hazmat Killer."

Not what I wanted to hear. "ID?"

"We can't get at her. The carousel is locked up tight. She's inside. We would never have found her except we heard the music, and we couldn't figure out why it was playing at 6:30 in the morning."

"Lead the way," I said.

The carousel is in the heart of Central Park, only a few tenths of a mile off Fifth, and unless a Parkie showed up in a golf cart, walking was the fastest way to get there.

"Grass is pretty wet," Bell said, stating the obvious. "I thought NYPD Red only got called in for celebrities and muckety-mucks."

"One of those muckety-mucks went missing Friday night, and my partner and I have been looking for her. As soon as you called in an apparent homicide, I got tapped. We work out of the One-Nine, so I got here in minutes. But if this isn't our MIA, I'm out of here, and another team will catch it."

"Casey and I volunteer," Bell said. "We clean up well, and if you really twist our arms, we'd even transfer to Red. Is it as cool as they say?"

Is it cool? Is playing shortstop for the New York Yankees cool? For a cop, NYPD Red is a dream job.

There are eight million people in New York City. The Department's mission is to protect and serve every one of them. But a few get more protection and better service than others. It may not sound like democracy in action, but running a city is like running a business—you cater to your best customers. In our case, that means the ones who generate revenue and attract tourists. In a nutshell, the rich and famous. If any of them are the victims of a crime, they get our full attention. And trust me, these people are used to getting plenty of attention. They're rock stars in the world of finance, fashion, publishing, and in some cases, they're actual rock stars.

I answered Bell's question. "Except for the part where I ruin a good pair of shoes tromping through the wet grass, I'd have to say it's pretty damn cool."

"Where's your partner?" Bell asked.

I had no idea. "On her way," I lied.

We were crossing Center Drive when I heard the off-pitch whistle of a calliope.

"It's even more annoying when you get closer," Bell said.

The closest we could get was twenty feet away. We were stopped by a twelve-foot-high accordion-fold brass gate. Behind it was a vintage carousel that attracted hundreds of thousands of parents and kids to the park every year.

It was hours before the gate would officially open, but the ride was spinning, the horses were going up and down, and the circus music was blaring.

"You can't get in," Casey said. "It's locked."

"How'd she get in?" I asked.

"Whoever put her there broke the lock," he said. "Then they replaced it with this Kryptonite bicycle U-lock. It's a bitch to open."

"They obviously didn't want anybody to wander in and mess with their little tableau," I said.

"We kind of figured that," he said. "Anyway, ESU is sending somebody to cut it."

"Not until the crime scene guys dust it for prints," I said. "I doubt if we'll find anything, but I don't want it contaminated by some cowboy with an angle grinder."

"Detective Jordan." It was Bell. "You can get a good look at the body from here."

I walked to where he was standing and peered through an opening in the gate.

"Here she comes," Bell said, like I might actually miss a dead woman in a white Tyvek jumpsuit strapped to a red, blue, green, and yellow horse.

"Damn," I said as she rode past us.

"Is that your missing muckety-muck?" Bell asked.

"Yeah. Her name is Evelyn Parker-Steele."

Both cops gave me a never-heard-of-her look.

"Her father is Leonard Parker," I said. "He owns about a thousand movie theaters across the country. Her brother is Damon Parker—"

"The TV news guy?" Casey said.

"The bio I have on him says he's a world-renowned broadcasting journalist," I said, "but sure—I can go with TV news guy. And her husband is Jason Steele III, as in Steele Hotels and Casinos."

"Holy shit," Casey said to Bell. "We stumbled onto the First Lady of rich chicks."

"She's a lot more than that. She's a high-paid political operative who is currently the campaign manager for Muriel Sykes, the woman who is running for mayor against our beloved Mayor Spellman."

"Rich, famous, connected," Bell said. "Six ways to Sunday, this is a case for Red. I guess we better get out of here before we blow our cover. Good luck, Detective."

"Hang on," I said. "My partner is running late, and I could use your help feeling out the crowd."

Casey instinctively looked over his shoulder at the deserted park.

"They're not here yet," I said, "but they'll come. The media, the gawkers, people in a hurry to get to work but who can always make time to stop and stare at a train wreck, and, if we're lucky, the killer. Sometimes they like to come back to see how we're reacting to their handiwork. You mind helping me out?"

The two cops looked at each other and grinned like a couple of kids who just found out school was closed for a snow day.

"Do we mind helping Red on a major homicide?" Bell said. "Are you serious? What do you want us to do?"

"Throw on some clean clothes, get rid of the smell, then hang out and keep your eyes and ears open."

"We'll be cleaned up in ten," Bell said, and they took off.

The calliope music was driving me crazy, and I walked far enough away from the carousel so I could hear myself think. Then I dialed my partner, Kylie MacDonald. For the third time that morning, it went straight to voice mail.

"Damn it, Kylie," I said. "It's 6:47 Monday morning. I'm 17 minutes into a really bad week, and if I haven't told you lately, there's nobody I'd rather have a bad week with than you."

CHAPTER
2

I FINALLY GOT a text from Kylie. *Running late. Be there ASAP.*

Not ASAP enough, because she was still among the missing when Chuck Dryden, our crime scene investigator, let me know he was ready to give me his initial observations.

They call him Cut and Dryden because he's not big on small talk, but he's the most meticulous, painstaking, anal-retentive CSI guy I know, so I was happy to have him on the case.

"COD appears to be asphyxiation. TOD between 1 and 3 a.m.," he said, rattling off his findings without any foreplay. "There is evidence that the victim's mouth had been duct taped and the marks on her wrists indicate she was handcuffed or otherwise restrained."

"Talk to me about the jumpsuit," I said.

Dryden peered at me over rimless glasses, a small reprimand to let me know that I had jumped the gun, and he wasn't ready for Q&A. He cleared his throat and went on. "The inside of the victim's mouth is lacerated, her tongue and the roof of her mouth are bruised, some of her teeth have recently been chipped or broken, she has fresh cuts on her lips, and her jaw has been dislocated. It would appear she was tortured for several days pre-mortem. Indications are that death occurred elsewhere, and she was transported here." He paused. "Now, did you have a question, Detective?"

"Yeah. Love that little white frock she's wearing. Who's her designer?"

"Tyvek coveralls," he said, not even cracking a smile. "Manufactured by DuPont."

"So we're looking at the Hazmat Killer," I said.

Dryden rolled his eyes. *A different shade of reprimand.* "What a god-awful name to call a killer of this caliber," he said.

"Don't blame me," I said. "That's what the tabloids are calling him."

"Totally unimaginative journalism," he said, shaking his head. "This is the fourth victim. All kidnapped, all dressed alike, and all bearing this oddly curious pattern of facial injuries. A few hours after the body is found, a video goes viral on the Internet where the victim confesses to a heinous crime of his or her own—and the best the New York press can come up with is the *Hazmat Killer*?"

I shrugged. "It's pretty descriptive."

"And highly inaccurate," he said. "Technically, it's not even a Hazmat suit. It's a pair of hundred-dollar Tyvek coveralls. What's more intriguing is that in the three previous cases the bodies were all scrubbed down with ammonia, which makes it almost impossible to process any of the killer's DNA, and that the Tyvek further prevents other traceable evidence from getting on the victim or the victim's clothes. At the crime lab, we call him the Sanitizer."

A satisfied smile crossed his face, and I was

pretty sure that he was the one who came up with the catchy handle.

"So you worked the first three cases?" I asked.

Dryden nodded. "The lead detectives are Donovan and Boyle from the Five."

"The Five?" I repeated. "Chinatown?"

"The first victim was an Asian gangbanger," he said. "The second body turned up in the One-Four, and the next was dumped in Harlem, but Donovan and Boyle caught *numero uno*, so they've stayed with the case. However, I imagine that Mrs. Parker-Steele, with her blue-blooded heritage, will go directly to the top of the homicide food chain, and she'll be turned over to the Red unit."

"Her blood may be blue," I said, "but her brother is famous, her husband is a billionaire, and her father is a zillionaire, so the operative color here is green. Mrs. Parker-Steele will definitely get the same five-star service in death as she was used to in life."

"So, then, I'll be working with you and your partner..." He paused, trying to remember her name.

He was full of shit. Chuck Dryden's brain operates like a state-of-the-art microchip. When he examines a body, he processes every detail. And when the body is accompanied by Kylie's sparkling green eyes, flowing blond hair, and heart-melting smile, it's forever stored in his highly developed memory bank. He knew her name, and like most guys who meet Kylie, she probably had a starring role in his fantasies. It happened to me ten years ago; only in my case, Kylie and I took it beyond the fantasy stage.

Way beyond.

But now she's Mrs. Spence Harrington, wife of a successful TV producer with a hit cop show shot right here in New York. Spence is a good guy, and we get along fine, but it gnaws at me that I get to spend fourteen hours a day chasing down bad guys with Kylie while he gets to pull the night shift.

"Her name is Kylie MacDonald," I said, playing into Dryden's little charade.

"Right," he said. "So this will probably wind up in her lap. I mean yours and hers."

Her lap? What are you thinking, Chuck?

"Yeah," I said. "I'm pretty sure Detective MacDonald and I will be tapped to track down this maniac."

Assuming Detective MacDonald ever shows up for work.

CHAPTER
3

"TAKE HER DOWN," Dryden ordered as soon as his team had clicked off a few hundred pictures of Evelyn Parker-Steele in situ. As macabre as it was, I imagined that the twinkling lights and brightly colored horses would make her crime scene photos more festive than most.

They lowered the body to a tarp near the base of the carousel, and I knelt down next to her to get a closer look.

"Looks like you found your missing person," a familiar voice said.

"You mean her or you?" I said, too pissed at Kylie to look up.

Kylie MacDonald is not big on apologies. That's because in her worldview, she's never wrong. "Hey, I got here as soon as I could," she said, stretching out the word *could*, so that it sounded more like *back off* than *I'm sorry*.

Now I definitely wasn't going to look up. "Did you happen to get a message that said we have a murder to solve?" I said, staring intently at the corpse.

"Yeah, I think you left that one about twenty-seven times."

"Then your phone works," I said. "So the problem must be with your dialing finger."

"Zach, there are about a hundred rubberneckers watching us from the other side of the yellow tape. Do you really think this is the best time for me to explain why I was late? How about you just fill me in on what I missed."

"Small update on that *we have a murder to solve* message. We now have four."

She knelt down beside me.

"This is the late Evelyn Parker-Steele," I said. "Evelyn, this is my partner, the late Kylie MacDonald."

I glanced over so I could catch her reaction. It's almost impossible for Kylie to look anything but beautiful, but this morning she was one hot mess. The mischief in her eyes, the sexy wiseass grin both gone, replaced by puffy eyelids and a tight-lipped frown. All the usual magic that made heads turn was now cloaked in gloom. Whatever had made her late wasn't pretty.

I felt rotten for coming down so hard on her. "Sorry I got pissy," I said. And just like that, I was apologizing to her. "Are you okay?"

"Better than her," she said, examining the victim's mangled teeth and disarticulated jaw. "This is nasty. She was alive when they did this. Were you serious about four murders? Where are the other three?"

"Dead and buried," I said. "The previous victims of the Hazmat Killer."

She already had latex gloves on, and she touched the Tyvek suit. "Anyone can buy one of these Hazmat outfits. How do we know it's not a copycat?"

"Chuck Dryden worked the others, and he says the forensics on this one have the earmarks of number four."

"He's probably right. The carousel fits the pattern too. When Hazmat Man dumps his victims, he likes to pick a spot that makes a statement. It's like his little touch of poetic justice."

"So what's the metaphor here? Parker-Steele's life was a merry-go-round?"

She shook her head. "Horses. Evelyn grew up on them. Show jumping, dressage, all that rich-girl equestrienne shit. Her family has a big horse farm up in Westchester County."

"So maybe he's just saying *screw you and the horse you rode in on.*"

"Let's go find him and ask. There's no question that this is our case. If anybody fits the Red profile, she does. You think Cates is going to ask us to work the other three?"

"Can you think of any other reason why she called and said the mayor wants to see us at Gracie Mansion?"

"The mayor sent for us?" Kylie said, smiling for the first time since she showed up. "When are we meeting him?"

I looked at my watch. "Twenty minutes ago. But hey, he'll understand. He keeps people waiting all the time."

"Damn," she said. "Why didn't you just go without me?"

"Cates is there," I said. "If we're both late, we can tell her we got jammed up at the crime scene, and she'll let it slide. But if I showed up on my own and told her my partner was MIA, she'd find a new team in a heartbeat."

Kylie took a few seconds to process what I'd said, and I could see that familiar look of appreciation in her eyes.

"Thanks," she mumbled.

Knowing Kylie, that was about as close to an apology as I was going to get.